THE NIGHT IS OURS

THE NIGHT IS OURS

Anne Hampson

This first world edition published in Great Britain 2005 by
SEVERN HOUSE PUBLISHERS LTD of
9–15 High Street, Sutton, Surrey SM1 1DF.
This first world edition published in the USA 2005 by
SEVERN HOUSE PUBLISHERS INC of
595 Madison Avenue, New York, N.Y. 10022.

British Library Cataloguing in Publication Data

Hampson, Anne
    The night is ours
    1. Mexico - Fiction
    2. Love stories
    I. Title
    823.9'14 [F]

    ISBN 0-7278-6224-3

Typeset by Palimpsest Book Production Ltd.,
Polmont, Stirlingshire, Scotland.
Printed and bound in Great Britain by
MPG Books Ltd., Bodmin, Cornwall.

One

It seemed a strange time to be haunted by that old affair, recalling a handsome, arrogant face, reliving an experience which until now had been long forgotten. Juley glanced at her husband across the firelit room, her brow furrowed. Why should she be wondering what he would say if she confessed that she had given herself to another man when she was only seventeen?

Barry was hunched up in his chair, staring into the flames, and she knew he was crying.

'Can't you ever forget it?' Immediately she spoke she cursed herself for providing an opening whereby he would inevitably subject her to distress.

'I shall never forget that you killed my mother.' His voice was flat; there was no hint of hatred and Juley felt that in spite of everything Barry still loved her passionately. Yet, ironically, he found it impossible to forgive her for the accident which had resulted in the death of his mother.

Juley remained silent, reliving a very different experience now as she saw herself behind the steering-wheel, the windscreen wipers working overtime to clear snowflakes falling so thickly that visibility was reduced to a mere few yards. The storm had come suddenly, unexpectedly, in one of those freak weather changes which often prove so dangerous to motorists.

Juley had risen that particular morning to sunshine and blue skies, so her shopping spree promised to be a pleasant diversion from the customary chores of a housewife, plus the added burden of caring for her mother-in-law, who, while in

1

good health generally, had suffered a stroke which left her unable to walk more than a few yards at a time. Juley did everything for her, and on that fateful day had even prepared her a midday meal, knowing her Christmas shopping would take her well on into the afternoon. She was looking forward to the complete change of scene, to being all on her own for a while, and especially to having her lunch in the 'Garden Restaurant' of the rather plush Angel Hotel.

'Juley, dear, take me with you.' The totally unexpected plea had brought an instinctive shake of Juley's head but her mother-in-law went on hurriedly, 'I shall be so bored, here on my own all day. I can sit in the car while you do your shopping. I promise I'll not be any trouble to you.'

Juley smiled affectionately. She had always adored her husband's mother and her plea soon weakened her resolve not to take the old lady out unless Barry was there to assist. It was so difficult, getting her in and out of the car, but Barry was now adept at it. Not so Juley. However, she did pause to consider the request and as she looked into the expectant blue eyes she had not the heart to refuse to take Mrs Allen with her.

It was on the way home that the accident happened. It was no fault of Juley's, nor in fact of the other driver. The road was treacherous, the bend acute. Both cars skidded, Juley managing to keep her car on its right side of the road but the other car crashed into it, the driver being helpless to control its course. Mrs Allen died two days later but by some miracle Juley escaped with a few minor scratches and a broken wrist. She did, however, suffer a great deal from shock, especially at the untimely death of the woman she had so dearly loved. The funeral took place only three weeks before Christmas, and Barry, who almost suffered a complete breakdown, and had in fact to be sedated for over a week after the interment, had harboured bitterness ever since. Why had Juley listened to his mother? Where was her common sense in taking on the task of getting her into

2

the car in the first place? Hadn't she promised never to take his mother out unless he was there too? Could she ever deny that she was wholly responsible for his mother's death? On and on it continued, with Juley's guilt complex becoming a heavier burden with every accusation and condemnation her husband made.

'He's always had this excessive adoration for Mother.' Sadie, his sister, said disgustedly when it seemed Barry's brooding bitterness would go on for ever. 'I used to wonder, before he married you, if he had an Oedipus Complex.'

'It's natural for a son to love his mother,' Juley said in his defence, and yet she herself had found his intense adoration difficult to understand. The bond was as strong after his marriage as before, and now that his mother was no longer with him he had changed into a brooding, morose and grief-stricken man whose only words spoken to his wife were those calculated to wound and denounce.

He spoke into the silence, just as Juley was about to ask, for perhaps the hundredth time, if he could forgive her.

'Mother had twenty or more years left, if it hadn't been for you. And you don't seem to care, to be in any way contrite even.'

'Barry, you don't know how I feel, simply because you won't listen to me. Do you suppose I don't miss her as much as you do? I loved her and wanted her to live to be a hundred.' She spoke the truth, despite the fact that the work would have become more difficult as the years went by. But Juley had regarded Mrs Allen as her real mother, simply because her own mother had died when she was born, and her father three years ago, only six months after Juley and Barry were married.

'If you wanted her to live then why did you expose her to risk?' Barry's voice was hoarse and very low.

'You're not being very sensible, are you? Did I know I was exposing her to risk? Of course I didn't, any more than I expected to be in danger myself.' It had often struck Juley that her husband had shown no concern whatsoever for his wife. It did not seem to register with him that the accident could have caused her death as well. In fact, had the other car skidded a second sooner, it would have hit the driver instead of the passenger in the back seat. 'Shall you and I ever be the same, Barry?' This vital question had hovered on her tongue countless times during the past five months, but she had not until now been courageous enough to voice it because she feared the answer. She looked at him intently, her big brown eyes unwavering as he raised his head to meet her gaze. His face was sallow, with the cheeks sunken and the mouth quivering; his hands were clenched in his lap and his eyes were bright, as Juley knew they would be, unnaturally bright. He looked ten years older than his age, she thought, remembering he had a birthday coming soon, his twenty-eighth. He was just a year older than his wife.

'I don't think so,' came the reply at last, the catch in his voice more like a small sob. 'No, we cannot ever be as close as we once were, not with this between us all the time.' There was flat resignation in his tone, and his shoulders sagged even lower. A great quivering sigh rose from the very depths of him and a silence fell like a smothering blanket over the cosy, oak-beamed room.

Juley said, tears stinging her eyes, 'You still love me, Barry—'

'Now is not the time to speak of love!' He spoke coldly, eyes glittering. 'It's all far too new, and crucifying. I – I – shall be years and years getting over – over it!'

She stared, wondering if Sadie was right, and he did have an Oedipus Complex. Yet her tender heart went out to him in his grief. He had always been so close to his mother, unlike Sadie, who had launched out on her own at eighteen, renting an apartment just as soon as she had obtained her first post as clerk in an office. She was all for independence, she had told Juley. She was not the kind of girl who cared for being 'smothered in love' she had frowningly said and added carelessly that her brother had enough filial emotion for the two of them.

'I'm going to bed,' Barry was saying into the silence at last. But as he rose from the chair, Juley, fighting for his happiness as well as her own, went swiftly to him, drew him back into the chair, and knelt beside it.

'I love you, darling. Please, *please* try to accept that it wasn't my fault. Mother wanted to be taken out, and you know she would have been so very bored, on her own all day—'

'There was no need to leave her all day,' he broke in harshly. 'Half a day would have sufficed.'

'I had my Christmas shopping to do,' she returned gently. 'You had said you didn't care for coming with me at the weekends as you wanted your Saturdays for relaxation, and so I decided to do the shopping for presents on my own. I planned to do almost all of it, so as not to have to go again and leave Mother.' She was pleading desperately for a return of the lovely relationship they had enjoyed before the terrible tragedy smashed into their lives as disastrously as that car had smashed into hers. 'You do still love me, Barry, and you also know that this can't go on indefinitely, you know it in your heart just as surely as I know it in mine.' She paused and then, in a voice low and desperately pleading, 'Come to me tonight, darling. Let us be together. Please, Barry.' She possessed an innate pride, and never dreamed she would ever humble herself like this, but when one's life's happiness is at stake, she thought, there is no room for pride. 'I'm pleading with you, my dearest, to be with me tonight.'

It seemed he would not be touched by her pleading, for he sat erect after pulling his hand from under the gentle fingers she had timidly laid upon it. Juley felt almost ill by the unnatural pounding of her heart as she waited, sure that their whole life's future happiness hung on this moment, as Barry stared into the dying embers in the grate, his mouth tight, his body tensed. Then suddenly he seemed to relax, and a smile vanquished all harshness on his lips. But it was a wintry smile, she realized. Nevertheless, it was a start and her own smile illuminated her lovely features – the high cheekbones and classical lines, the enormous brown eyes so widely spaced below delicately curving brows. He looked at her, aware of the full, generous mouth, quivering just a little, and the hope glowing in her eyes. A sigh escaped him; he moved at the same time as she did and their arms came about each other as their lips met. Juley went limp in his embrace. She would comfort him tonight. And once the ice was broken, then surely they would be real lovers once again.

Sadie's eyes were glinting and her mouth was set as she faced her sister-in-law across the café table. Juley had phoned her at work to ask if she would join her for lunch, and so they were eating at the Happy Crêpe, a small select café close to Sadie's office where everything one ordered was wrapped in a delicious crêpe.

'You're saying he's still harbouring a grudge, after you and he had – well – got together again?'

Juley nodded. She had puzzled herself by seeking out her sister-in-law, but she felt she had to talk to someone or she would go mad. If only she could return to work, get back to the busy routine of being a private secretary – the work she had been forced to give up when her mother-in-law had the stroke. But going out to work was impossible now . . .

'I naturally believed we'd be happy again,' she said at last brokenly. 'I thought that normality would return to our marriage, but it was only the once. The next morning he was as horrid with me as ever.'

'And that's six weeks ago.' Sadie was absently playing with a small silver vase holding a posy of flowers. 'You're becoming desperate, naturally?'

Again Juley nodded her head, and trembling fingers spread through her russet-brown hair, brushing it back from her high, intelligent forehead.

She hadn't told Sadie everything, not yet. Nor could she

6

understand her reticence, not when the main reason for this meeting was to impart her news. At least, that was the rather vague idea in Juley's mind when she asked Sadie to meet her. Vague, yes. Everything was vague just now, but how else could one expect it to be?

'I'm having to accept that Barry and I will never be the same again, Sadie,' she murmured, desperate unhappiness in her voice.

A flash of fury brought a heavy frown to Sadie's eyes.

'While I'm fond of my brother, I feel at this moment in time that I could give him a piece of my mind he'd not forget in a hurry! He's crazy to act like this! Doesn't he realize that his marriage could break up? Doesn't he also realize that what is done is done and no amount of pining can bring our mother back?' She was furious with him, and scared of a separation. She cared for both Barry and Juley, cared a lot, and she could not even contemplate a separation and, perhaps, a divorce. It was unthinkable when the two had been so perfectly happy for so long. She sat in silence for a time, then spoke her thoughts aloud.

'Juley, what do you think of going away for a little while? I'm sure it would bring Barry to his senses because he's bound to miss you.'

'Go away? Where to?' How would she live?

'I don't know where to,' Sadie had to admit, but she went on to say that she believed it would not have to be for long at all. 'Barry will come after you sharpish,' she predicted optimistically. She glanced down at the crêpe stuffed with crab that lay untouched on her plate. 'Have you any money?'

'A bit – but Barry and I have a joint account.'

'You can still draw some out. And if it did happen that Barry waited a bit before asking you to return, you could get a job. I'll bet your old boss would find you something in his office.'

Juley hesitated, wondering again why she was now reluctant to disclose to Sadie that she was pregnant. She had been to see the doctor only yesterday to make absolutely sure. It was ironical that she and Barry had been trying for a baby for the past two years without success, and now that they were estranged she was to have his child. Obviously she had considered telling him, sure the news would soften him, make him look forward to the new life instead of brooding on the past. But she was prevented in some way she failed to understand, prevented from saying anything about the baby yet.

'You might have a point,' she found herself saying, rather to her surprise, 'about my going away, I mean. As you say, Barry is sure to miss me.'

Sadie said an idea had just come to her. 'You remember that ancient aunt of Joan's – the one who lives by the sea?'

'Yes, she had you and Joan staying with her once.' Joan was a very good friend of Sadie's. They had gone about together until a few months ago when Joan began going steady with the man she had recently become engaged to.

'Well, she writes to me now and then, and always says she wishes she has a visitor, and when am I coming to see her again.'

'But she wouldn't want me, a stranger.' Although seriously discussing the possibility of going away for a while, Juley had a sinking feeling in the pit of her stomach at the idea of parting from the husband she so dearly loved.

'I know she would want you,' stated Sadie with conviction. 'Can I phone her this evening and suggest you go and stay with her?' She cut into her crêpe at last, but held the piece suspended on her fork as she looked at Juley across the table. 'Give it a try,' she urged. 'I'll bet Barry will be after you within a week.'

The confidence in her tone cheered Juley but she was not so confident that she could envisage his seeking her out within a week. It all depended on just how deep his resentment against her went, mused Juley as she found herself saying, 'Yes, I'll give it a try.'

'Good! I guess this lunch date will prove to be profitable.'

*   *   *

But Sadie had reckoned without the possibility of her brother's turning to someone else for comfort. He believed he was gravely injured anyway, without the added upset of his wife's going away and leaving him all alone.

And it so happened that, by sheer coincidence, he ran into an old flame only four days after Juley had gone to stay with Joan's aged aunt, an old flame with whom he had enjoyed a torrid affair before she'd gone to work up in Scotland. Now she was back and Sadie, on calling on her brother to see 'how the land was lying', as she told Juley on the phone before she went, was stupified to find Greta Worthing in the kitchen – Juley's kitchen! – cooking dinner for two.

'What the hell's going on here?!' she was swift to demand, blue eyes flashing fire. 'Barry, what is this woman doing in this house?'

'You know Greta of course.' For the first time since his mother's death he seemed cheerful. 'She's being kind enough to make herself useful until Juley decides she's had enough and comes running back.'

Infuriated that he could speak of his wife like that, Sadie was speechless, unable to assimilate the fact that her idea had gone sadly awry. Barry, it would appear, was not in the least pining for his wife. On the contrary, he looked almost happy.

'You do know where Juley is,' she managed at last, her voice quivering with rage as she watched Greta, a most satisfied smirk on her face, turning two steaks which she had drawn from under the grill. 'She left you her address – I know because she told me.'

'I do have her address, but no intention of going down on my knees begging her to come back.'

'She won't be expecting you to go down on your knees!'

'Barry, darling, you did say you liked yours medium to well?' from Greta as if she just had to interrupt. 'Dinner won't be more than another five minutes,' she added with a significant glance in Sadie's direction.

*　　*　　*

9

'I played merry hell,' Sadie was telling Juley the following evening when, having decided she must see her sister-in-law, she took a day off work to travel down to Devon. The following day was Saturday, soe she planned to stay with Juley and the old lady till Sunday afternoon, there being a train back to Chester at three fifteen. 'It's incredible. Barry must have taken leave of his senses!'

Deathly pale, and with her nerves quivering, Juley stared dully at her sister-in-law, unable to speak for the moment. She seemed to have become dazed by the information brought to her; she felt herself to be drifting into a vacuum where all thought and movement were denied her. When at last she was able to speak it was in a dry, cracked monotone, startlingly different from the more familiar musical voice which everyone who knew her found so very attractive.

'I – I believed he loved m-me, but now I'm beginning to – to wonder.' What would become of her should Barry fall in love with his old flame? The baby would have to be fed and clothed. Oddly, the obvious course evaded Juley's consciousness. Yet even if it had occurred to her that this was certainly the time to tell her husband about their child she would instantly have dismissed the idea. She needed time to think, to watch and wait, to discover what Barry would do if she did not return just yet. Perhaps she was foolish, allowing the affair – if at this stage it could be called an affair – to develop to that point where the other woman was in a position to snatch her husband from her.

'You must go back without delay.' Sadie's tone was urgent. Plainly crestfallen, she was guiltily aware that it was her suggestion that Juley should leave her home, which had left it wide open for another woman to enter it. 'I'm so sorry I persuaded you to leave, Juley.'

'Don't apologize.' Juley put a shaking hand to her throbbing temple. 'It's fate. I'm beginning to think that Barry thought more of his mother than of me, and if that were the case then there was no future for us anyway. I adored her as you know, and wanted her to be with us for a long time, but I'd never have been happy knowing that, with Barry, his mother came first.'

'Certainly a wife should come before anyone else in the world,' agreed Sadie, still overwhelmed by guilt. If only she had left Juley to sort out her own life instead of putting an idea into her mind that had failed miserably.

Looking at her, as they sat on the patio of the comfortable Victorian house in which Juley had come to stay, Juley read Sadie's mind and was swift to say, 'Don't blame yourself. I came of my own free will, remember.'

'But at my instigation.'

'It was your idea, granted, but I had no need to act upon it. In any case, it might prove to be a lesson I am learning now instead of later.'

'A lesson?' frowned Sadie, eyes wandering momentarily to the large disused barn and ancillary outbuildings which had once formed part of the old farm worked by Aunt Emma's grandfather. Today all the land had been sold off for the housing estate which had crept almost up to the old lady's back door. 'What do you mean, Juley?'

'If Barry was going to be unfaithful to me I'd rather learn about it now than at some future date.'

'Don't be silly!' flashed Sadie in angry tones. 'There's no question of my brother's being unfaithful to you. This will all blow over and you very well know it.'

Juley looked at her. She was desperately trying to assume a confidence she did not feel. Yes, Sadie was well aware of the risk, with Greta in the house with Barry, and Barry feeling so bitterly resentful, blaming his wife for the death of his mother.

'I feel I want to be entirely alone . . .' Juley spoke her thoughts aloud, then had to continue, as Sadie was looking questioningly at her. 'If I were quite alone I might be able to think clearly, estimate the probable consequences of my leaving home.'

'You ought to go back at once,' urged Sadie.

But all Juley returned to that was, 'I'll think about it . . . yes, I'll think about it.'

Two

'Greta was kind enough to look after me, that's all.' Petulant, and at the same time on the defensive, Barry faced his wife as she stood with her back to the stove. She had automatically gone to the kitchen, just to see if everything was as she had left it. Strange, she thought, how possessive a woman could be about her kitchen, especially as it wasn't exactly the place where she was her happiest. She had timed her arrival home for three o'clock in the afternoon, so that she would be there when Barry came in from work. But he'd had a day off, so was at home when she arrived. She stared at him now, a few minutes after noticing several changes had been made in the kitchen, silly little things which should not have irritated, but they did. Why should Greta have moved the kettle to the other plug, or the set of jugs to another shelf?! Juley's fists tightened with emotion but she contained her anger, not wanting to quarrel with her husband. He said, 'You chose to go away, to leave me. It could have been a permanent separation for all I knew. How was I to know what was in your mind?' His tone was crisp and cool and she flashed him a glance.

'This is my home and you shall not bring other women into it!' She was pale with anger but her voice was steady and without passion. 'Just tell that woman she is to keep away – or else.'

'Or else – what?' There was an arrogance about him now, and a sort of sneering challenge which filled her with foreboding.

Nevertheless, she was able to look him in the eye and answer calmly, 'Or else I might throw her out.'

A smile of amusement took the arrogance from his mouth.

'What makes you so confident you could match her strength?'

'Are you on her side?' Juley was no longer angry; she was alert to the seriousness of her position. 'You're surely not going to see her again, now that I'm back home.' Should she tell him about the baby? It would certainly make him answer in the way she wanted him to, but she kept silent and he told her deliberately that he would be seeing Greta that very evening.

'And tomorrow evening,' he added slowly, stressing every word. 'In fact, Juley, your leaving me could lead to the end of our marriage. You see, with Greta there is not the constant reminder of the untimely death of my mother. With you it is there all the time. I am faced with it every time I look at you, and so—'

'Barry,' she broke in with sudden desperation, 'you love *me*! Don't deny it – you can't truthfully deny it!'

He turned away as if unable to meet the challenge in her lovely eyes, eyes that were far too bright owing to the tears gathering behind them. It was an eternity before he spoke but at last she heard him say, 'I shall not deny it, Juley. I do love you and always will. But I'm finding it impossible to forgive you for my mother's death. He stopped abruptly and swung round to face her. His head was bent as if in defeat and hopelessness but although his mouth trembled owing to the depth of his emotions, he could not absolve her from blame regarding his mother's death. 'During those days you've been away,' he continued when she did not attempt to speak, 'I felt so free from the grim atmosphere which seemed to have overshadowed this house since Mother was killed in an accident that never should have involved her because she ought not to have been in the car.' He stopped again, this time to redden at his wife's expression which clearly accused him of forgetting that *she* was also at risk. He shrugged after a moment and went on, 'It was all so different while you were away. I was not so weighed down with grief.' He paused as if carefully considering the words yet to come. 'When I met Greta again it was all the old times, the good times, that I was recalling, not that terrible accident. And when Greta and I had a meal together it was wonderful – so pleasant and free from the smothering atmosphere that now exists when you and I are alone.'

'So it was . . . wonderful.' She swallowed convulsively, very sure that she could not mention the baby now.

'The total absence of tension within me.' His glance of apology appeared ludicrous to Juley. 'I knew a lightness I hadn't known for the past months.'

'In other words,' interposed Juley in a tight little voice, 'my very presence oppresses you.' It was not a question but obviously he had some comment to make. He nodded and said she was quite right: her presence did oppress him, all the time.

It was a long time before Juley spoke. She had walked into the living room, the charming, tastefully furnished room which was mainly her creation, as Barry had no bent for decor or design when it came to planning a room. He had followed her and was standing with his hand resting on the mantelshelf, staring broodingly at her.

'Do you want a – a . . . ?' For a small interval silence descended again as Juley swallowed to clear the pain from her throat. 'You want a divorce?' The words came at last and she strove valiantly to stem the tears which threatened. What about the baby? Their baby?

'I wouldn't make such a drastic decision as that without some further thought.' Barry gave a deep sigh as he turned towards the door. 'We must both consider all the implications,' he recommended presently. 'One thing is certain: we can't go on as we have been doing, not indefinitely.'

'But it's your fault entirely!' she cried. 'You haven't tried to forgive me!' She remembered that Sadie had stated categorically there was nothing to forgive. Her mother's time had come; it was fate and certainly nothing to do with Juley. But such was the persistence of her husband in his condemnations that by now Juley had reached that state where she genuinely believed she really was to blame, and so it was forgiveness she asked. 'Why haven't you tried, Barry, tried to forgive me?'

'For killing my mother? Juley, when will you realize it isn't something one can forgive in a matter of weeks or even months. It could take years.' And with that he turned and left the room.

Juley sat down on the sofa, put her face in her hands and sobbed hysterically into them.

'What shall I do – whatever must I do now?' She had no one to turn to other than Sadie but she could not bring herself to go to her husband's sister for help in her plight. If only she was able to work . . . Maybe she could get a job for a while – but where would she live?

Desperate, and feeling she had not a friend in the world, Juley wished she could die, escape the stress and uncertainties that loomed so darkly before her.

But soon she was bravely telling herself that her situation was by no means unique; other women had faced a similar situation. Yes, she would try to get a job and somewhere to live, but she would never ever tell Barry about the baby, never as long as she lived.

She stared at the doctor in silence, the very blood in her veins seeming to have frozen solid. Her mouth was dry, a result of the suffocating pain in her throat. She spoke at last, to murmur brokenly, 'My baby, doctor . . . ? What about my baby?'

There was another silence, tense and extended, while Dr Blount toyed uncomfortably with the report on the table in front of him.

'Juley,' he said at last in a sternly inflected tone, 'y
must tell your husband—'

'No! Do you suppose I shall let that woman bring up
baby? Call her Mother! Barry is intending to marry he
soon as the divorce is through, and if I tell him about Ja
he'll want him.'

'Barry is his father,' broke in the doctor gently. 'And
that you are – are –'

'Dying! Can't you say it – and you a doctor!' She w
her wits' end, faintly hysterical under the weight pres
down upon her, heavier and heavier. She had survived
ordeal of living alone through her pregnancy, having ref
to win Barry back by using the one weapon which cou
all probability have made him drop the idea of divorce.
had told Sadie she had no wish to see her any more, ma
it appear she was bitter because she happened to be Ba
sister. Sadie, puzzled and yet hurt to the point where
took exception to Juley's behaviour, had said all right!
would not see each other again! And she had stalke
head in the air. To Juley it meant she was able to hide
Sadie the fact that she was pregnant. She had manag
get a job and had worked for a while, living in the
she had shared with Barry, as he had been the one to
after deciding he wanted a divorce. He was living with
in her flat but had instructed his solicitor to tell Jule
must sell the house and let him have his half share.
having lived more meagrely than ever before in her lif
saved hard, so had been able to foot the expenses of
the baby. Barry had, however, made her a small allov
sent via the solicitor, so this had helped.

Then suddenly she had begun to have headaches a
birth of her baby and as they became severe the
arranged for her to see a specialist. The result was t
learned she had about six months to live.

'If you don't tell your husband,' Dr Blount was
'then I shall.'

17

Glassy-eyed, she lifted her face to look at him.

'I shall never hand James over to Barry, so you needn't think you can make me.'

He drew an impatient breath, brushing a hand through his sparse white hair.

'Juley,' he said with some impatience while plainly trying to be gentle, 'you must know there is only one course open to you under the circumstances. You should have told Barry long before this, before the baby was born, and you know it. Barry can claim his son once his mother is – dead. So why not let him have James now? Then you can do something with the time left to you.'

She could only stare in bewilderment. What could one plan for a six-month lifetime? And what did he mean by asking her to give up her baby to a man she was not even married to? In any case, Greta would have something to say about taking on a baby – another woman's child. Perhaps even when she and Barry were married she would not want the child— Juley halted her train of thought, tension rising as she whispered vehemently to herself, 'I shall *not* give him up! I shall keep him till the very end!'

The doctor stirred restlessly; she knew he, too, was under strain but he spoke to her curtly, clipping off his words.

'I repeat, Barry must be told that he has a son.'

'And if I don't tell him, you will, you say?' She stared directly at him with a challenging look. He frowned and looked troubled, as she hoped he would because she had no wish that he should be tempted to contact her husband. He said, far more gently now, 'Don't do anything silly, my dear. Promise me.'

'And don't you contact Barry.'

His frown deepened.

'Then you will contact him?'

'I shall think about it.' She was white to the lips, every nerve within her quivering. 'I'll phone you in about a week's time.'

'A week?' with a lift of his bushy eyebrows. 'Why so long?'

'It's not a decision I can make in a hurry.'

He looked at her suspiciously and said on a very troubled note, 'Are you planning something, Juley?'

'Such as?'

He tapped the report which the specialist had sent to him earlier that day.

'When people become desperate they are liable to act illogically. They do things they never would do—'

'Like taking a life? Dr Blount, I am not thinking of killing my child. I'm his mother and I love him.'

'I wasn't suggesting you would kill your baby. But your manner – it worries me. I believe you are going to act in some foolish way.'

She stood up, taking her handbag from the table where she had placed it on entering the consulting room.

'I shall act in a perfectly logical way, I assure you.' She paused a second. 'I shall do what I consider best for my baby. Good afternoon, Doctor.'

There was nothing else for it, decided Juley in desperation. James would have to go to his father. The decision had been reached after long sleepless nights followed by days of anguished uncertainty and misgiving. When first she had told the doctor she would phone in a week's time, Juley had some vague idea of trying to have her baby adopted, fobbing the doctor off in some way while negotiations were going on. But that course was fraught with difficulties, not least of which was that in any event the father's consent would have to be sought and given. Adding to Juley's troubles was the fact that the headaches had grown more severe and were recurring rather more frequently than before. So it seemed she ought to begin making concrete plans for her baby's future. For although she had been given six months, Dr Blount had stressed the possibility of the end coming much sooner than that. She could not risk the calamity of dropping dead and leaving James uncared for until someone happened to notice such things as milk left on the doorstep, or other signs that something was amiss. Had her neighbour, kind Mrs Furbishly, been at home all the time it might have been different, but the old lady spent more than half her time visiting her three daughters in turn. Moreover, she had no idea that Juley was ill. Juley could not have said why she was reluctant to confide in her neighbour; all she did know was that she would not be happy with too much sympathy.

Her decision having been made, Juley wept and wept, seeing Greta with her baby, perhaps not treating him right, especially if and when she had children of her own. Barry would not be there all the time to see his son was treated properly, and with affection. What kind of child would James become if he were deprived of his birthright: love? And later, what kind of a man would he become? All these heartsearchings naturally brought floods of tears, resulting in Juley becoming ill in other ways than the brain tumour which was to kill her before very long.

Pale and thin-faced, she did not realize just how troubled her neighbour would become. Mrs Furbishly had of course known Barry – in fact, she was living there when they took over their house; she had watched with interest all they did to beautify their new home, and then shown horror when the split came and she saw another woman going in and out of the house while Juley was away. But soon it was Barry who left and Juley became rather close to her neighbour, who was kindness itself. When repeatedly questioned as to how the split had happened, Juley said, 'It was the accident. Barry blames me for his mother's death.'

Mrs Furbishly was disgusted by his attitude but assured Juley that he would soon come to his senses and want her to have him back. Well, she had been wrong in her supposition. Barry had decided he wanted to end the marriage.

He was in love with Greta. Mrs Furbishly now did not have one good word for the man she had initially liked so very much.

Having firmly decided to see the doctor and tell him of her decision, Juley went to ask Mrs Furbishly to have James for an hour or two. It was a request not often made, as Juley had a fervid passion to make the most of every single moment of what life was left to her, and that, at this time, naturally included having her baby with her all the time. But when she had to visit the doctor, or had some heavy shopping to carry, she would ask this favour of her neighbour.

A frown instantly appeared on the old lady's brow when she opened the door.

'Are you ill, child?' she asked concernedly, opening the door wide as a silent invitation for Juley to enter the hall. 'You're so pale – as though you haven't been sleeping or eating.' She paused but only for a second. 'Something's wrong, isn't it? Money worries? If so, get that husband of yours into court, and quick sharp! He must know that a baby is expensive.'

Juley went in and the door closed behind her. James was in his pram, sleeping in the sunshine and Juley automatically looked through the window as she entered the sitting room. She had not told her neighbour that Barry had been kept in ignorance of the baby; luckily he was living forty miles away on the other side of town now, so there was little chance of Mrs Furbishly seeing him.

'It isn't money,' she answered, eyes again wandering to the pram on her front lawn. 'I wonder if you will have James while I go out?'

'You know I will.' A pause followed as the older woman's eyes took the direction of Juley's gaze. 'Nothing wrong with him, is there?'

Juley shook her head.

'James is perfect, Mrs Furbishly. 'Just perfect—' Her

voice broke and she was sobbing into her hands. 'I'm sorry about this,' she quivered even as the old lady's arms came about her.

In a soothing voice Mrs Furbishly said, 'It's becoming too much for you, child. If only you had parents living – or a mother at least. What is to be done?' No answer because Juley was still crying. 'When James is at school it will all be much better for you, dear. You'll be able to take a part-time job, maybe.' She went on, talking of the future, a future Juley would never see. At last, in control of her emotions again, Juley offered another apology and glanced at the clock.

'I must rush,' she said and although it was plain that Mrs Furbishly was puzzled, she did not ask where she was going, much to Juley's relief. 'I'll be back by four o'clock at the latest,' she was saying a few minutes later, having wheeled the pram on to her neighbour's lawn. She bent to kiss the chubby face of her sleeping child, then hurried away before Mrs Furbishly should see the tears.

The doctor was not at his surgery.

'I can't think what has happened.' His dispenser glanced worriedly at her watch. 'He knew you had an appointment.'

'I'll have to make another.' Juley turned at once; she wanted to get away before the doctor came – if he came. And the reason was that she had the sudden desire to delay the parting with her child.

It was later that afternoon that she decided to begin clearing out drawers and cupboards, destroying papers, snapshots, even the wedding album was put with the items to be burned the next day at the bottom of the garden.

And then the snapshot came to light, tucked into the envelope containing her birth certificate and her parents' marriage certificate.

'Charles . . .' How had this snapshot survived when all the others had been thrown away when she became engaged to Barry? Strange that it should have become tucked away in this envelope. Perhaps it had somehow got into the envelope before the certificates. What did it matter how it had come to survive? she thought with an impatient frown. She gazed at the face, while memories flowed in, and a blush brought colour to her pallid cheeks. 'Charles, where are you now? Do you ever think of that night? Are you married? Happier than I? Have you a baby like my little James? Suddenly she felt icy cold; she dropped the snapshot on to the dressing-table and rubbed her hands together . . . only to revive another memory, that of Charles's warm strong hands enclosing hers to give them some of their heat. She stared, fascinated now, at the dark, arrogant features, the straight classical nose and obstinate chin, the bronzed skin – and those dark, piercing eyes below straight black brows. His mother was Mexican, his father Irish. A mixture that had produced both strength and fire, a temper swift to ignite and just as swift to die, an imperiousness, a mastery. So much character in one man. 'How old are you now?' He was a mere twenty-one at the time she was just seventeen. So he was now approaching thirty, she mused. Still in the very prime of life. She could imagine the maturity given him by the added years. Lines, perhaps, and a hint of grey in that very dark brown hair – yes, it was almost black, she remembered, and how thick – so exciting to handle, to run fingers through! That mouth . . . her own lips quivered as she recalled,

'This night is ours whatever else happens. Come to me, dearest.'

She tried to cut her thoughts but found herself living again the rapture, the flight to paradise. And suddenly she was admitting that nothing Barry had given her could come anywhere near the ecstasy she had experienced with Charles Burke. She had known why Charles had taken her. He had wanted to make her pregnant so that his father would have to give his consent to their marriage. Not that Charles needed

23

it as he was old enough to please himself. It was Juley who had brought the affair to an end, and she would never forget Charles's fury. She had half expected him to do her a physical injury, such was his anger. He had been willing to defy his father and marry the girl he loved, but even at that early age Juley had had sufficient common sense to realize that the day would come when Charles would regret what he had sacrificed, as old Mr Burke was a millionaire several times over, owning a castle on the shores of Lough Corrib, another home in Florida and a mansion in Spain. His business was linen and glass which he shipped to almost every corner of the globe. It was a vast concern, the Burke empire, and to Juley there inevitably must eventually be some regret on Charles's part should he impulsively marry her against his father's will and lose his entire inheritance. Mr Burke had said quite categorically, when he spoke to Juley after having summoned her into his presence, that should his son marry her he would cut him off without a penny.

'What do I care?' scoffed Charles, who had met Juley at a garden fête when she had tripped up and literally fallen into his arms. For him it was love at first sight, but for Juley, who had never had a boyfriend before, the next few weeks were ones of confusion and uncertainty, a situation helped by the suspicion that Charles's father, whom she had not even met at that time, would never approve of her as a suitable wife for his son. But Charles was certainly a man to be desired, and admired. Handsome in a severe kind of way, he was well over six feet tall, with the physique of an athlete in his prime. He walked with the air of a king and often, seen in a pensive mood, he seemed unapproachable, too stern and arrogant, too godlike for mixing with mere mortals. But with Juley he was all passionate tenderness, and now as she gazed down at his photograph, she saw that same tenderness as he looked into her camera. 'What do I care for the old man?' he had repeated. 'Let him cut me off. We'll manage. I'll make my own way in life with you by my side.'

24

It was the idyllic dream of a youth madly in love, Juley's friend had convinced her.

'Think before you act, Juley,' she had warned. 'The day must surely come when Charles will regret his foolhardiness. It is up to you to guide him, to prevent him from ruining his life.'

And although Juley did have suspicions that her friend was a bit envious of her, Juley took heed of her advice and told Charles she could not marry him. He appeared not at all perturbed at that time, and it was later that Juley realized he had planned to bring about a situation where marriage would be imperative as his father would assuredly insist on it on learning that Juley was pregnant.

And that night . . . The night Charles's car broke down on that lonely mountain road, so conveniently close to a small stone cottage standing unoccupied and owned by the man on whose land it was: Mr Burke's. Warmth met Juley as she entered and she knew that Charles had been there earlier. He had lit a fire then let it go out; there was a sofa, and even soft cushions on it.

Half in love with him as she was, despite her determination to avoid heartbreak, Juley found herself ignoring these signs, and welcoming the shelter of the cottage. Charles had seemed to accept her decision anyway, so she had nothing to fear, she told herself. Later, as she went over Charles's attitude and behaviour, she knew his acceptance was assumed, that he was *not* resigned to losing her. On the contrary, he meant to marry her, and in his own imperious way he had made his plans.

'This night is ours,' His words came drifting back through the opening mist of memory and everything became vividly clear. The words began ringing over and over again in her mind and almost angrily she thrust the snapshot into the pile which was to be burned the following morning. 'This night is ours . . .'

*　　*　　*

'Dead?' Juley shook her head in a stupified way. 'Barry . . . dead?'

Dr Blount seemed almost unable to add more to what he had already said. Juley was aware that Barry, having moved, had changed his doctor, but somehow, it would appear, word of the accident had come to her own doctor's ears. His tone was hoarse and low when he eventually explained what had happened. Barry and Greta had been to a party and both had had too much to drink. The car had crashed into a tree. Luckily no other vehicle was involved.

'James,' murmured Juley in a cracked little voice, 'where will he go now?' The fact of her husband's death was registering only in the way it affected her child. She was as yet unable to assimilate all the other aspects of the tragedy, the cutting short of Barry's life in much the same way his mother's had been cut. And if Mrs Allen had not died then neither would Barry have died because he would not have been in that car with Greta. Such was fate, and Sadie would say what has to be will be.

Juley did not examine her feelings as they applied to her love for Barry; she still loved him, she told herself, but yet her whole mind was occupied with her baby and what was to happen to him now. 'Oh, God, Doctor, whatever am I to do!' She felt she was bordering on insanity, because she wanted to scream, against fate and what it was doing to her and James. 'I'm desperate now – *desperate*, can't you see!'

He had come prepared, and the tablets did calm her quickly. He made her sit down, spoke softly to her, assuring her that he and his wife would make sure James was cared for should anything happen to Juley in the very near future.

'However,' he went on soothingly, 'we are not expecting anything calamitous to occur yet, and so we can discuss James's future in a week or so, when you have recovered from this added shock.'

She looked up at him through eyes glazed by anxiety and

bewilderment. Why were these things happening to her? What had she done to deserve all this distress?

'I'm at my wits' end,' she cried, unable to sip the tea the doctor had made for her, in her own kitchen. 'I wish James had never been born!' She did not wish that at all, yet conversely, she was thinking that all would be so much more simple if she had only herself to worry about.

'I know just how you are feeling, Juley. And my wife has asked me to take you back to our home, to stay for a while. I can take James's cot and pram in my shooting brake.'

She looked at him, suddenly aware that he had no knowledge of her sister-in-law's existence. She and Barry had registered with him on their marriage, when they had settled in his area, but although Christian names were soon being used by him, he was not on that kind of footing where the couple had made any confidences, or references to relatives. He knew of Mrs Allen, naturally, as he had attended her after she had come to live with Juley and her husband, but Sadie had never been mentioned to him. However, as Juley would have to get in touch with her now that her brother was dead, this meant that Sadie would learn about the baby. Perhaps she would be willing to take him. The possibility was cheering in the midst of Juley's depression and confusion of mind. She declined the doctor's offer, telling him she had a sister-in-law with whom she would immediately get in touch.

'A sister-in-law?' Dr Blount looked amazed. 'Then why haven't you solicited her help before now?' Are you not friends?'

'We were, but I didn't want her to know about the baby. She'd have told Barry—'

'Who should have been told anyway,' interrupted the doctor, frowning as Juley shrugged off the rebuke.

'It wouldn't matter much now, would it?' she said logically.

A sigh escaped him.

'I suppose not. Well, can I contact this sister-in-law for you?'

She shook her head.

'I'll phone her as soon as you've gone. She'll be devastated about Barry . . . I wonder why she hasn't phoned me already. She must surely know of the accident?'

'I got to know from Barry's doctor. You see, we were in contact when Barry changed his doctor after moving away. So Dr Meredith immediately phoned me, only an hour or so ago, so perhaps this sister of Barry's does not yet know of the accident.' Dr Blount looked down at the untouched cup of tea. 'Try to eat something,' he advised. 'And do make use of your neighbour. She sounds as if she'll be a great help to you—'

'She's away from home, Doctor,' cut in Juley, a flatness in her tone. 'I could have done with her help and sympathy now . . .' She shrugged her shoulders. 'She often goes away, visiting her daughters.'

When Juley phoned Sadie's number it was to hear the reply: 'Miss Allen does not live here now. She got married and left the same day for Australia. I'm the new tenant. Sorry I can't help. I don't even know her married name.'

Another shock. Juley cursed herself for not keeping in touch.

'So you don't have her address?' A useless question, decided Juley but went on to add, 'I'm her sister-in-law and must find her.'

'Sorry, no. I'm merely the tenant who took over when she left. I've rented this flat through a house agent. He might know more about your sister-in-law. I'll give you his name and address.' This she did and Juley took it down. But the agent knew no more than the woman to whom Juley had spoken.

'From what I gathered at the time,' he said, 'there was some haste as her fiancé had obtained a post in Australia, so they were married quickly and went off the same day.'

'I see. Thank you.' As she replaced the receiver Juley wondered what would happen next, and suddenly she was afraid, desperately afraid that she would die before she had made provision for her child. So much was happening. Her stars were all in the wrong place, she thought.

'Perhaps I'll find Sadie's address among Barry's belongings . . .' The idea of going through them was far from pleasant but of course it had to be done. However, it was a wasted journey for as Barry was living in Greta's flat it was her mother who took possession, and she refused Juley entry.

'It should not be difficult to find her,' Dr Blount assured Jule. 'Leave it to me.'

'But if she's over there, and newly married, she won't want to be saddled with a child who isn't hers.'

The doctor looked steadfastly at her.

'You don't want James to have a father who might not treat him as his own son, is that it?'

Tears gathered; angrily she swept them away with the back of her hand. Tears hadn't done her much good up till now, she thought, bringing out a handkerchief.

'I don't know what to do!' she cried, desperately striving to see some flicker of light in the black void around her. Was there no way out of her dilemma? 'The headaches are getting worse and I don't think I shall last much longer.'

'The stress is causing the headaches to increase, but if you could get James settled you would find they would not be so frequent, at least, not at this stage. Later, yes . . .'

'You believe that?'

He nodded his head.

'Yes, in fact, I'm sure of it.' He paused and a gravity came over his face, and a hint of anxiety too. 'I have a solution, Juley,' he told her at length. 'No, don't interrupt just now. Let me say a little more. I have a couple coming to see me to find out about adoption. They are suggesting I help them, because they are unable to have a child of

29

their own. Both have consulted another doctor and their case is hopeless; they can never hope to have a child of their own.' He paused to watch her expression. She was nodding slowly but tears had brightened her eyes. He knew his point had gone home. 'They are definitely intending to adopt a baby.'

Juley shut her eyes tightly, stemming the tears that were ready to flow. How she loved little James! And to let him go, to strangers, was something that would tear the very heart out of her . . . but she knew she had at least to consider this proposal and she heard her own voice, so low and indistinct, telling the doctor that he could arrange a meeting between this couple and herself.

'I will, my dear,' was his ready and relieved reply. 'They are charming; you'll find no fault with them. They are so kind and loving towards one another—'

'Then they might not have enough love for my baby!' Distraught now, she scarcely knew what she was saying.

The doctor returned gently, 'You'd rather they were a happy couple than otherwise.' And somehow that produced a smile.

She said, 'Of course I would. Please arrange the meeting soon . . .' She swayed in the chair. 'I'm going!' she gasped even as the doctor came to her side. 'Oh, please God, don't let me go until I have my baby's future settled.'

'And now,' Dr Blount was saying with a smile, 'you must think what you are to do with the time left to you.'

'It's about four months, you say?' So calm now after the trauma of Barry's funeral and then the handing over of her baby to the charming couple who, she knew for sure, would love him as if he were their own. He wasn't legally adopted yet, as this took time, but the Donnellys, Mary and Oliver, were fostering James and, reluctant as she had been to let him go just yet, Juley had allowed the doctor's persuasion, and her own common sense, to

30

prevail. The couple might just apply for another baby, the doctor had pointed out and this swiftly finalized Juley's decision. And now she had about four months, so she felt she had been given a bonus which, Dr Blount advised, should be used in trying to find contentment and peace of mind. But before she could think of herself there was one thing troubling her.

'How long before the adoption can be arranged?' she wanted to know. 'You see, if I did happen to die soon, before the papers were signed, then the Authority would take James and he'd be brought up in care and I do not want that for my child.'

His admiration for her concern was apparent as the doctor replied, 'I'm working on it, Juley, so don't trouble yourself like this. In view of the circumstances – that you have so little time left – we are sure of being able to get the adoption papers through without the usual waste of time.'

'Then I can put the house in the hands of an agent, and try to sell it, as you've advised?'

'Certainly sell it if you can. It was on the market before Barry died and you did mention that a couple were keenly interested in buying it.'

'That's right. The agent is very keen to let them have it.' She gave a small sigh. 'You advised me to get the money and then go off somewhere for a holiday, but when I think about that course, I – I get frightened. Surely I'd be better staying around here, where I can be sure of help when – when the t-time c-comes . . .' Her voice faltered to an unsteady halt and it was not difficult for the doctor to read her mind. Help, as she called it, would not do her much good when at last the time did arrive. She gave another deep sigh and looked at him with a dull expression in her lovely eyes. 'A holiday isn't the answer,' she told him decisively. 'If I could get a job – sort of housekeeper or something like that, I'd take it and get away.' She had suddenly realized it would be a crucifying experience were she to see her baby with its new mother. 'I ought to get away, Doctor,' she added finally and he nodded in agreement.

It was to transpire that two circumstances made Juley's life a little easier.

'And not before time,' had been the doctor's grim reaction. 'If anyone needs a bit of luck it is you.'

'You must have worked hard to get the adoption through so quickly.' The desolation seemed to have evaporated with the news given to her and she was immeasurably grateful to Dr Blount for his sustained assistance. 'He's now legally adopted by parents who already adore him.' Her voice caught but bravely she managed a smile, much to her doctor's satisfaction. 'And the house sold – and now this job you've found me. I must tell you this, though, I'm not telling my employer about my health, for even though she only wants temporary help, I'm sure she'd not be taking me on if she knew the true situation that I'm in.'

Dr Blount nodded his head.

'I agree, and that is why I haven't mentioned anything to Mrs Greatrix. Though she's bound to realize something's wrong eventually.'

'Of course, but if I have four months, or even three . . .' She paused to reckon up and decided she had only about three and a half months, that was, presupposing the specialist's conclusion was correct. She caught her lip and bit it cruelly – an unconscious action, and the pain inflicted was nothing to the agony of heart and mind. To die before she was twenty-six years old. To be parted from her child . . . but she should be thanking God for the parents who now had him safely in their care, legally adopted.

The doctor was saying, 'Mrs Greatrix says she needs help only for about eight to ten weeks.'

'It's a long way to go,' she murmured almost to herself.

'Cumberland? Yes, I suppose it is.'

'Companion to a lady whose regular companion is visiting

relatives in Canada.' She glanced up. 'You heard of Mrs Greatrix through a friend, you said.'

'Yes. I remember the lady's name came up quite casually, so casually that I can't remember how, but I do recall that it immediately struck me that the post was just made for you.'

'It was fortunate.' She pushed a hand through her dark hair and he noticed the healthy sheen and gilded highlights and a silent sigh escaped him. Such a beautiful girl, and so young . . .

Juley and her future employer took to one another instantly. Examining the older woman's features, Juley saw fine classical lines, severe yet compassionate, a wide, full mouth and determined chin. The straight nose was rather too large for beauty, but the features were, overall, most attractive and Juley wondered why she had never married again after being widowed at only thirty-four years of age. Mrs Greatrix, surveying the young woman whose recommendation had come through her doctor, found herself faintly puzzled that such a lovely girl should be interested in a post which was to last a mere couple of months or maybe a little longer. Mrs Greatrix could not help but appreciate the perfection of a face which, at the same time, gave the impression of sadness, even deep grief. She decided now was certainly not the time to question the girl and steered the conversation on to the matter of the duties she would expect of her.

On hearing the 'list' Juley could not resist saying, 'You do not appear to need a companion, Mrs Greatrix.'

The curving eyebrows were instantly raised.

'I strike you as totally self-sufficient?'

A small nod accompanied Juley's answer.

'Yes, as a matter of fact, you do, Mrs Greatrix.'

'Neverthless, I have periods of loneliness, even depression. That surprises you, I see. Perhaps I shall tell you my story one day . . . and you might tell me yours,' she added without having had any intention of doing so.

A startled glance assured the older woman that she was not mistaken in sensing a mystery.

'I cannot imagine your being depressed.' Juley was not affording her the chance of steering the subject on to personal lines.

'Everyone becomes depressed sometime, Mrs Allen.' She hesitated, a faint line knitting her brow. 'I must ask you a question – just one.'

'Yes?' Juley's nerves became alert. 'I hope it isn't too personal, Mrs Greatrix.'

A smile resulted from that.

'You don't talk about yourself, is that it?'

'I prefer not to.' Juley hoped her tone was not too chilly.

'I shall respect your wish. Nevertheless, I am asking if you are separated from your husband – perhaps divorced?'

The doctor had told his friend that Juley was widowed but it was doubtful if this friend had mentioned this to Mrs Greatrix.

'I'm a widow,' returned Juley briefly.

'Ah . . . so that is the reason for the sadness in your eyes.'

Juley said nothing. She was half inclined to bring the interview to a halt but at the same time she had taken a liking to the woman and knew she would be happy working for her – well, as happy as was possible under the circumstances.

Mrs Greatrix spoke at last, with a note of apology as she said, 'You puzzle me, my dear. However, I do know when to mind my own business. You can start right away, I believe?'

'Yes.'

'Tomorrow?'

'I'd prefer a couple of days, Mrs Greatrix. When I said "right away" I really meant within the next few days.'

'Friday, then? Can I expect you the day after tomorrow?'

'I can manage that, yes.'

'Good. I'm sure you and I shall get along famously.'

'I hope so. It isn't for long.'

'Maisie will probably want to stay on for as long as I will let her.'

'Ten weeks, you mean?'

'If I let her stay on a little longer than that you won't mind staying with me?'

Juley shook her head and said without thinking, 'It can't be much longer. In fact, it could be—' Abruptly she broke off, eyes wide with consternation.

'It could be – what, Mrs Allen— Darn it! Can I call you Juley?'

'Of course; I prefer it.'

The subject was changed by that diversion and soon Juley was being driven to the railway station by the woman's uniformed chauffeur, Tim.

'Safe journey, madam.' He touched his cap. 'You'll be back on Friday, I believe?'

'That's right.' She smiled at him, then turned away. And although her heart was heavy at the parting with James, it was certainly lighter for her meeting with Mrs Greatrix.

Three

'Mexico?' Juley looked at her employer with a question in her eyes. 'But I thought I'd be here all the time. You're saying you want to go to Mexico and I'm to go with you?' Her thoughts winged to Charles, whose mother had been Mexican.

'I've a sudden urge to see my sister. She's married to a wealthy Mexican and they live in a beautiful mansion called the Hacienda Morelos. We write to each other regularly, and she's been wanting me to pay her a visit for some long time now. Maisie was not the kind of companion to take. She is not a sociable woman, nor is she young like you. So I'm taking advantage of this situation and visiting my sister.'

'You need me with you?'

'Of course. Who would dress my hair, iron my clothes, talk to me?'

'I guess your sister will want to do some talking. How long is it since you last saw her?'

'Four and a half years.'

'That's a long time.' She and her employer were sitting in the large, luxuriously furnished living room and the view was over Lake Windermere. The past two weeks had been ones of adjustment for Juley and she had been surprisingly happy and at peace. Her headaches were few and far between – in fact, she had had only two, neither severe – since coming to work for Mrs Greatrix. She had the tablets in plentiful supply, of course, because she knew the pains would become more frequent as the weeks went by. She

36

found herself living for each day, and within a few minutes of her employer's decision to go to Mexico being voiced Juley was eagerly looking forward to the complete change of scene. It was something new to occupy her mind, taking it away from reality. Mexico! Again it came back to her that Charles's mother had come from that country. She had gone to Ireland with her parents, for a holiday, and had fallen in love with an Irishman: Charles's father. But only six years after making her home in lovely Connemara she died, leaving her son to be brought up by nannies and by a father who was stern to the point of callousness. A big, blustering man whose personality had overpowered Juley on that one brief visit she had made at his request. To a girl of seventeen the sixty-year-old Irishman with his iron-grey beard, powerful shoulders and pugilistic features had seemed like a giant bent on her destruction. She sometimes wondered if it was fear of him as a father-in-law that had helped in her decision to give Charles up. Charles had tried over and over again to see her after she had given him up, but Juley's father saw to it that his daughter's mind should not be changed.

'When shall we be going to Mexico?' she found herself asking, faintly bewildered by the persistence of her thoughts regarding Charles. But she supposed it was only natural, the association being there.

'Soon. I never waste time once my mind is made up. It's profitless to dally or have doubts. I suggest we go as soon as we can get a flight. See to it at once, Juley. You might be lucky and get us a flight for tomorrow.'

'Tomorrow!'

'Why not? If you succeed I'll phone Agatha and let her know what time to expect us.'

'Will she be ready? I mean, won't she want some warning of more than a few hours?'

Sarah Greatrix laughed.

'She's like me, does everything with speed. She'll not

want any more warning than a few hours. It isn't as if she has any preparations to make,' went on Mrs Greatrix by way of putting Juley in the picture. 'She and her husband have eleven servants at the hacienda and four gardeners. It's an eighteenth-century building, very magnificent with vaulted ceilings and wings enclosing quadrangles . . . But why am I describing it all to you when you'll be seeing it tomorrow?'

Juley had to smile. Her employer was so sure they would get a flight. And as it happened, they did, and so within forty-eight hours of the decision being made Juley was in a magnificently furnished bedroom adjoining that of her employer, preparing herself for a dinner party, the like of which she would never have dreamed of being invited to. It was Don Ramos de Morelos's birthday and over thirty guests were to dine at the hacienda that evening.

'Sorry I threw you in at the deep end within your first few hours,' grimaced Mrs Greatrix. 'I'd completely forgotten it was my brother-in-law's birthday. However, you'll enjoy the company. I know I shall.' Juley had been unpacking for her, but with that finished they had been sitting on the flower-strewn verandah to which the window of Mrs Greatrix's room opened out. Juley had a similar verandah and she guessed that these apartments, four in all, were in fact for married couples. Other guest accommodation seemed to run into dozens of rooms, from what Juley could see from the stroll along the maze of corridors on the first floor of the mansion. 'What do you think of my sister's good fortune?'

'In marrying Don Ramos? I think he's something special.'

'Not as special as some of the men you'll meet this evening. Mexicans are handsome and no mistake!' She glanced at her companion with what could only be described as a mischievous expression. 'You might get yourself a rich husband like Ramos,' she added, which was exactly what Juley had expected her to say.

She said nothing, and after getting her employer ready she went into her own room to take a shower and put on a dress, which she feared would be totally inadequate for the occasion. But although she had pointed this out to her employer Mrs Greatrix had merely pooh-poohed the idea, saying that Juley could carry off anything and look like a lovely English duchess. A blush flooding Juley's cheeks had brought a laugh from the older woman, who had then thought to ask how long Juley had been widowed. Her consternation was apparent when she learned that the bereavement was so recent, but Julie had been honest enough to admit that she and Barry were already on the verge of divorce when the accident happened. In that case, declared her employer, relieved, she ought to be looking out for someone else.

'You look wonderful!' she exclaimed when Juley eventually came from her room. She had decided on a long black velvet skirt and white lace blouse. She looked very young – innocent and vulnerable, her pale cheeks adding to the impression of ethereal beauty and simplicity. 'Regal, yet so youthfully pretty.'

'Thank you, Mrs Greatrix.'

Juley was embarrassed but it eased the moment when her employer said impulsively, 'Call me Sarah, dear. I'm not at all partial to hearing Mrs Greatrix all the time.'

'I'll try,' from Juley with a smile. 'But you are my employer, not my friend.'

'I'm trying to be both, my dear,' returned Sarah with an odd inflection. 'Yes, I am trying to be your friend as well as your employer, Juley.'

The dining saloon was like fairyland with candles everywhere, flowers among them and crystal and silver gleaming on a table set with fine embroidered linen and Sèvres porcelain. Sarah had taken Juley in, just for a preview, she said, before they went along to the main salon where aperitifs

were being served. Juley was introduced to several nota-
bles and found herself attracting her fair share of attention
from two young Mexicans, both of whom seemed to find
her especially attractive. She sat with a glass in her hand
watching smiles which revealed gleaming white teeth; she
heard flattering comments, and decided that these two,
Pedro and Ricardo, were flirts, nothing more.

Ramos came to her, all smiles, and asked how she was
liking her new job. He was curious but restrained, unlike
his vivacious wife who sailed across the room, caught Juley
by the arm, and propelled her towards a tall, immaculately
dressed man who at this moment had his back to them,
being in earnest conversation with Senhor de Samados, one
of the district's wealthiest coffee producers.

'Charles!' The name rang out and he swung around.
'Charles, meet Juley from England. She's companion to my
sister and they both arrived today . . . Is anything wrong?'
She glanced from one to the other, saw the last vestige of
colour drain from Juley's face, saw Charles gape and stare
before making a rapid recovery.

'Juley . . .' He looked her over from head to foot. 'Well,
imagine meeting you here. Companion, you said, Agatha?'

'You two know each other?'

'We – we used to,' stammered Juley, wishing she could
escape into thin air, though she had no idea why. She was
recalling vividly that night and knew instinctively that
Charles was thinking about it, too. The snapshot. Was it a
sort of omen, her finding it like that? And what of her
thoughts when she and Barry were arguing that evening?
Charles's face had drifted before her eyes, a picture from
the past, recalled without her own volition. She had later
put the snapshot to be burned, but it had fallen out of the
pile, on to the grass, and instead of throwing it on to the
bonfire she had put it in her pocket. What had made her
keep it?

'You're looking very fit and well, Juley.' Charles's deep

voice broke into her thoughts and she managed a faint smile at his words, wondering how he would feel were he to know that although she looked well, she was dying. 'The world must be treating you kindly.'

Kindly? Well, at least she had only one thing on her mind now. Was it only a few short weeks since she had had so many burdens weighing her down? There had been Barry's funeral to be arranged, the adoption on her mind, the house to be sold, and the uncertainty of what to do with the short time left to her. She felt lighter now than for a long time and this was reflected in her smile. The colour was returning to her cheeks and she was at ease with him. He had changed little in appearance, apart from the fact of his growing a bit older, collecting a few lines of maturity that only added to his attractions. The grey in his hair she had imagined had not appeared. His hair was as thick and healthy as ever. He was slender and lithe and bronzed to the colour of well-matured teak.

'I'm fine,' she responded, aware that her hostess was no longer at her side. She had left them to go over to guests who had just arrived. 'You, Charles, what are you doing in Mexico? Visiting relatives?'

He was shaking his head even before she had finished speaking.

'I live here,' he said. 'I've been here for over three years.'

'You have?' She felt a pain coming on and put a hand to her head. 'You own a business, or something?'

'I inherited an estate from my maternal grandmother. It was unexpected.' He stopped, then asked, 'Are you ill, Juley?' No concern, just the normal question anyone would ask. 'Your eyes, they seem tired all at once.'

'I do feel a bit dizzy – something I ate on the plane, I guess. If you will excuse me . . .' She turned and left the room as quickly as she could. Her bed was calling; she took two tablets and lay down, her head throbbing, her heart accelerating with fear. Death was terrifying and for one wild moment she wished it would come at once, so that she could drift into that sweet oblivion where no pain exists.

'Oh, God, help me to bear it.' She turned instinctively as the words left her lips. Sarah was there, in the doorway, having missed her soon after she had left the room. Charles had said he believed Juley was not too well. 'Sarah – my head aches abominably.'

'You've taken some asprin?' Her eyes darted to the bottle on the bedside table.

'A kind of aspirin – yes.' She reached out before Sarah could pick up the bottle. 'I'll be down in a few minutes'. Please leave me. I'm all right, really,' she added on noticing Sarah's deepening concern.

'I can't leave you, not when you're like this. Is it very bad? Shall I bring a doctor?'

'No, I don't need a doctor!'

'Why the vehemence?'

'I don't care for doctors, that's all. I'll be OK in a few minutes when the tablets have begun to have an effect.'

'So you are prone to these headaches?'

'I do have them now and then – er – migraine, you know. Lots of people are affected.' She was fearing a further and deeper probe and added with a deliberate hint of anger, 'I shall be all right, Sarah. There isn't any need for all this fuss.'

'Dinner will be served quite soon.'

'I'll be down – please leave me. I do appreciate your concern but there isn't any need for it, I assure you.'

The older woman sighed then, with resignation.

'All right, but if you aren't down in ten minutes I shall know you're needing a doctor. Pains are always warnings, remember.'

No need to be reminded of that! Juely took another tablet and lay down again. She was beginning to think clearly again, and quite naturally it was to her unexpected meeting with Charles that her thoughts turned. He lived here, in

Mexico, he had said, having inherited an estate from his grandmother. What had happened that he had not gone into his father's business, as the old man had planned? Was his father still there or was he dead now? And Charles, was he married? It did not seem as if his wife was here tonight.

At last she sat up, glancing at the clock and knowing her employer had meant what she said.

'I feel fine now,' she was telling Ramos a few minutes later when she was again in the main salon. 'It was nothing really, just one of those sick headaches which one sometimes gets.'

'Effect of the long flight. I told Sarah it would be that but she does fuss sometimes. She was all set to bring in our doctor.'

'It's nice to have someone concern themselves about you.' She was speaking in defence of Sarah and Ramos nodded in agreement.

Charles came up and Ramos said, 'I'll leave you in good hands, Juley. Charles is our most eligible bachelor. Juley is a widow, Charles.' He chuckled and went off, leaving Juley blushing and Charles with an expression of mocking satire.

'Always the matchmaker is our Ramos,' he commented. 'But you, Juley, is it right that you are widowed?' His manner was impersonal. That night might never have happened. It meant nothing to either of them now. She let Charles take her arm and lead her to a sofa by the window. 'Yes, I'm a widow,' she said, turning to him. But he was not looking at her and she saw his firm features in profile. Strong as ever, and perhaps a little more stern and arrogant. 'My husband died in a car accident a few weeks ago.'

'Only a few weeks?' He did turn then, with an expression of interrogation in his dark eyes. 'What are you doing here, Juley?'

She paused but a moment before telling him most of the story, leaving out her condition and that she had a child who was now adopted. She would have liked to tell him about James, but if she had done so she then would have had to explain why he was adopted.

'So the world didn't treat you kindly. You've had some very bad luck.'

'Yes.' She was hurt inexplicably by his suave indifference. Yet what did she expect? Eight years had gone by since that night, since he wanted her for his wife. Many things had happened to them both, things that could only widen the gap she had made when she turned him down.

'You've taken the post only for a couple of months or so?' He seemed to be trying to understand something. 'Wouldn't it have been better to have taken a permanent post and tried to reorganize your life?'

A faint and bitter smile touched her lips. Reorganize her life? What life?

'I thought the change might take my mind off things,' was all she said in response to his question.

'But you say your marriage had already broken up, before your husband's death, so you can scarcely be heartbroken over the break up.'

'No, I'm not heartbroken,' she agreed. 'But I've had several shocks in the last few months and this post seemed to be a godsend. I'm glad I took it. Sarah is wonderful to me.'

'It brought you here,' he mused. 'Quite a coincidence, isn't it?' The dark eyes scrutinized her face, her throat, and the fine slope of her shoulders, then focused on the curves of her breasts and her colour heightened. His lips curled and his eyes were mocking. 'Shy, after being married?'

She returned stiffly, 'Your stare embarrassed me.'

'You still have the most beautiful curves of any woman I know.'

'Charles . . . don't—'

'Remember that night?' The inflection in his voice was unfathomable.

Startled, she stared at him, not having expected him to

refer to it. In fact, the manner he was adopting, that of polite but cool indifference, made it seem impossible that he had recalled it.

'One never forgets anything like that, Charles,' she said gently. 'At least, a woman doesn't. A man might – probably in most cases he does.'

'And after what happened between us you refused me.'

'It's a long time ago, Charles,' she reminded him gently. 'I rather thought you'd have been married by now, with children growing up.' Her face was towards him; she saw his eyes flicker with interest – interest in her, not in what she had been saying. And when he spoke it was automatic in his reference to her words.

'Children, eh?' And he fell silent, still looking at her, his eyes moving from her face to the delicate curves of throat and breasts, then he was looking into her eyes again and she remembered her conviction that his intention, on that fateful night, was to give her a child so that his father would, being a devoutly religious man, agree to the marriage. 'You didn't have children, it seems?' added Charles and there was but the merest pause before Juley answered him.

'No,' briefly and she swiftly lowered her eyes as she had never found it easy to lie.

'Why did you throw me over, Juley?' His tone was soft and accusing. She was again startled by the question she had never expected. 'My father's dead,' he went on before she could reply. 'He died of a heart attack.'

'He would have cut you off if I'd married you. I couldn't let that happen to you, Charles. There was so much at stake, as he was such a wealthy man.'

'He cut me off anyway.'

'He—!' Juley stared in disbelief. 'He cut you off – without anything?'

'Without a penny. I even had to get out of the house.' A bitter smile hovered for a moment, as Charles looked deeply into her eyes. 'So you see, throwing me over gained me

45

nothing.' He paused and the moment became intense. 'I guess destiny never did have anything planned for you and me, Juley.'

She glanced away, something painful turning in her heart. Charles was her first love; to him she had given her virginity . . .

'I'm so sorry about your father doing that to you,' she quivered at last. 'Why did he cut you off – his only child?'

'We never did get along. I had no intention of being dictated to and a major row was inevitable. He said I was too much like my mother, a foreigner, undisciplined. I left him and travelled for a while, then took a post as manager of a wine-producing estate in Portugal. I went back home when my father had a stroke; he died shortly afterwards and I was told by the lawyers I had no home. Everything was left to charities. I travelled again and it was while I was in Spain that I had word that my grandmother had died and left me her estate here. She had produced mainly coffee and wine. The wine-growing side has progressed beyond all expectations. You see,' he added becoming enthusiastic about his subject, 'quality wines were not possible here in Mexico until the advent of modern technology.' He paused in thought. Juley waited, having no comment to make. 'It was owing to my being interested in wine that my grand-mother decided to leave me everything she owned. It would have gone to another grandson, though, had he not died. As I said, the inheritance was quite unexpected.'

'Your father,' she began, frowning heavily, 'couldn't he accept that you had a will of your own?'

'That was something he could not allow. All who came into contact with him had to bend to his wishes. His servants were cowed and far too humble in my opinion.' He shrugged carelessly. 'It's all water under the bridge now. Even had I not had this stroke of good fortune I still would have made my own success in life.' He changed the subject abruptly. 'What shall you do when this job with Sarah is finished? I understand she has a companion and you are merely filling in while she takes a holiday?'

'That's right.' What would she do later? he had asked. 'I'm not bothering to make any plans at present,' she went on in an expressionless voice. 'I live each day as it comes along.'

'That's the philosophy of the aged,' he frowned.

Or those with a similar short expectation of life . . .

'I suppose something will turn up,' she told him with a smile.

'How long is Sarah staying here?'

'I don't know. Only a week or two, I expect.'

Charles was about to say something else when the butler came to announce that dinner was served. He spoke in Spanish but Juley understood. She noticed that Spanish was spoken a good deal, but in consideration for the visitors English was spoken as well. Charles said, in answer to a question from Juley, that he had not found it too difficult to pick up enough Spanish to be able to converse.

'I'd picked up some while I was in Spain,' he explained, 'and so it was fairly easy to gain some degree of fluency after I'd been here for a few months. You'll find that everyone here tonight is bilingual,' he added, offering his arm as they went into the dining salon.

He had been put directly opposite her and she felt that lightness come over her again. The pain in her head had gone completely and she felt so well that it was hard to believe what fate had in store for her.

'Enjoying the party?' Charles asked the question after the second course had been served.

'Very much. It's all so new and exciting. I'm very lucky—' She broke off abruptly, feeling she had turned pale. Her eyes seemed to be drawn to Sarah, who was lower down the table on the same side as Charles. She spoke to him again after dragging her gaze from the all-compelling one which seemed to have a vital question in its depths. 'It's a pleasant, unexpected surprise to have someone here whom I know, and can talk to.' Strange that there had been no awkwardness and, on her part, little or no embarrassment. If ever she had envisaged a meeting between her and Charles she felt trepidation, recalling their last encounter and his fury at her refusal to marry him. He'd said that her father would have given his consent and so, he'd told her harshly, there was no excuse for her refusing to marry him. He did not know of her meeting with his father, and of the old man's threat. And yet, he had cut his son off anyway. So it had all been for nothing. She was not sure she would have married Charles, had it not been for that threat, but neither was she sure that she would have refused him. But as he had said just a short while earlier, it was all water under the bridge – all of it, and nothing could be changed.

The dinner party was thoroughly enjoyable for Juley, for although Charles's attitude towards her alternated between semi-indifference and friendly interest – both of which were somewhat disconcerting – she was happy, able to forget the dark destiny that awaited her.

'You two appear to have much to talk about.' Ramos made the smiling observation and it was Sarah who responded.

'It was such a coincidence, your having known one another years ago. You must tell me all about it, Juley.' She stopped, eyes narrowing as she noticed the glance that passed between the two, with Juley uncomfortable under the mocking amusement of Charles's smile. Sarah said slowly, 'But maybe you won't tell me all about it. After all, you did warn me you disliked talking about yourself, didn't you, my dear?'

Juley coloured, even more profoundly aware of Charles's amusement. But he was faintly surprised, too, by Sarah's comment and later he was to ask Juley why she disliked talking about herself. But for the present, Ramos spoke, telling Charles to have cognac with his coffee. The party was now back in the main salon, where after-dinner coffee was being served from silver pots, with four manservants in attendance. Charles shook his head, murmuring a polite refusal.

'I've had wine with the meal and as I'm driving I'll give the brandy a miss.'

'Why drive?' from Ramos. 'There's plenty of room here. Stay the night. There's no reason why you should drive home tonight.'

After sending Juley an oblique glance Charles accepted the invitation without pause.

'Thank you, Ramos. I will stay. But I must be away very early in the morning as I've work to do. I'll try not to disturb anyone when I leave.'

'We'll put you in the same wing as Sarah and Juley. There's a door at the end of their corridor leading to a veran-dah, so if you use that you can't possibly disturb anyone.'

So it was settled, and after Charles and Juley had finished their coffee he suggested they go outside.

'I don't know about you, but I find it excessively hot in here.'

She hesitated, but in that authoritative way she had once been so used to, he was already propelling her towards an arched doorway leading to a perfumed courtyard. Flowers sprayed downwards from a turreted wall made of coral lime-stone with marble columns at each end; coloured lights gave soft and subtle illumination, hidden as they were among the foliage of bougainvillaea vines. The moon rode full and high, lording it over a million stars, its silver luminescence filter-ing the lacy cirrus floating in the deep purple of a Mexican sky. A night for romance . . . something akin to an electric current pulsed through Juley's veins as her hand was taken in a strong, cool one and fingers caressed, gently, excitingly. Memories flooded in; she felt intoxicated, stripped of the power to think of anything but that night . . . and this one.

'Why have you brought me here?' Her voice was unsteady, her heart beating far too rapidly for comfort.

'To talk of old times. And I also want to know what you've been doing with yourself all these years. And then I shall tell you my story – although there isn't much to add to what you already know.' He looked down at her and his smile was wonderful in her eyes. 'I've been rather more expansive than you, my dear. And, also, what did Sarah mean by saying you disliked talking about yourself? Have you something to hide?' His voice was deep and authoritative. vibrantly timbred, and the very nearness of him was disturbing. Juley felt she was proceeding willingly towards the edge of a precipice.

She said with an effort at carelessness, 'I've told you my story, and there isn't anything of importance to add. I told Sarah I disliked talking about myself because I sensed a curiosity about her and decided to put an immediate brake on it.'

'So you do have something to hide?' He looked at her speculatively, noticing the slight deepening of colour in her cheeks.

'Why do you say that?' she asked warily.

'Simply because, had you nothing to hide, there would have been no need to put this brake on Sarah's curiosity.'

She had to laugh.

'Your particular brand of logic will gain you nothing,' she told him. 'I shall not talk about myself.'

'Not even to me?' It was a subtle question and a faint accusation. He had guessed she had a secret which she meant to keep. She made no answer, and after a small silence he moved and she found herself going meekly where she was led – towards a hammock-lounger, cushioned and wide, low to the ground. It was nevertheless suspended from a shiny-foliaged lime tree whose perfume filled the air. They eased themselves into the cushions, danger in the way Charles was helping her, his hands warm and strong, his breath clean and fresh against her cheek. Expectancy thrilled over her, not unmingled with a sort of exquisite fear, and she made an attempt to take a grip on her emotions. But all was geared for romance, the sky dramatically overflowing with light, and on the sweet-scented eddy of a breeze there floated the potent tang of the sea, while high in the dome of the sky clouds in moonglow appeared like lace spun by some fairy hand. Subtle lights of rose and amber shimmered from some hidden place beneath the eaves to scatter colour on to a bed of flowering cacti, deepening the rose-red blooms.

Charles was beside her and she caught the scent of body lotion mingled with the heady male odour she could even now remember. He spoke into the deep silence.

'You've said there isn't anything of importance to add to your story, but you haven't told me all, Juley.' His hand had caught hers. She offered no resistance when his lips touched her cheek.

'What makes you so sure?' she asked curiously.

'You haven't had time.'

She laughed and said, 'It just depends on how much there is to tell.' A hint of couquettishness edged her voice, quite unknown to her. 'I've had a dull life.'

'You could have had an exciting one.'

'How can you be so sure?'

'We were so happy together. It could have continued . . . for the rest of our lives.' His voice was suddenly hard, inscrutable, and she thought: he can't still love me. No, his love much have died long, long ago.

Turning towards him she asked, 'Why are you talking to me like this, Charles? I'd have thought you'd hate me.'

'Hate is a strong emotion, and I feel no strong emotion where you are concerned.'

Deflated, she fell silent, but when Charles made no attempt to break the silence she inquired tentatively, 'What kind of a life have you had, Charles? Surely you've been in love?'

'Not in love, no.'

51

'You haven't a girlfriend?'

'Oh, yes, I do have a current friend.'

'But nothing serious?'

'That I can't say.' He paused speculatively. 'Perhaps it will be serious one day.'

Suddenly she felt flat, dejected, as if the evening were going to disappoint her after all. It had been so pleasant up till now.

'Is your home far from here?' she enquired at last.

'Not too far, about twenty miles.'

'You're a friend of the Moreloses?'

He nodded his head.

'Yes. We've been friends almost from the time I came here. Agatha and Ramos were great favourites of my grandmother.'

'She was a widow?'

'Had been for over fifteen years. I visited her on occasions and she seemed glad to see me but never extended an invitation for me to visit her regularly.'

'And yet she left you all she had.'

'I was fortunate. I have over a thousand acres of vines, and five hundred under sugar. It's a very prosperous estate and had been expertly run by my grandmother's estate manager.' He was not bragging about what he owned, just stating facts. 'The house is charming, Juley. You must come along for dinner one evening before you return to England.' His voice had lost its previous hardness; it was gentle now, and profoundly attractive to Juley's receptive ears.

'I'd like that,' she returned eagerly. 'You want Sarah as well?'

His lips twitched.

'If that is what you want. Wouldn't you feel safe if you came alone?'

'It wasn't that,' she laughed. 'I was just thinking that Sarah would like to see your house.'

'Then my invitation includes her.' Charles had somehow

edged closer and she could feel the steely hardness of his thigh against hers, his warm breath against her cheek. His intention was being made blatantly clear to her but he was proceeding slowly, affording her a fair chance of withdrawal before it was too late, before she was aroused to the point of no return.

For Juley it was as if time hung suspended for moments of indecision before shooting backwards so that it seemed only yesterday that she had lain naked in his arms, a rush of joy spreading through her heart. Children both, she mused, playing the love game which for her was the first time, the glorious experiment. Her thoughts reeled forward to remind her of the brevity of the time left to her. And she told herself she had nothing to lose, but everything to gain by living this hour, and another, and another . . . if Charles wanted her. But she had no wish to sully even an affair by a swift and anxious interlude which must, of necessity, be all too short. The quick impersonal gratification of a desire was not for her at this time in her life when every moment should be one of beauty. Charles spoke into her meditations, his breathing more than a little pronounced now, his hands more venturesome. He was no longer the inexperienced boy of that special night, but a man of the world whose knowledge of women must surely include their weaknesses.

'Juley,' he whispered close to her ear, 'you must be missing a lot now that you are widowed.' It was a question, not very tactfully put and she stayed his hand before it reached the tender curves of its target. 'Juley . . .' His voice became thicker, his thigh against hers warmer than before, his whole manner more urgent. All he desired was swift relief, easement from the tension strongly setting up within him, brought about by his action in bringing her here, to this most romantic place, and then deliberately making close contact with her body, so close that the fine linen of his slacks and the soft velvet of her skirt were no adequate barrier to the erotic heat of his body which he so easily imparted to hers. He would be satisfied with an urgent, animal-like assuaging of his desire and she supposed he believed she was ready and willing to accept a similar release. But although her own desire was growing strong within her – not aroused by anything Charles had done, but rather by the memory of that night – she again stayed his roving hand. 'Juley – you must want sex. It's well known that—' He stopped for some reason and she finished for him,

'. . . a young widow is an easy target for a womanizer. Is that what you are trying to say, Charles?' There was dignity in her manner and her lovely voice was placid.

'You're not repulsing me, yet you know what I want. Isn't that proof that you are now missing something vital in your life?'

'I did mention that Barry and I were separated for several months before the accident that made me a widow.' She had no wish to talk of Barry, nor even recall anything in her life except that night. It seemed to be the only thing of importance that had happened in her life until this moment when she was close to Charles, with his arm about her shoulders and his cheek touching hers.

'Are you going to let me love you?' His hand had freed itself from the restraint of hers. It was warm and soothing on her breast. She quivered and lay against his chest. 'You are!' Triumph rang even in the whisper. 'Lie down, Juley. I'm afraid the "bed" is going to rock a bit—'

'Charles, not here. It's too risky. Someone could come out because, as you said, it became very hot in there.' She coloured painfully as she laid her head against the lapel of his dinner jacket. 'No, not here . . . there are too many lights as well.'

'You say, not here.' He held her from him, surveying her critically. 'Where, then?'

She paused, swallowing hard, preparing to utter words

which must surely arouse his contempt – but what did it matter what he secretly thought of her? That was the least of her worries, for whatever his opinion of her he would never voice it; he was too much the gentleman. And he would enjoy his affair with her, and treat her gently and with affection.

She managed at length to say, though in a rather hollow little voice, 'In my room, Charles. I just couldn't here.'

He held her further away and she lifted her eyes. His were narrowed, puzzled, but in no way contemptuous.

'You're inviting me to sleep with you tonight?'

She nodded, wishing her throat was not so dry that she could scarcely speak. She managed to whisper, in the same hollow tone,

'Yes, Charles – I'm inviting you to – to sleep with me tonight.'

Four

The sun was effectively penetrating the long velvet drapes as Juley stirred, then wakened fully. Luxuriously she stretched her naked body beneath the covers and a sigh of contentment fell from her lips.

'What a glorious day!' She leapt out of bed, grabbed a dainty nylon robe and eased herself into it, moving towards the window at the same time. Opening the drapes, she looked out on to the satin sheen of morning spreading over the magnificent gardens of the hacienda. Statuary and fountains, colourful parterres and sunken gardens flaunting an incredible variety of exotic flowers. Tall palms swaying gently in the zephyr of a breeze allowed sunlight to escape through their spidery foliage to create shimmering patterns and mosaics on wide, manicured lawns where not a single weed dared raise its head.

Opening the window, Juley stepped out on to her verandah. She was so happy she felt almost light-headed. What a transformation of her attitude towards the life left to her! Never would she have believed she could cast off the depression of the past few weeks, those weeks before she came to Sarah. It was a miracle that she had obtained the post. And now she was able to forget what was in store for her. She had *some* life left to her, and she meant to live it to the full!

Charles had talked before leaving her in the early hours of the morning and she was left in no doubt about his wanting an affair with her. She just had to mention his girlfriend and he admitted she would be unhappy if she found out about his affair with Juley.

'But an affair like this is not of the kind that lasts for any length of time,' he remarked casually. 'As with you, it is for me just a diversion, pleasurable and satisfying, but transient if only because, firstly, you will not be here for very long, and secondly, you will marry again in any case – and I rather think I shall, one day.' He was calmly telling her not to expect an offer of marriage, and she did ask herself how she would have felt if circumstances had been different and this fate was not hanging over her. But then she was remembering that the 'affair' would never have come about had she had a lifetime before her. It was the urgency of gaining every moment of what was left to her that had thrust her into having an affair with the very man who had so long ago robbed her of her innocence. 'We must arrange some way of seeing each other regularly while you are here,' Charles had said firmly. And he had added, 'Tell me, what are your future plans?'

'I have none. I'm interested only in the present.'

'Strange,' he murmured almost to himself. He was getting dressed and Juley was propped up on her elbow, watching him.

'The present is all that matters, surely?' She saw him pick up his jacket and wished she could put back the clock . . . to when she was taking it off. But now he was putting it on; he would go back to the room he'd been given, ruffle the bedclothes to make it appear he had slept there, then soon he would be on his way home. 'None of us knows what will happen tomorrow,' she added when he looked at her. 'So why not think just of the present, and enjoy it?'

'You're suggesting one should not plan ahead?' He gazed at her with an unfathomable expression. That he was puzzled by her philosophy was plain, but he would never in a thousand years guess the reason for it.

'Plans often go awry,' she smiled and he came close to the bed.

'Juley,' he said softly, his hand reaching out to caress her cheek, 'you're being mysterious again. I've already said you puzzle me, and now you are adopting the kind of philosophy that is not at all logical.'

'Not logical in ordinary circumstances—' She halted abruptly, though aware that she had said too much for him to let it pass without comment. What on earth had brought forth those words she never had any intention of uttering?

'Ordinary circumstances?' His frown was heavy, his dark eyes penetrating. 'Just what is this mystery?' he demanded. 'I hate being perplexed in this way. Come out with it. We're close now and shall be for the next couple of weeks at least, so let us not have secrets from one another.'

'It's nothing,' she prevaricated, curling her fingers into his hair as he sat down on the edge of the bed. 'You say we mustn't have secrets from one another, but you have secrets from me.'

'Not many. My life hasn't been in any way out of the ordinary – but I suspect yours has.'

She shook her head.

'I was married, and living a rather humdrum life when I look back on it now.'

'No excitement with the man you chose instead of me?' His voice carried a ring of irony. 'No wonder it broke up.'

'It wasn't because of me. I still loved Barry, but as I told you, he couldn't forgive me for involving his mother in the accident which brought about her death.'

'There was nothing to forgive,' he retorted in a hard tone. 'We die when our time comes. It's written in our destiny before we're even born.'

True. Juley's own belief was that one could never hope to escape what had been mapped out for one, mapped out in some mysterious way which no one would ever be able to understand.

'I wish Barry had thought like you,' she sighed. 'If he had, then he'd not have been in that car.' She stopped rather abruptly owing to the amusement appearing in Charles's eyes.

'We've just agreed – well, it appears you are in agreement with me – that our fate is mapped out for us, so Barry was fated to be in that car.'

'I suppose you're right.'

Charles became thoughtful for a space.

'Did it not occur to you that you were better without a man who professed to love you while at the same time blaming you for something unavoidable?'

'I shouldn't have listened to his mother's plea.'

'Her time had come,' he almost snapped. 'That is why she died, because her time had run out.'

Her time had come . . . Juley's face blanched as for one fleeting moment her own doom was inscribed on her brain in huge black capitals. Charles, swift to spot the change in her face, asked anxiously if anything were wrong.

'You've gone white – you are ill?'

She shook her head and smiled.

'No, I'm fine – and happy,' she added, which was true for the picture was now blotted out from her brain. 'Oh, dear, you will have to go, and I do want you to stay.'

His gentle hands cupped her face.

'There will be other times,' he assured her. 'As I've said, we must find a way of seeing each other regularly.' Although he smiled, making her whole world rosy, she sensed an underlying curiosity and knew he would persist in his intention of learning more about her. Well, he would never elicit her full confidence; he would know soon enough what she was hiding. Meanwhile, there was pleasure to be had and she meant to live each day to the full.

She came in from the verandah, still thinking of that conversation and Charles's firm assertion that they would find a way to see a lot of each other for the time she was here in Mexico. Charles was going to phone today asking her out to lunch. She had told him Sarah was not too demanding and seemed to want a companion only when she was alone. Now that she was visiting her sister she appeared to be fully occupied, needing Juley not for companionship but merely to do her hair and generally take care of her clothes.

'Juley!' The call interrupted her thoughts, swinging them from Charles to Sarah. 'Get me a cup of tea, dear. I can't stand that maid, Rosita, and if I ring you can be sure she'll be the one to come up . . . Juley, open the door.'

Juley raced to the door, cursing herself for not remembering to unlock it earlier, when Charles was leaving. Could she now turn the key without making a sound? Charles had managed it last night, she recalled, gingerly putting her fingers to it. But to her consternation Sarah had become impatient and now she was turning the handle and tugging. 'What . . . ?'

Juley turned the key, colour rising.

'I must have locked it without thinking,' she offered unsteadily.

'Locked the door between your room and mine.' Sarah's glance was puzzled. It moved for some reason to the other door, the one opening out on to the wide, balustraded corridor. 'Is that one locked, too?'

'Er – no . . .' It had been until Charles left but she hadn't troubled to get out of bed to lock it after him. And now it looked very odd indeed that the main door was unlocked while the communicating door was locked.

And Sarah might have read her thoughts for she said curiously, her gaze never leaving Juley's flushed face, 'I find it very strange that you would lock this door, Juley. You say you locked it without thinking but I cannot imagine your doing it.'

'I – I did, though. I'm sorry.'

'It does not call for an apology,' was her employer's rather dry rejoinder, 'just an explanation.' And with that she turned back into her own room, her diaphanous neglegée flowing. Juley drew a deep breath and immediately went over to the bed and turned one pillow over so that the uncreased side was upwards. How fortunate that Sarah had not noticed the bed!

She called out, 'I'll not be long with your tea.' She was conscious of a pain in her head and took a pill. Then she went off to find a maid who would give her a cup of tea.

When Charles phoned later Sarah happened to be with Juley when the message was brought to her by one of the manservants. Juley and Sarah were strolling along a shady path between two borders of exotic shrubs whose colours had made Juley gasp and stop to admire flowers she had never even heard of, much less seen.

'A phone call for you?' Sarah looked interested. 'Now who could it be?' She followed Juley into the house.

'It's Charles.' Juley felt guilty, uncomfortable. 'He would like to take me out to lunch.' She coloured up and was angry with herself because of it.

'Would he, indeed?' with a lift of her eyebrows which did nothing for Juley's discomfiture. 'This is sudden. Has he fallen for you?'

'I shouldn't think so. He has a girlfriend.'

'So I believe. Agatha mentioned her last evening. Well, off you go on your luncheon date – and good hunting. I'm sure this girlfriend would have to be something exceptionally special to be able to compete with you.'

Juley's colour fluctuated but she let that pass without comment.

'What time must I be back?' she asked. 'Shall you want me before it's time to get ready for dinner?'

'I don't think so.' Sarah was eyeing her with a curious expression, 'Why? Are you expecting to be out all day?'

'No – it's just that I want to be sure not to inconvenience you.'

The older woman produced a faint smile. She was look-ing particularly attractive and graceful this morning, dressed in black with white trimmings and accessories. Her hair was newly washed and blown dry by Juley, and as usual, she was superbly made-up. From the first Juley had envied her the ability to use cosmetics with such pleasing results. For herself, Juley merely used a blusher and lip-rouge, with the occasional application of eye make-up.

But today, as she prepared for the date with Charles, she took more than average care and was rather pleased with the result. She chose to wear a finely knitted cotton skirt and top, short-sleeved and with red trimmings on the neck, waist and hem. Soft beige leather sandals and handbag matched the colour of the suit and a red Alice band hold-ing her newly washed hair in place gave her an exception-ally youthful and unaffected look. A perfume spray provided the final touch of simple elegance before, darting a glance at the clock, she swung the handbag on to her shoulder and hurried out to where Charles was waiting in the forecourt, standing beside his low-slung sports car, chatting to Ramos. She paused to appreciate the superb appearance of the man: the height, the lithe physique with its broad shoulders and narrow waist. He stood erect and proud, so it was arrogance and complete self-possession which came through to impress deeply and at the same time to disturb in the most inexplicable way. That he was remarkably attractive was without question, and Juley marvelled that he had not been 'caught' long before now. After all, he was only twenty-one when first he'd wanted to marry.

He looked at her and she smiled. It lit her eyes and he seemed to give a little gasp but then he was smiling too, and so was Ramos. In fact, his eyes never left her face as she made her way towards the car. After saying, 'Have a good day,' Ramos went back up the flight of stone steps and disappeared into the house.

'You look perfectly stunning.' Charles had the door open

for her. 'We have an audience,' he informed her and she turned her head. Sarah and Agatha were at the sitting-room window. 'Already they'll be coupling our names.' He closed her door and went round to the driver's side.

'What about your girlfriend?' Juley was asking as they drove away from the hacienda along a winding, tree-lined drive towards the road.

'Mari? What about her?' He was so casual, indifferent, that Juley felt sure he was not yet in love with the girl. 'What do you mean?' He turned left after waiting for a car to pass.

'If, as you suspect, our names are to be coupled she isn't going to be very pleased.'

'That,' he returned quietly, 'is an eventuality that will be dealt with if and when it arises.'

She had to laugh.

'You're obviously not too concerned that she might throw you over if there's gossip about you and me. You appear almost callously casual about her feelings.'

Charles turned his head to look at her in profile.

'You don't seem too concerned, either – about the gossip which might arise.'

Juley shrugged her shoulders. His puzzlement was obvious.

'It will be a new experience for me to be gossiped about, but not one that will trouble me unduly.' She had nothing to lose, she could have added, but of course refrained.

'Who's being casual now?' he queried in bantering tones.

'Gossip can't hurt me, especially as I shall be leaving here and never seeing any of these people ever again – except Sarah, of course.' She glanced through the side window. It was a lovely sunlit day with clear blue skies and colour everywhere. Suddenly she shut her eyes tightly as a deluge of despair threatened to drag her down to the depths of hopelessness, and a stab of real fear touched her heart. This was one of those devastating moments which had been so familiar during the past months of anxiety and confusion. She had so often become smothered by the nearness of her end. She thought now of her dear little baby and of the fact that he was settled in a home where he'd be nurtured and loved – and this suddenly opened up the cloud to let the sun burst through again. Thank God for the relief!

'Leaving . . .' There had been a long silence so the word came as a surprise and Juley swung her head around. Charles's features were taut in profile, his fine mouth tight. 'You haven't asked Sarah yet when she'll be wanting to leave?'

'No. We've only just come. I expect she'll stay at least a fortnight.'

'It isn't long, having come all this way.' Charles swung the car from the main road on to a much narrower one lined with lime trees and tall pines. Fields on both sides were sown with corn, and away in the distance rose the sepia foothills of the higher peaks. There was a loneliness here, a sense of isolation from the rest of the world. The silence would be complete, she knew, if the car engine were to be switched off. An ache caught her throat, a tightness beyond her understanding. Nothing about her seemed real or solid; even her own body was floating above all that could be described as earthly. Surreptitiously, and only after a glance at that set profile had assured her that its owner was fully absorbed in driving, she felt in her bag for the box of tablets she always carried and a sigh of relief escaped her. She knew the pain was about to start and for one panic-stricken moment she could not remember putting the precious box into her handbag. 'I said it isn't long.' Charles's repetition jerked her from her almost drugged state and brought her back to her surroundings.

'Two whole weeks – not long!' The exclamation was out before she stopped to think. Charles's head shot round and she saw the frown between his eyes.

'You feel that two weeks with me is long enough?'

'I didn't mean it like that at all.'

'Our affair will be over in two weeks. Is that what you are telling me?'

'You said yourself that it'll end when I leave here.'

'I don't remember.' He was suddenly away from her, preoccupied, broodingly pensive. Whatever the motive that had precipitated him into embarking on an affair with her, the desire to have it continue for longer than two weeks was without doubt very strong. Would they somehow contrive to have it continue right to the end? How would Charles feel then, when she died? Juley did not care to have her thoughts drifting in that direction and so she began to speak, voicing an opinion on the beauties of the scenery and the softness of the sunlit terrain through which they were passing.

'How much longer – I mean, where are we going?' she enquired finally. There didn't appear to be any restaurants out here, in this vast region of countryside most of which was open, with crops flourishing in what must be excellent soil.

'We are going to my home. It isn't far now. I said I wanted you to see it.'

'Your home . . . oh . . .'

'What does that lack of enthusiasm mean?' He turned his head. She had expected humour in his expression but there was merely a question.

'There isn't any lack of enthusiasm,' she argued. 'I shall love seeing your home. I'm so glad you were in your grandmother's favour, Charles, because it was awful of your father to leave you out of his will.'

'I'd have got by. It isn't money that makes for happiness.'

'It's people?'

'Yes, people, not possessions. But even people let you down. However, one faithful friend is worth a ton of gold.' The very seriousness of his manner was bound to affect her and it did, in a profoundly deep and emotional way.

Her voice was infinitely gentle as she asked, 'Have you never had a faithful friend, Charles?'

'One. My dog.' His voice was suddenly bitter and his mouth took on a harsh uncompromising line. His tone was pitched low when at length he added, 'Faithful friends, it has been said, are as rare as hothouse plants in the Arctic.'

'Not quite as rare as that,' she contradicted, still in the same soft and gentle tones. 'This girl – Mari – tell me about her? She must be nice for you to be interested in her. How old is she? What's she like? Where does she live? Is she Mexican? Does she come from a big family?' The string of questions broke the spell of brooding gloom that had descended on Charles and he burst out laughing.

'Which question shall I answer first?'

Juley caught his amusement and her mouth curved into a smile.

'How old is she?'

'Twenty-eight, a year younger than I.' He was slowing down and neither spoke again until he had swung the car through intricate wrought-iron gates and begun travelling along an avenue of sapodilla trees, their glassy, oval leaves catching the sunlight, their white, bell-shaped blossoms shedding an intoxicating fragrance on to the warm, balmy air. Flowering bougainvillaea abounded beneath the tall trees, offering further shade, colour and perfume, pleasantly breaking the lush, blue-green monotone of the fields beyond. 'She's dark,' continued Charles presently, 'of Indian stock originally but somewhere there's been the white man's influence, so that she is strikingly beautiful in an exotic kind of way.' He paused to concentrate on his driving and Juley thought: she sounds just the kind of woman to go to a man's head. Beautiful in an exotic kind of way . . . 'she lives close by,' added Charles, 'on the adjoining estate, in fact, so it would be convenient if we were to marry, especially as she is an only child who will inherit a vast fortune along with the estate.'

He spoke in a brisk and businesslike voice which convinced Juley that if he did marry the girl it would not be wholly for love. But she hoped he would have love in his life as well. Hadn't he just said that happiness depends on people, not possessions?

The hacienda, called Casa Verano, rose in patrician splendour that left Juley gasping with admiration the moment she stepped from the car. She had thought that the Ramos residence must be the superlative, but the magnificence of the Casa Verano's beauty even surpassed that of the Hacienda Morelos. Charles, standing close to her, watched in some amusement as she remained, as if rooted to the spot, apparently mesmerized by what she saw.

'It's . . . beautiful,' she declared in an awed voice. It's much more appealing than the home you had in Ireland – there's no comparison!'

'I'm glad you like the Casa.' He spoke with an unfathomable inflection in his tone. 'It is styled on similar lines to Ramos's house, but it is slightly older and larger.'

'Yes, I see what you mean – the two storeys and wings surrounding quadrangles. The front elevation is different, though, much more imposing and tasteful. I adore the marble columns! And the gardens . . .' She swung around to take in the sunken rose beds and parterres, the borders bright with zinnias and marigolds and the showy plumbago with its friendly blue blossoms. A hedge of bougainvillaea and hibiscus flaunted its beauty in the sunshine, while among the flowering trees growing in the massive lawns were the beautiful frangipani and the royal poinciana with its clusters of flaming-scarlet blossoms and fern-like leaves. The pink and yellow poiu rose next to the African tulip tree, branches and foliage mingling, and the backcloth was a magnificent traveller's palm. More borders met her eyes as she turned yet again, to meet another enchanting view, and then there was the lake with ibis and herons and wild ducks with gorgeous plumage that shone translucent in the sun's golden rays; hummingbirds and dragonflies added more variety and colour to the scene, and the chirping of cicadas completed the picture of something out of a fairy tale. Turning again, Juley looked up into her companion's face, her own now pale, her mouth quivering slightly. She could not have analysed the emotion that welled up within her; it was partly a yearning and partly the hopelessness which had been so familiar not so long ago, before she and Charles had met again. Yet there was something else affecting her which she could not explain. Was she envious of the girl who would probably become mistress of this lovely establishment? The girl who had a life before her, as Charles had a life.

Juley smiled in response to the amused curve of Charles's lips. He reminded her that beautiful as this home was, he had only his grandmother to thank for his being its owner. He took her arm and guided her up the wide steps to the front door. It was opened by a butler in immaculate black who said unsmilingly, '*Buenos dias, senhora.*'

'It's just a greeting,' explained Charles as she turned to him questioningly. 'Casco has bidden you good day.'

'Good morning,' she returned shyly.

Charles led her into the drawing room, which, he said, was called by his grandmother the Crimson Velvet Room on account not only of the upholstery of the chairs and sofas, but because the walls were covered with a Regency-type satin paper with gold and red velvet stripes. Much silver, and beautiful English porcelain were plentifully scattered about, on antique tables, in cabinets and on shelves above the pelmets. A room of exquisite taste, decided Juley, and yet cosy and lived-in. The kind of room where one could relax completely, find peace after a hard day's work or a long and tedious journey.

'You're pensive.' Charles seemed to be asking if she regretted her decision not to marry him. Was he hoping she was realizing what she could have had? But no; he was not like that at all. In any case, as he was certainly not in love with her now, he must be glad she'd made that decision. He now had an opportunity of marrying a wealthy woman whose estate adjoined his. Yes, he must be glad she, Juley, had turned him down.

'It's so beautiful here. It is such a peaceful room; that is what I was thinking. A "something special" room to which one would automatically come on entering this lovely home.' She was oblivious of the wistful shadow that lay in her eyes, but profoundly aware of a sudden feeling of turmoil which made her ask herself if she was falling in love with Charles. Not that it would matter, so long as he did not fall in love with her. It was unlikely. He had told her the affair was temporary, although it did seem he would like it to last for more than the two weeks which Juley had mentioned as being the period of the visit.

They had lunch in a small dining room situated in the south wing of the casa and then Charles took her back to the room she had admired and it was here that they had their coffee and liqueurs.

Juley leant back against the soft upholstery and breathed a sigh of contentment. The months left to her had so recently appeared to be fruitless, a time of fearful waiting with only oblivion at the end. But now she was uplifted, having Charles as her lover. She felt she could now meet her end unafraid because of these weeks of happiness which had miraculously been bestowed on her by a relenting fate.

In response to some magnetic draw she lifted her head to meet the intense scrutiny being given her by Charles. His expression was unfathomable, but a nerve pulsated strangely at the side of his throat, as if he were in the grip of some powerful emotion affecting nerves he could not control. What was he thinking as he held her eyes, held them by some irresistible magnetism! It seemed an eternity passed as they stared at one another, neither finding anything to say. His mouth was set, the line of his jaw as rigid as granite. But there was something different in his eyes, something more than the magnetism that held hers inexorably. A disturbing emotion set Juley's nerves on edge; she seemed to be drawing closer to Charles . . . but the physical intimacy had nothing to do with it. It was a relief when a manservant tapped at the door and the spell was broken.

'Come in.' A slight frown creased Charles's brow as if, for him, the interruption was certainly not welcome.

'Senhorita Mendosa is here, *senhor.*'

The hint of a frown was swiftly erased.

'Show her in.'

'*Si, senhor.*'

The man went out and Juley sent Charles an enquiring glance, but he was already saying, 'Mari. I thought she was away from home but she must have returned sooner than planned. She's been visiting a great-aunt of hers in England.'

'Mari . . .' Juley was conscious of a sudden flatness within her.

Charles's girlfriend was the last person she would have had intrude into this pleasant and intimate scene. 'England? She is part English, then?'

He nodded, smiling.

'She does have English blood in her veins, just as I have Mexican in mine, but her connections are rather less strong than mine. This great-aunt, as she calls her, is rather more distant even than that.'

'Where in England does this relative live?'

'Lyndford, I think.' He stopped. 'Isn't that where you lived with your husband?'

'Yes – it's not far from Chester.'

'What a strange coincidence.'

'It certainly is,' agreed Juley, her thoughts winging to James, and his new parents. They lived in the next village to Lyndford and so it was possible that this Mari, perhaps while out walking or in a car, had actually seen her baby

70

being pushed in his pram— Juley cut dead these meditations, self-consciously aware that her thoughts were silly
and irrelevant. Yet, in some unfathomable way she was
affected by the coincidence of Mari's relative living so close
to where her baby was now living with his new parents,
and she was one day in the not-too-distant future to recall
how she was being affected, because heartbreak was to come
to her almost equal to what she had experienced on parting with her baby.

A minute or so later a tall, self-assured girl was being
shown into the room. Juley was introduced, a smile coming
to her lips. It was ignored. The other girl, to say the least,
was cool and distant, appearing to resent the visitor Charles
had in his home.

'Juley is companion to Agatha's sister,' explained Charles,
who had risen from his chair to take Mari's silky suede
jacket from her. Juley, appreciative of good and well-
designed clothes since coming to work for Sarah, admired
the way the matching skirt moulded itself to the girl's svelte
figure, and the subtle way the blouse accentuated the delicate curves of her breasts and finely sloping shoulders. The
raven hair was taken back in a bun, so that the earrings of
sapphires and diamonds could be seen and appreciated in
all their sparkling glory. A necklace and bracelet completed
the matching set and Juley guessed their value at many times
what she herself could have earned in five years. 'She's here
because Sarah – Mrs Greatrix – is visiting her sister.' He
smiled affectionately at her, sweeping a hand towards a deep
armchair. 'Coffee?'

She shook her head, offering a wintry smile in response
to his affectionate one. She turned her immaculately coif-
feured head to enquire of Juley, 'Are you enjoying your stay
in our country, Mrs Allen?'

'Very much, thank you.' A feeling of inferiority came
upon her, with the result that she wanted to get away. She
felt flat, so very disappointed that the girl should have

chosen this particular time to call on Charles. She said, trying to ease her own discomfiture, 'Charles tells me you've been to England.'

Mari merely nodded her head and it was to Charles that she spoke.

'How does Mrs Allen come to be here, on her own? You said she was employed as companion to Agatha's sister.'

'I invited Juley to lunch.' Charles's tone was rather clipped. 'You see, we knew each other some years ago—'

'You knew each other? You are old acquaintances?' Without giving him time to answer, she added something in Spanish and Juley felt her colour rise as embarrassment grew. She was also angry at the girl's manner, speaking to Charles as if she, Juley, weren't there at all.

Charles replied to what was said in Spanish, then immediately reverted to the language which Juley could understand.

'Juley's been married, but is now a widow, her husband having met with an accident just a few weeks ago. She took this post in order to get away from familiar surroundings for a while.' He was adopting a charming manner towards her but Juley did wonder if he had sensed the girl's hostility. 'Mrs Greatrix lives in the Lake District of England but she suddenly decided she wanted to visit Agatha, so that made an even greater change for Juley.'

'I see,' with almost arrogant coldness. 'It was most fortunate for Mrs Allen to have found an employer who just happened to be coming on a trip like this.' She was plainly resentful, decided Juley again. The feeling was mutual, since Juley was resentful of Mari's appearance, her intrusion into a happy time, with the intimacy between her and Charles. All had been set for a pleasant afternoon as Juley was sure Charles had no intention of taking her back to the hacienda until the very last moment possible. Now, however, this chill had enveloped the room and Juley was pondering a way in which she could ask Charles to take her back. Mari's hard voice interrupted her thoughts and in answer to the girl's enquiry as to how long she and her employer would be staying she said she had no idea.

'It all depends on Mrs Greatrix,' interposed Charles, whose tone now carried an edge of curtness. 'I can't imagine that Mrs Greatrix will be making it a particularly short visit. She hasn't seen Agatha for several years, and added to that, she has all the time in the world, having no obligations back home – not from what I have gathered.'

He sent Juley an interrogating glance and she said quietly, 'Mrs Greatrix doesn't have any commitments that I know of.'

A frown marred the smooth beauty of Mari's forehead.

'So you could be here indefinitely, then?'

'Not indefinitely,' was all Juley offered as she turned to Charles. He was sitting with his back to the wide, high window and was staring at Mari through half-closed eyes. It was a measuring look of which the girl was completely unaware since her own eyes were focused on Juley's rather pale face. She missed nothing even though her very dark eyes were unmoving. She saw the finely contoured features, the high cheekbones and wide, intelligent brow, and the expressive brown eyes beneath, haloed by thick, incredibly long lashes. She was aware of the gleaming hair of russet brown, with natural highlights of what resembled spun gold as it caught the sunlight streaming through the window behind Charles. 'I'd like to go now, Charles.' Juley smiled at him but in her eyes he saw disappointment . . . and sadness too, but little knew that she was thinking that here was a gap in her happiness, caused by the intrusion of his girl-friend. 'Mrs Greatrix might be needing me,' she added and she saw his eyebrows lift a fraction. He knew very well that Sarah had said she did not need Juley until it was time to dress for dinner.

To her surprise he said, with a swift glance at Mari, 'You told me you could stay out all day.'

73

'Yes, but—' it was her turn to throw Mari a glance – 'I feel I should be leaving.'

He seemed far from pleased. Juley sent him a winning smile in order to make him feel better because by now he appeared to have noticed Mari's attitude. He rose from his chair and to Juley his silent sigh was obvious.

'Must you go?' he asked even while seeming to be resigned.

'Yes,' she nodded. 'I had better get back to Sarah.' She saw him cast another glance in Mari's direction but merely shrugged. Juley asked if she could go to the cloakroom as she wanted to wash her hands.

'Of course.' Charles walked to the door and she followed, profoundly conscious of two dark eyes following her, eyes glittering with dislike.

Juley was away no more than five minutes, since she was anxious to get away as soon as possible. She expected Charles would get one of his manservants to drive her home, since it was not feasible that he would leave Mari here alone. Juley had her hand on the ornate door knob of the salon when the mention of her name brought an instinctive pause. The door was already ajar and she heard quite clearly, '. . . this girl, Juley. And do I have to have a reason for calling like this, unexpectedly? How was I to know you would be entertaining an old flame?' Mari added something in Spanish but reverted to English again as she went on, 'I was bored sick with my aunt and her imaginary disorders, so I cut short my visit. She'll cut me out of her will and leave everything to Stephen but I don't care. I don't need her fortune when I've one three times as large of my own.'

What a way to talk! Juley could scarcely believe her ears. She made to open the door but paused. It was not nice to listen, she admitted, but her curiosity was natural seeing that she had been a part of the topic.

'You're not in one of your best moods today, Mari. What is wrong?' Charles voice was so quiet that Juley barely caught it, so she had no clue as to whether or not it carried affection in its tone. She rather thought it could have tolerance in its depths, but then again Charles might be chiding the girl. 'Are you sure you don't care about your aunt's fortune? Shall you be happy if she does leave it all to your cousin?'

'Charles, I can't keep going over to see her when I dislike her so much! It's becoming a chore, so why should I punish myself like this?'

'You only visit her twice a year,' he reminded her gently. 'I'd continue to do so if I were in your position, for although her fortune is only one-third of yours, it is still a very large one and I don't feel you will be happy if you lose it simply because you don't want to put yourself out for these two visits a year.'

'You're so mercenary, Charles,' came the complaint and it brought forth a surprised sort of laugh.

'I like that,' he admonished. 'If anyone is mercenary it is you. I often wonder if it is me you're interested in or what my grandmother left me.'

'Don't be silly! You know I love you and if you had nothing I'd still want to marry you.'

'Even if you had nothing too?' he queried softly and again Juley had to strain her ears. She felt she should open the door and go in, but just as the decision was made she heard her name mentioned again.

'Never mind that, Charles. Let's get back to this friend of yours. I don't care for the idea of your inviting her here. What would you say if I invited an old flame to lunch?'

Again he laughed.

'Do you have old flames, my dear? What have you been keeping from me?'

'Nothing, and you know it! But this woman—'

'Shall we leave her out of it?' There was no missing the arrogant and masterful inflection and Juley could easily imagine Mari's lifting her head and throwing him an angry glance.

75

'You're very puzzling at times, Charles.' A small silence ensued before she went on, reverting to the subject of her aunt as if the old lady were still on her mind, 'you know, I don't think Aunt Evelyn will leave her money to Stephen, not when I recall something she said to me one time when I was over to see her. She hadn't wanted Stephen to take up medicine. She'd wanted him to be an artist, like her husband, and Stephen certainly had talent, so she considered it a terrible waste for him to choose to become a doctor.'

Juley sensed a sudden impatience as Charles replied, 'Stephen had every right to please himself. He's making a name, from what I have heard, and read in the newspapers.'

'Oh, yes, I admit that. He specialized in brain surgery and has performed some spectacularly successful operations which is bringing him much publicity; he's plainly in the forefront in his particular kind of surgery.'

'He's one of the top neurosurgeons in Britain, and well on his way to even more fame. I read recently that his latest operation had been termed a miracle—'

Juley scarcely heard the last sentence because, having seen a movement at the far end of the hall, she quickly pushed open the door and entered the room in which the two had been talking.

'I'm ready.' She smiled at Charles as she passed him to pick up her handbag. 'You have someone to take me home?'

'I'm taking you home. Mari is just leaving.'

'Oh, but I think you ought to stay—'

'Sorry to push you off like this, Mari,' he broke in before the protest could be finished. 'I'll give you a ring later. We'll probably go out to dinner somewhere.'

Mari's dark eyes glinted as they rested on Juley for a moment and it was plain that the girl's hostility towards her had increased owing to Charles's behaviour. Juley was naturally embarrassed but refrained from voicing another protest as she strongly suspected Charles would not be over patient at the suggestion she be taken back to the hacienda by someone else, or by taxi.

Charles showed Mari out himself and when he came back he told Juley to sit down. Then astounded her by saying they could now continue their little chat.

'Perhaps we shall have more coffee made.' He pulled at a bell-rope by the side of the fireplace and soon there was a silver tray on the table and the manservant was pouring out two cups of steaming hot coffee.

Juley had already protested about his treatment of his girlfriend and now she repeated, when the man had gone, 'Mari, Charles – you weren't very nice—' She was silenced most effectively by Charles striding across the room and kissing her hard on the mouth.

'Surely you knew it was my intention to make love to you today,' he said with a sort of mocking satire which, added to the question itself, brought the hot blood washing into Juley's cheeks.

'I – I—'

'Before you begin to stammer out a lie, Juley, I'm stopping you.' He pulled her to her feet and for several minutes she thrilled to the mastery of his hard mouth and the nearness of his body. His hand was warm and gentle on her breast. He whispered in tones edged with ardour, 'We don't want that coffee, do we?' His ardour was increasing and so were Juley's heartbeats.

She found herself saying tenderly, 'No, Charles, we don't want the coffee.'

Then a shyness came over her, and a hint of fear. How could they get to a bedroom without one or more of the servants seeing them? Her face was buried in his linen jacket with the result that her words were muffled. He tilted her face with a finger beneath her chin and she saw eyes lit with amusement.

'I have a suite above here,' he told her after kissing the tip of her nose. 'We shall go up there and make love without

77

fear of interruption. It is more than anyone's job is worth to intrude unless I ring. I work up there, you see.'

'But won't they – suspect something if I go up there with you?' Shyness was still with her but her heartbeats were restored to normal.

He held her by the shoulders, towering above her, his finely chiselled mouth lifted at one corner in a half smile of amusement. His eyes danced, too, as he slowly shook his head.

'Does it really matter what anyone thinks? In any case, they'll not know we aren't talking business since I often take business associates up there.'

She went meekly with him, embarrassment mingling with pleasurable anticipation. And it was so simple once they were in the privacy of the delightful suite with the 'hall' door closed as well as that of the sitting room-cum-study with its satinwood bookshelves, its massive desk and the comfortable sofa with its matching chairs, all upholstered in a brightly flowered material which came as a surprise to Juley who would have imagined he would favour something more plain and conventional. Her feet sank into the carpet as she walked around, going at last to the window to appreciate the panoramic view of hills and a valley, of cultivated fields and, far beyond all this and to the east, the sea shimmering in the bay, smooth as silk and with many yachts and other craft silhouetted against the sapphire blue of the Mexican sky. She swung around, a wistful expression in her eyes.

'You have a beautiful home, Charles. You must be very proud of it.'

He flipped a hand carelessly.

'No credit due to me, remember. This all came to me on a plate, mine for the taking. I'm grateful, and yes, I do feel the natural pride of ownership, but I can scarcely claim any credit, can I? Now, had I made all this through hard work and sustained effort . . .' He tailed off, flipping a careless hand again. 'All I can do in gratitude to my grandmother is to keep it all as she would wish it to be kept, and to run the business efficiently.'

She looked at him across the room. The self-effacement made him all the more attractive to her. But, for some reason she could not explain, she had to mention Mari even though she knew she was risking a rebuff.

'Charles, your – er – association with Mari. She's wealthy – you told me that and so did Agatha. Shall you marry her? I'm asking because – and I expect you will perhaps be angry at what I am about to say – you don't seem to be in love with her.'

A few silent moments passed before he spoke. And when he did there was no sign of the anger she had anticipated.

'Mari and I are well suited in several ways, Juley. No, I am not wildly in love with her, nor is she with me, although she would have me believe she is. Mari wants the status of marriage but she has been very choosy. You see, she'll never marry a man who had no fortune. I suppose it is natural with a wealthy woman for her to fear being married for her money.'

'And so she wants to marry you?'

'Oh, yes, she wants to marry me. It is I who am the tardy one. I expect I shall make a decision soon – once you have gone.' He looked steadfastly at her. 'I intend to enjoy our affair, Juley. Perhaps I can call it my last fling, the final sowing of my wild oats.'

She lowered her lashes. Stupid to want to cry. Charles was giving her life! For a part of the time she had left – oh, so short it was becoming! – she could be happy, happy with the man in whose arms she could even forget what was her lot, for the time was *now*! And 'now' was beauti-ful. How long would Sarah stay? Juley felt she must know; she would ask her as soon as she got back to the hacienda. Yes, she must know just how long her affair with Charles was to last. Her eyes strayed to the sofa, and

Charles, smiling at her thoughts, told her quietly that there was another room in this suite. And he led her to it, taking her by the hand. It was his rest-room, he said . . . but the divan was a double one.

He said at last, 'You're the most beautiful and tempting woman I have ever made love to. How you do tempt me when all I want is to proceed slowly.'

'We were far too eager,' she agreed and a low laugh escaped him.

He began to caress slowly and she employed her gentle hands, too, in a prolonged interlude now of lazy love play, stimulating gently, without haste, enjoying the relaxation from the primitive ferocity of a short while ago. His fingers ignited the flare of passion and her breathing, like his, became erratic in the quickening momentum of their locked bodies. She smiled in the midst of her passion. It was good to know how deeply she attracted him, even though it was no more than a purely physical attraction. She thought, womanlike: One night, in the future, when he is with Mari, the memory of me will intrude and he'll remember how wonderful it was. But suddenly this idea became a dragging, smothering weight which she had not the strength to combat. And with the dark burden of depression came a sick and agonizing headache resulting in a little moan, which Charles quite naturally took for a plea and he lifted his body to get on top of her.

'No, Charles! Please – no! – I'm – I'm— Oh, God!'

'Juley, what's the matter? You can't want to change your mind now. Silly girl, how can you be scared when we've only just made love?'

'You don't understand . . .' She put her hands against his chest, trying to thrust him off.

'No,' grittingly, 'I certainly do not understand!' And with that he sought what he wanted, disregarding her struggles, believing her to be teasing. Certainly he had no idea she was earnest in her desire to get away from him. His hands were gripping her shoulders, his hungry mouth parting her pleading lips with ruthless mastery; he was acting as he believed she wanted him to. Defeated, but with her head still throbbing with pain, she abandoned the struggle. For she felt his first shudder of rapture as the final volcanic burst of pleasure drew close. He uttered her name in laboured tones, throaty and hoarse, and then fervid urgency took full possession of him. And Juley, despite the excruciating pain, arched her supple frame to help him, ensuring his ecstasy was complete. But then the tears were flowing, as he lay still beside her, drained of strength, languid in the sublime aftermath of his soaring flight to the very heights of bliss. Another little moan fell from her lips, and now Charles was alerted, aware of the dampness of her tears on his chest. He shot up to a sitting position.

'Juley! My God, child, you're ill.'

'It's my head,' she quivered, holding a trembling hand to it. 'Oh, Charles, I'm in such dreadful pain!'

'Dear Juley, why didn't you tell me—? But you did. Why wasn't I taking heed?' He slid from the divan, went to a small wardrobe and took out a dressing gown, which he immediately donned. 'You look ashen. Shall I call a doctor?'

She shook her head.

'In my bag, there on the table . . .' She pointed but slid from the divan just the same. 'If you would get me a glass of water, please.' He went at once while she found the tablets. He stood over her while she took them, an odd expression on his face. 'I'll be all right in a few minutes,' she assured him with the hint of a smile. So urgent had been her need for the tablets she had not heeded the fact that she was still naked. Charles took up the sheet and wrapped it around her. 'Thank you.' Her eyes kept closing with the pain.

He said with an unfathomable expression, 'Do you carry those tablets with you all the time?'

'Er – yes. Most women carry a few aspirins around with them. You never know when you're going to need one.'

'You have these headaches regularly?' She guessed he was recalling the previous evening, when she had gone to her room with a headache.

'It's the flight – jet lag, and probably the meal I ate on the plane didn't agree with me.'

'You're not very convincing.' His eyes were intent, probing. She lowered her lashes and heard him say, 'There's so much about you that I can't fathom. If you're ill why can't you say so?'

'I'm not ill. The pain's going.' She managed to inject a light and careless note into her voice. 'I'll get dressed. I could drink that coffee now, and I guess you could, too.'

He looked suspiciously at her, brows darkened.

'You're very adept at changing the subject,' he told her curtly, then took up his clothes and went into the bathroom.

When they had drunk the coffee, freshly made and brought in by the same manservant who had brought the other, untouched pot, Charles said he would drive her home.

Not much was said and Juley stared from her window, her thoughts not on the scenery but on the idea of confiding in Charles, telling him everything, that is, the two important things she had left out of her story. Her baby and his adoption; she felt she could easily tell about that, but if she did she would also have to tell him the reason for her act. One could not be told without the other and while she would very much like to talk to him about her baby son, she rejected the idea on account of the fact that she could not bring herself to tell him of her illness. It would be unbearable to have him pity her. He would, she felt sure, insist on Sarah knowing, which meant the whole household would know, and all would be pitying her, and probably feeling awkward in her presence; she could well imagine it all and she could not face it. No, for these last weeks left to her she wanted to live normally and the only way she could do that was to keep her secret close. She was happy in her relationship with Charles and should she confide he might feel he could no longer make love to her . . . for fear of her dying in his arms.

And Charles's love-making was all that made life worthwhile; it was a bonus she had never dreamed of a few days ago. It had imbued her with a new vigour, given her a reason for throwing off the black vision of her fate which had, until she came to Sarah, and consequently met Charles, been constantly with her, blotting out every last ray of sunlight.

But now the sun was shining for her . . . and life was good.

Five

Juley registered some considerable surprise when Sarah said there was a letter for her.

'A letter for me?'

'It's on the table in the hall. I left it there when Agatha handed it to me.' Sarah was in the garden, reading a book. Juley had been in her employer's bedroom, pressing some clothes and tidying out drawers. It was almost a fortnight since they had come to the hacienda and Sarah showed no signs of wanting to leave. As intended, Juley had asked her how long they would be staying and received the vague reply that Sarah did not know.

'I'm enjoying it here and I know you are, so we'll stay for a while.'

Juley's affair with Charles had been made easy and Juley often wondered if her employer's offer of so much time off was because she knew what was going on.

'What are your plans for today?' she added before Juley could go to find her letter. 'I did say you could have the whole day to yourself.' Sarah put her book on her lap and looked up at Juley. 'I mean it, my dear. It's at your disposal.'

'Thank you very much. You're exceedingly kind to me and I do appreciate it.'

'Gratitude isn't necessary. Is Charles taking you out? I expect you phoned to tell him you were free for the day?' There was little expression in the voice but keen interest in Sarah's eyes as they continued to fix themselves on Juley's face.

'Yes, I did phone him. He wants to take me to Mexico City.'

'An outing you'll thoroughly enjoy; I can guarantee it.' The blue eyes twinkled as she asked if Juley was intending to wear something pretty. 'That leaf-green dress with the lacy collar and cuffs is extremely flattering, I thought, the other day when you had it on. Off you go, dear, and make yourself attractive for him.'

Juley coloured, then had to laugh.

'There's nothing serious, you know,' she said. 'Charles is spoken for.'

'They're not engaged.'

'Unofficially, I should think.'

Sarah drew a breath and said almost shortly, 'Off you go, and put on that dress – and don't forget the perfume – the one I gave you suits you— All right! I'll not say another word.' And she picked up her book, ostensibly to read, but she watched Juley's slender figure until she entered the house.

The letter was from Dr Blount, to whom Juley had sent a picture postcard the day after her arrival at the hacienda.

Letty and I were pleased to receive your card telling us you were in Mexico. It will be a nice experience for you. Let us know when you will be back in England as we would like you to stay with us. In the enclosed envelope are a couple of snapshots. My wife said we ought not to send them but James's new parents particularly wanted you to know that he is thriving . . .

There was more but she could not read on just yet. The envelope was still in the larger, thicker one and Juley had not realized it was there. Now she withdrew it, her heart beating rather too fast for comfort, and her hands trembled visibly.

'My baby . . . my beautiful baby . . .' Tears inevitably

gathered behind her eyes, blurring her vision as she stared at the first snapshot. Chubby and laughing, his tiny feet in the air, James had been in a lovely shining pram when the picture was taken. 'How his hair has grown! It looks so thick – and it's going to curl, I think. Are you going to have curly hair, darling? And what a lovely smile you have,' she quivered on looking at the second picture. 'I'm sure you'll be very handsome one day—' She choked on the words, rubbed her eyes and looked again at the second snapshot. This time James was lying on a fluffy blue rug that had been spread on a lush green lawn. He was naked in the sunshine, eyes alight and obviously focused on the person taking the picture. 'You will never know me, know th-that I brought you into th-the world and would have loved you so much, my darling, and cared for you so very well—' Again she stopped and the tears washed on to her cheeks unhindered by the handkerchief she had taken from her pocket. 'But you are happy,' she managed after a while, 'and I'm so very grateful that you will always be with these good people who love you as if you were their own . . . Oh, why do I cry so, when I should be happy that you, my little son, are so happy, and always will be?'

She felt she could not go out with Charles today. She just wanted to sit quietly by herself and look at these snapshots of her child, the baby she had been forced to give away, and in these moments of agony she felt the wrench as if it were only an hour that had passed since she parted with him. No, she would not go out with Charles— But already he would be on his way, so there was no way she could get in touch to stop him coming. She was in her room and she glanced in the mirror; her face was flushed, her eyes swollen and moist. What must she do? Sarah had always maintained that she, Juley, had no need of artificial aids but after bathing her eyes and washing her face she set to and applied eyeshadow to her lids, hoping it would detract from the eyes themselves. She used the blusher on her pallid cheeks, and applied rouge to her lips. Not too bad at all. And perhaps it was wise to go out anyway. If she sat here, staring at the snapshots, she would be crying all the time.

But she could not leave them, so she put them into her handbag. It was as if she must have them for comfort even while she knew without any doubt at all that every time she looked at them she would be in tears.

Charles subjected her to a critical scrutiny and said baldly. 'You've had one of your headaches again. Does Sarah know about them, because if not, it's time she did.' He was all mastery and authoritative; she was quick to tell him she felt fine and had certainly not had a headache.

'I really do feel fine,' she reiterated when it seemed he was far from satisfied. He was holding the car door open for her and she slid into her seat. 'I'm very much looking forward to this trip. Sarah said I'd thoroughly enjoy it and I'm sure I shall.'

He stood for a moment after closing the door, an unfathomable expression on his handsome face. His manner was disturbing; she hoped he would not tell Sarah she had these headaches. She'd had two in the past week, so it was not surprising that he was beginning to disbelieve her when she said it was 'nothing'. Just a normal headache which was always cured by a couple of aspirins, she told him.

He observed when he was in the car beside her, 'If you haven't had a headache then you've been crying.' His hands on the wheel were idle as he waited for her comment. 'Your eyes are swollen,' he added rather crisply when she did not speak.

'Loss of sleep.' Her voice carried a casual ring. 'For some stupid reason I didn't sleep too well last night.'

'I see . . .' His tone was sceptical and brusque. 'Perhaps you should rest, then, instead of coming on this trip.'

'Charles,' she chided with an attempt at banter, 'you're being horrid with me!'

'And you are being dishonest with me,' he countered curtly.

'Please don't ask me questions,' she begged after a moment of considering, wishing she could be open with him and that she could proudly show him the snapshots of her dear little son. 'You and I agreed to have this affair; we both enjoy it but have accepted there's no permanency about it. So don't let us probe too deeply into each other's private affairs.'

Silence followed as he started the car and steered it towards the avenue of lime trees.

'Your words have only deepened the mystery. However, I'll do as you suggest; we'll make a pact not to worry our heads with the problems of the other.'

She was relieved by his agreement; she had nothing more to worry about. He would not question her again. But obviously he was extremely curious – and he was a man of keen perception, so although she would not be questioned directly, Juley decided she would have to be on her constant guard against any clever manoeuvre he might decide to make in order to satisfy his curiosity.

He fell silent; she hoped he had not been too vexed by her plea and she leant back, relaxed, but her mind on the snapshots in her handbag. How she wanted to take them out! To look and look, to hand them to Charles and say proudly, 'This is my little son. Isn't he beautiful—?' She jerked with pain shooting through her head; the blackness of fear enveloped her, so that she could scarcely breathe. The pain were coming more often now . . . and one would herald the end. She found herself clutching the door handle, relieved to notice that, having entered an area of rather heavy traffic, Charles's whole attention was on his driving. But she could not take the tablets without water, so she willed the pain to cease. Mind over matter. It was said there is nothing one cannot do if one really makes up one's mind. The pain *could* be made to go away. And miraculously it began to ease. By the time they were in the city, strolling down a narrow street with Spanish-style houses, the pain had gone completely.

'This is charming!' she exclaimed when, having turned into the thoroughfare known as Paseo de la Reforma, they were walking along an avenue of ash trees and eucalyptus where, at intervals, there were wide circles of monuments where people sat on stone seats chatting or having their shoes cleaned by barefoot boys with cheeky grins on their not-too-clean faces. 'Aren't I lucky, seeing all this!' The exclamation came forth spontaneously, her head lifting so that she could look into his face. His smile was enigmatic but she could see the admiration as his dark eyes swept from her gleaming hair, tousled by the breeze, to the slope of her shoulders and then lower and lower till he had absorbed the beauty of her whole body. A nerve twitched in his throat; his face became a mask devoid of expression and his pace increased, so that she had to give a little skip now and then to keep up with him – that was, until he saw what he had done and he then slackened his pace again but his eyes swept over her figure once more and with dancing eyes and a voice that teased she said laughingly, 'It isn't any use looking at me in this sexy way, Charles. You can't do anything here.'

Charles gave a gust of laughter, told her she was a minx, then added challengingly, 'Can't I?' and without more ado he took her face between his hands and kissed her hard on the lips. 'There are shady places around here that I know of, so don't you tempt me, my girl!' He took possession of her hand and they strolled along in companionable silence. She sighed contentedly. This was living! And later, if they left the city early enough, Charles would make a detour on the way back so they could spend an hour or so at his home, where his body would provide her with forgetfulness and pleasure indescribable.

After a while she asked if they could go to the shops.

'I heard Ramos and Agatha talking and it seems Sarah has a birthday coming soon. I didn't get the date but they were discussing having a party for her. I'd like to find her something really nice, something – different.'

'Another birthday party.' He paused in thought and she flicked him an upward glance from under her lashes, noticing a slight frown between his eyes. She wondered if he were thinking that, were he to be invited – which was of course a foregone conclusion – then Mari would be invited also, now that she was back home. 'Yes,' murmured Charles, 'we can go to the shops. We'd best go by car, though.'

The shopping area proved to be a vast region sprawling out in all directions but the most exclusive and expensive shops were situated in the Avenida Francisco Madero and it was to this part that Charles took her. She bought a tooled leather handbag and six embroidered handkerchiefs to put into it. Then Charles was looking at a solid gold bracelet that had caught his eye and Juley stood beside him, slanting him an oblique glance and wondering if he would buy this for Mari in the hope that she would like it. Juley rather thought she was the kind of girl who would prefer to choose things like jewellery herself and not have a 'surprise' as most women would wish.

'What do you think of this?' he asked Juley.

'It's really beautiful. Mari should like—'

'I want to buy it for you.'

He took her arm to guide her into the shop but she drew back saying before she had time to think, 'No, Charles, it isn't worth it for the short time . . .' And too late she tailed off, with Charles already looking at her with the most odd expression, puzzled as much by her fluctuating colour as by the words she had so inadvertently uttered. 'You know wh-what I m-mean,' she added wishing she did not stammer so. 'You and I – we're going to say goodbye quite soon and – well – a bracelet like that . . .' Again she let her voice trail to silence, profoundly aware of his bewilderment.

90

'Short time, you said?' His penetrating gaze disconcerted her and she lowered her eyes, cursing herself for the slip. 'Surely a present like this is one to keep for a long time,' he added slowly at last. 'What has our goodbye to do with it?'

She moved uneasily, looking up into a steely gaze as they stood there, by the glittering window of the best jewellers in the city. 'It's such an expense—'

'An expense. But there isn't a price on it.' Again that slow deliberate manner of speaking.

'It will be expensive, though,' she replied defensively.

'Which has nothing to do with you. I want to buy you a present and you've said you like it. Also, I noticed you looking at a bracelet very like this in that other shop along there.' He flipped a finger to indicate the shop. He was puzzled and she had the uneasy conviction that his suspicions were growing to a point where he could very well consult Sarah to ask if she knew anything about the 'mystery' which Charles knew existed. Juley decided, under the circumstances, to appear eager, since it was a certainty that Charles intended buying her the bracelet.

'I do like it – I think it's beautiful – and I'd love to have it from you as a present, Charles.'

The purchase was made and they left the shop with the velvet-lined box in Charles's pocket.

'And now for some lunch,' he suggested briskly. 'Let us drive back to the centre of the city.' This was the *Zocalo*, the very heart of the town, the main square officially known as the Plaza of the Constitution. Here, Charles told her, the Conquistadores destroyed the splendid Aztec monuments, then erected their own palaces on top of the remains. Recently,' continued Charles, aware that she was avidly taking it all in, 'workmen digging in an area behind the cathedral unearthed a ceremonial stone weighing over eight tons. This stone was used five hundred years ago by the Aztecs. The workmen were immediately taken off the site and the archaeologists moved in; the result is that many more relics of the Aztec Empire have been discovered.'

'Isn't it interesting? I'd love to stay here and see what other finds come to light.' She stopped rather abruptly, aware that she had quite forgotten, for that moment, just how little time was left to her. She had visualized the excitement of learning about ancient finds which would be periodically made on this fantastic archaeological site.

'What made you stop so quickly?' They were arriving at a car park and as the car slowed down he turned his head to ask the question.

'Well – it's just that I shan't be here, shall I? When Sarah decides to leave that is the end of my visit to Mexico.'

He brought the car to a standstill. Juley was assisted out and no word was spoken by either of them.

Charles took her to a hotel built on the lines of an Aztec temple where the restaurant overlooked exotic gardens and two swimming pools. In a cocktail lounge, which was in effect a verandah, with colourful flowers abounding, they had aperitifs and, after a lunch of *ceviche* – fish marinated in lime juice and seasoned with chilli, tomato, oregano, and garnished with olives and avocado – then strawberries and cream to finish off with, they sauntered along to the Museum of Anthoropology. It was the finest museum in the world, Charles said as they entered.

'So obviously we'd need much more than the couple of hours we have if we wished to see everything,' he said with a grimace. They saw the famous Aztec Calendar Stone carved only a few years before Columbus set sail from Spain; they saw the model of the Great Temple which once stood on the site of the *Zocalo* at the time of the arrival of Cortés with his destructive Conquistadores. Juley, fascinated, could have stayed on for hours but the afternoon was passing swiftly and she had to be back at the hacienda in good time to help Sarah with her lengthy preparations for dinner. So, mused Juley, there would be no going back to the casa today.

'It's been a wonderful day, Charles,' she smiled as they left the museum and walked slowly to where Charles had parked the car. The smell of cakes newly baked brought the suggestion that they have afternoon tea before driving home.

'Have we time?' asked Juley doubtfully.

'We can spare half an hour or so.'

She knew he was doing it for her, to add one final touch, one last pleasure to a memorable day. So she agreed and once inside the café the waiter came to say they would have to wait a few minutes for a table.

'If you would like to sit here until we are ready –?' He had led them into a small lounge and indicated a low sofa. 'We will not keep you long.' With a flash of white teeth he was gone and they sat down, but it was only a matter of five minutes before another waiter approached to say the table was now ready.

'Are these yours, Juley?' She had preceded Charles but swung around as he spoke. He was holding the two snapshots, looking intently at them. Her breath caught. She had opened her handbag to bring out her diary, intending to make a few notes as she and Charles waited for their table. The snapshots had somehow fallen out without her noticing, but she could not imagine how it had happened. But it had, and Charles, looking up from the pictures, was now regarding her questioningly. In a panic, the kind which deprives one from thinking clearly, she shook her head and said no, they did not belong to her. He shrugged and laid them on the arm of a chair. She saw a waiter pick them up and drop them into a waste-paper basket. She bit her lip, hesitating in a fervour of suspense, wondering what to do. How stupid it was to have lied when, had she stopped to think, she could have said yes, they were hers, saying the child was that of a friend. So simple . . . but she had panicked and acted impulsively. Charles was showing some surprise and puzzlement at her pausing there instead of proceeding to the table in the wake of the waiter. She had an inspiration then, realizing it would be a simple matter to excuse herself once she got to the table, saying she wanted to wash her hands. This she did, and hurried back to the lounge, only to find, to her consternation, that the basket had been taken away. She asked a passing waiter where it was. He spoke very broken English but she was able to understand that the contents of the basket had been put on a fire.

'Fire?' puzzled, as she glanced around. 'Where is this fire?'

It was in the kitchen, she learned, and as the man had pointed she sped away in the direction indicated. She must regain possession of those precious snapshots – she must! She entered the kitchen, oblivious of the stares of the cooks and other staff who were working there. She stopped dead, staring at the basket which was standing empty beside an big iron cooking stove.

She went to the powder room, weeping, and at the same time cursing herself for her carelessness in the first place, and then her stupidity in disclaiming ownership of the precious snapshots. To have had them in her possession for such a short space of time. Now they were gone beyond recall, burned in that stove, along with the rubbish which had been in the basket.

It was some time before she felt ready to join Charles, her tears having left their mark. But although he stared at her strangely, he made no comment as she sat down opposite to him.

He was obviously remembering the pact they had made earlier: not to probe into one another's private affairs.

Six

The loss of the snapshots preyed on Juley's mind so much that she had no sleep that night. Earlier, Sarah had shown curiosity as to who had sent the letter and Juley had said it was from a friend. And as she added nothing else to this Sarah had become rather cool, so it was a relief to Juley when the trying evening came to an end and she was in the privacy of her bedroom. But she could think of nothing else but the loss of the photographs, and the fact of their being burned, along with rubbish, only made matters worse. They had become treasures during the short time she had had them, and for some quite illogical reason she felt a deep anger against Charles for being the one to pick them up. Had it been a waiter, and had Charles not been there, all would have been well. The fact that Charles certainly would have been there made no difference. She blamed him for the loss of her precious photos.

'What is the matter with you?' he demanded curtly when, the following day, she could scarcely be civil to him. 'Are you becoming tired of the affair? If you want to terminate it you have only to say so.'

Casual and uncaring . . . He had spoken words to startle her, words which revealed the almost indifferent attitude he had towards their relationship. Yet this attitude was contrary to the fact of his buying her that lovely bracelet, to his tenderness, to his flattery – oh, yes, and to much more in his behaviour towards her. That he did not love her she could accept – and was glad he did not love her as he could not be hurt when the end came – but that he was indifferent and casual to this extent she could certainly not accept. But looking at him she saw a hard uncompromising countenance and fear rose within her. He was the most important person in her life and should he call a halt to the affair she would wish to die immediately, since she would have nothing left to live for. His charm, his companionship, his love-making . . . All were so vitally important for making her diminishing days happy, for helping her not to dwell on the ordeal soon to come, an ordeal which, in times of depression before she met Charles again, here in Mexico, she had wished was over and done with. 'I asked you a question, Juley!' His tone was icy cold as was the expression in his eyes.

She answered hastily, 'Of course I don't want to terminate our affair. I'm sorry, Charles, for being horrid with you.' She turned a wistful face towards him. 'You see, something happened to upset me. But I'm all right now.'

'Something happened? Was it yesterday?'

'Er – yes, it was, as a matter of fact.'

She hoped he would remember their pact, and refrain from any further questions, but he did say, a little testily, 'Can't you tell me about it? Has it something to do with Sarah?'

She shook her head.

'Sarah's marvellous with me. She gives me so much time off.'

'And you know why, don't you?' His anger melted under the amused curve of his lips. 'It's plain to see she's matchmaking. Your employer would like to see something develop from this friendship and so she is playing her part by giving you ample free time.' He and Juley were at his home, where he had brought her to spend the whole day. 'She's going to be disappointed when it comes to an end, I'm afraid.'

She nodded in agreement.

'I guess she is.' Juley paused a moment. 'There's something I must ask you, Charles, and it's rather personal.'

The dark brows lifted as if as a reminder of their pact and she coloured faintly. He said pointedly, 'Yes? But I believe we made a promise not to ask one another questions.'

'I remember,' she acknowledged, but went on to say it was rather important, and in any case, it was not really touching on the deeply personal.

'Go ahead, then,' encouraged Charles but there was a moment of hesitation before Juley spoke what was in her mind.

'It's about Mari, and of some importance to me. I don't like hurting people and she's not going to be happy if she ever finds out about us.'

'She doesn't have any suspicion, and I can't see any reason why she ever should. You see, we never have done much together during the day – mainly because I'm usually working in my study for several hours, and she has her various social activities like bridge and tennis and some charities with which she is periodically involved. We usually see each other about three or four evenings a week, and on occasions we've spent the whole of a Sunday together.'

'So it's all right, then, our having this affair. It won't hurt her, because she'll never know?'

Charles regarded her in speculative silence for a space, and for the very first time she had the impression of contempt lurking beneath the rather blank exterior.

'You say you don't like hurting people, but you are willing to have this affair. It seems to be a case of "what the eye doesn't see the heart does not grieve over", yet, somehow, the part you are playing doesn't fit your character as I see it.'

She lowered her lashes, his words having gone home, a reminder of her own self-condemnation. Willingly to indulge in an affair with a man another girl hoped to marry was what only a bitch would do, so what must she say to him? He was studying her, a flicker of interested enquiry in his stare, waiting to see how she would react to his comment.

She heard herself say at last, 'You're thinking that I'm not a nice person, basically, aren't you?'

'So you acknowledge to yourself that what you're doing isn't quite the thing?'

Something made her laugh; she thought it was the last three words.

'This is a very strange conversation, Charles.'

His eyes lit up with amusement, but she sensed that hint of contempt to be there as well.

'We're both thinking only of ourselves,' he stated. 'The physical attraction we have for one another is far more important than doing the honourable thing, which, under the circumstances, would be to resist temptation – which would be a pity seeing that we can give one another so much pleasure. After all, life is for living, every moment of it if at all possible.'

Every moment of it . . . If only he knew!

He had made a matter-of-fact statement carrying no hint of contrition or regret for being unfaithful to Mari.

'Going back to what you said a moment ago,' he interposed into her musings, 'neither of us is a nice person, basically.'

'But we like each other despite that fact.' She laughed again and he joined in. 'Shall you remember me, I wonder, when all this has been over and done with for, say, a year?'

Charles lifted his brows and rejoined with assumed pain, 'Are you suggesting I could forget anything as pleasurable as this in only a year?'

'You'll probably be married to Mari.' She had no idea of the bleakness that had entered her voice, nor of the yearning expression shadowing her eyes. And they completely escaped Charles's notice.

His stare became narrowed and penetrating.

'You don't care a fig, do you, whether I remember you or not?'

Somehow she was startled by the question, since it could mean that it was a matter of importance to him how she answered it. Was he just a little bit attracted to her in a way other than the purely physical? He must never come near to falling in love with her. No, she must ensure that nothing like that should happen as he must not be hurt.

So she laughed and replied lightly, 'Frankly, Charles – no, I don't care a fig whether you remember me or not. As far as I am concerned you can forget me the moment we say goodbye.'

A silence followed, hostile and cold. She shivered, hugging her arms. She looked through the window on to a scene of beauty and good taste, on to exotic grounds filled with sunlight and colour, where marble statues looked more like gleaming silver and where fountains playing over ornamental pools stole rainbow hues from the sun to scatter them over the aquatic vegetation. A scene of blissful peace and tranquillity . . . but in Juley's heart lay tension and conflict, for although one part of her genuinely hoped Charles would not fall in love with her, the other yearned desperately for a place in his heart and in his memory.

She was in love with him. No longer could she deny what was so vitally alive within her . . . and her love was far, far deeper and stronger than it had been all those years ago, when she was able to give him up, just because his father wanted it that way.

Charles's hard, cold voice interrupted her meditations and she brought her eyes from the window and looked at him.

'Well, you've made it abundantly clear as to just where I stand. But it is of no matter. As you have so often reminded me, this is only a temporary diversion for both of us.'

'I'm sorry if I said something you don't like, Charles.'

'Forget it,' he snapped, then uttered a low laugh, mirthless and brief. 'How did we manage to become so serious?'

She made no reply. She was recalling his saying, just a short while ago, that Sarah was going to be disappointed when the association between them came to an end. That did not tally with the possibility of his having begun to fall in love with her, and she sank back into the chair with a sigh of relief. Charles was merely amusing himself before he settled down to married life and becoming a father. He had said himself that this was his last fling, the final sowing of his wild oats.

For a change, Sarah wanted Juley to be with her for the whole day on the following Tuesday. So Juley phoned Charles, whose disappointment was undisguised as he heard her say she would not be seeing him at all that day.

'We're going into town,' she went on, 'as Sarah wants to do some shopping.'

'What about tomorrow?'

'I'll phone you when I find out whether she needs me or not.'

'Her birthday. Have you found out when it is?'

'Yes, a week today. Agatha's giving a party for her. I expected her to do so. I think your invitation went out today.'

'A week today . . . So you'll not be leaving until after that. Probably she'll decide to stay for at least another fortnight.'

'She hasn't even mentioned going home. She seems settled, and is certainly enjoying herself. She and Agatha have been almost inseparable. I suppose it's owing to their not having seen one another for so long.'

'Well, it's good news that she's settled for a time. I'll wait for your phone call.'

'It could be this evening.'

'I'll be in. Mari's coming to dinner.'

Juley went quiet. Mari and Charles dining in the candlelit intimacy of that lovely room. Flowers and soft music . . . She caught her lip, biting till it hurt. If only she had not fallen in love with him. But she was in love in a way which made her feelings for Barry seem a weak and worthless emotion by comparison. This was real, vital, deep as the ocean, wide as the sky. It filled her being to the exclusion of all else and she prayed that the time predicted as left to her would not be cut short.

Agatha drove them to town and it was when Sarah, having decided on impulse to go with her sister to the hairdresser's and hope she would get service even though, unlike Agatha, she had no appointment, left Juley to her own devices, that she ran into Mari, the latter having come to town for an interview with her bank manager. This having been conducted, she dropped into a little open-air café for a cup of coffee. Juley had the same idea, and chose the same café – a coincidence since cafés abounded. The two met, said hello and sat down at the same table. Juley was not over-pleased but she could scarcely say no when Mari smilingly suggested they share a table. The girl was more friendly than at that other meeting and within minutes the aversion Juley had felt was rapidly disappearing.

'Are you enjoying your holiday?' Mari took a cigarette from a gold case after offering it to Juley, who said she did not smoke.

'It isn't a holiday as such,' she corrected, watching her take out a matching gold lighter. 'I'm Mrs Greatrix's companion as you know. But my stay here has been most enjoyable.'

'You've been around?'

'A bit,' answered Juley guardedly.

'Mrs Greatrix goes out, I expect. And you go with her?'

'She's with me now – but has gone off to have her hair washed and set.'

The older girl's eyes narrowed suddenly.

'It so happens, Mrs Allen,' she murmured with slow deliberation, 'that I've seen you in Mexico City with Charles. I've also learned that you are a regular visitor to his home.'

Juley's nerves tensed, and she knew some of the colour had left her face. It struck her forceably that her affair with

Charles could come to an abrupt end if Mari threatened to give him up, since she felt sure that, however casual he appeared to be about his association with Mari, he did intend to marry her one day.

'We knew one another years ago,' she said defensively. 'We merely chat, and he has shown me his home—'

'Many times,' snapped Mari. 'Perhaps you can explain why?'

Juley lifted her chin.

'I don't quite understand what you are getting at, *senhorita*.' The white-aproned waitress was at the table and Juley gave her order for coffee. Mari gave hers in Spanish.

'Charles and I are practically engaged to be married.' The girl drew on her cigarette and inhaled deeply. 'I expect you know, because everyone up at the Ramos home knows.'

Practically engaged? Well, perhaps it was true. Juley swallowed the painful little lump which had risen in her throat.

She said a trifle huskily, 'Yes, I did know – at least, I know that you and Charles have an understanding.'

'Charles has told you?'

'Things he has said give me the impression that you and he will marry one day.' She wished she had not come into this café, and was in two minds about making some excuse and leaving.

But the coffee was arriving and she felt she could scarcely get up and go now.

'I'm glad you know how it is with Charles and me,' Mari was saying with a sort of acid sweetness. 'Our estates adjoin, and so we became friends almost as soon as Charles came to live here, in Mexico, having inherited the casa and all that goes with it.'

There was an air of arrogant superiority about the way she spoke of Charles's inheritance which brought Juley's hackles rising. However, she feigned a degree of friendliness and said conversationally, 'I expect you are invited to Mrs Greatrix's birthday party?'

'Of course. Charles will be picking me up and taking me to the hacienda. I must find a suitable present.' She inhaled, tapped the cigarette against the ashtray and then took a sip of her coffee. 'I don't suppose you could give me an indication of what she likes?'

'She loves perfume – and it doesn't matter which because she tries them all.' Juley laughed at the recollection of Sarah's using no less than three different perfumes at once. 'Then there are things like evening bags. She likes many changes, to go with what she happens to be wearing, and I can safely say she would like a black one as she was telling me that she ought to be getting a new one as she has had the one she uses far too long.'

'Thanks. I'll get a bag, then. It is so difficult, buying presents . . .' She tailed off, her attention caught suddenly. 'You are wearing a lovely bracelet. That must have been a present. From your late husband?'

Startled by the question, Juley felt the colour rise in her cheeks, and saw Mari's eyes narrow to mere slits. Juley marvelled at the cool collected way she was able to voice the lie: 'Yes, from Barry, on our second wedding anniversary.' But she spoke rather quickly and noticed Mari's mouth compress.

'It looks quite new,' observed the older girl tautly. 'You must rarely wear it.'

Juley moistened her lips.

'I haven't worn it much up till now,' she replied, glad to be telling the truth this time.

But she was unprepared for Mari's smoothly spoken, 'Up till now, eh . . . ?' She inhaled again, her eyes still narrowed. 'How long have you had it, Mrs Allen?'

Juley had a sudden impulse to tell the truth; it would certainly be less harrowing than groping around for another lie. Still, it was only a white one, since it formed a complement to the lie already told.

'Two years.'

'I see.' The dark eyes sought the gleaming gold again. 'So you were married for four years?'

'Yes, that's right.'

'You're young to be widowed, Mrs Allen.'

'It was through an accident.'

'Very sad. Have you any children?'

Yet another lie. Once again Juley wished she had not been so unlucky as to choose this particular café.

'No –' She shook her head, thinking of the two lost snap-shots. 'No, I didn't have any children.' Mari was watching her closely and Juley felt sure her cheeks had reddened. Quickly she lifted her cup to her lips, uneasily conscious of the other girl's continued stare, and of the silence which was heavy and, somehow, ominous. Why should she feel like that – as if Mari could harm her in some way?

'That,' murmured Mari smoothly, 'was fortunate for you, since you will have more chance of marrying again if you have no encumbrances – for children are encumbrances when second marriages are contemplated. No one wants someone else's children, do they?'

'I wouldn't know, *senhorita*.' Juley's voice was cool, to say the least. Her former dislike of the girl was rapidly returning. 'Nor does it interest me since I shall not be marrying again.'

'Of course you'll marry again. You're far too young to remain single for the rest of your life.'

The rest of your life . . .

'I'll not argue with you.' Juley finished her coffee and picked up her bag. She was ready to leave but Mari spoke again, to ask what part of England she came from.

'I know you live in Cumberland now,' she went on with an unexpected smile which revealed perfect white teeth and the tip of a pink tongue. 'Charles mentioned it one night, but that isn't where you're from originally?'

It would seem that Charles had not mentioned that she, Juley, came from the next village to where Mari's great aunt lived, and Juley had no wish to mention it either, yet how could she evade the question? Another lie? No, it was quite unnecessary. Mari's look of surprise was not unexpected, nor her swift remark that this was very close to the place so recently visited.

'What a coincidence! Small world, isn't it?'

'Very.' Juley rose from her chair. 'I'm sorry, but I have to be going. My employer will be waiting for me if I don't hurry.' And with that she managed a thin smile, lifted a hand and swiftly made her escape. What an ordeal that had turned out to be!

Yes, quite literally it was an escape, but Juley was perturbed nevertheless. It would be disastrous if Mari should learn she'd had a baby . . . Yet how could she? This sudden fear was absurd, Juley admonished herself. Hadn't Mari told Charles she might never go over to England again?

Once again Juley felt she had to ask Sarah when she would be going home.

'Not yet. Do you want to leave, my dear?' The subtle inflection could not be missed, but it could be ignored.

'No, of course not,' airily and with a smile. 'I just wondered, that was all.'

'You and Charles . . .' Sarah tailed off, her eyes amused. 'He does have a girlfriend, you know.'

'Yes. Mari; we've mentioned her before.' Juley hoped she was appearing to be calmly indifferent. 'Charles and I are not becoming serious, if that is what you are hinting at.'

'Charles,' returned Sarah with a wide significant stare, 'spends far more time with you than with this Mari girl.'

'Mari sees him almost every evening.'

'Does she know of your – er – friendship with her boyfriend?' That was bluntness and no mistake, so much being revealed in the hesitation. Juley felt uncomfortable, wishing she were one of those quick-witted people who always had an answer ready.

'What makes you suppose it is an affair?' was all she

could muster and a laugh issued from her employer's lips.

'The absence of an indignant denial is significant,' she commented, with another laugh at Juley's obvious discomfiture. 'However, I haven't mentioned an affair.'

'You hinted at at, though.'

'You mystify me, Juley. Oh, I respect your desire for privacy as to your personal affairs, but you and I do happen to have become rather more than employer and employee, and I'd love to know more about you.'

'There's very little *to* know, Sarah.'

'But,' pronounced the older woman with slow deliberation, 'that little is, I am sure, the most important part. What you have already told me about yourself is nothing.'

Juley paused then said with a direct look, 'I'm glad you respect my wishes, Sarah.'

'Little wretch! You care nothing about my woman's curiosity!'

Juley had to laugh.

'You once said you'd tell me your story but I never pressed you – nor even reminded you until now.'

The merest pause followed before Sarah smiled and said, a faraway look in her eyes, 'I was madly in love with my husband, Juley, and still cherish his memory to the extent that I shall never marry again. I have a child – a daughter—' She stopped, a frown knitting her brow and it seemed that she would not continue, but eventually she did. 'She's bad, Juley, as bad as they come.'

'Bad?' Juley shook her head in pained protest. 'How could any child of yours turn out to be bad? In what way do you mean?'

'Every way.' For a moment Sarah's eyes were infinitely sad. 'At only eighteen she got in with a crowd of undesirables, drop-outs, and she went off to Australia with some of them. They dressed in rags, stole to live until thrown out of the country by the government, deported. She takes drugs; she sleeps with men—'

'Oh, don't say such things!' begged Juley. 'It's hurting you . . . Oh, I wish I'd never reminded you of the promise to tell me all about yourself! I'm sorry, so very sorry.'

'It's nice of you, child.' She looked at her steadily in the eyes before letting her own wander over Juley's figure. They were standing by an ornamental pool where waterfowl preened themselves, their glorious plumage iridescent in the sunshine. A peaceful view with marble statues standing guard by fountains sporting rainbow colours – it was all so much like Charles's home, thought Juley. All luxury and comfort, yet here was a sad story not at all in keeping with the beauty surrounding the woman who was telling it. 'If only she'd been like you, my dear. Ever since you came to me I've wished you were my daughter instead of her. What a wonderful relationship we'd have had, a happy future. I'd have had my own child with me when the time came for me to die—'

'No!' The one short word burst forth, and Juley was on the verge of tears. 'No, it wouldn't have been like that at all. It *couldn't* have been. It would have been more sadness for you—' She stopped, aware that she was mystifying her listener. 'You see, Sarah, I could never have been your daughter, could I? So it isn't logical to dream of what might have been.'

'You talk in a strange way, Juley. What is this sadness I'd have suffered if you had been my daughter? You'll not talk about yourself.' She shook her head resignedly. 'Let us change the subject. But I will say this finally before we do. One day you might in fact want to confide. Well, I'm here, Juley. I want you to keep that in mind.'

Juley nodded, emotion causing a constriction in her chest. Would the time come when she was ready to confide? She had received another letter from Dr Blount telling her the house was sold, the money in the bank. He knew it was for James, he said, but for the time being it must be available for her when she left Mrs Greatrix's employ on the return

107

of Maisie. It had crossed Juley's mind that she might be denied the full time given – estimated, rather – by the specialist, in which case there would be the possibility of the final pain coming while she was still here, but on the other hand, she might have a little more time, in which case, should she have left Mrs Greatrix, she would need some money for entry into a nursing home.

She said, in an attempt to throw off the depression that had descended on her, mainly owing to Sarah's sad story, 'Let's talk about your party. I'm really looking forward to it, but I suspect I shall feel dowdy, as I did at Ramos's party.'

'Dowdy! you looked perfect, as you always do. Charles obviously thought so,' she added with a deliberate lack of expression in her voice. Juley wondered if she was remembering that locked door between their rooms. 'But if you really feel like looking extra special allow me to buy you a dress.'

Colouring at the suggestion, Juley shook her head, albeit a trifle apologetically since it was a charming gesture for Sarah to make.

'It isn't necessary. I'll find something.'

'Let me, dear. I'd very much like to buy you a present, and what could be more fitting, than a dress for my birth-day party?'

Again about to refuse, Juley paused. The offer was sincere; its acceptance would afford immeasurable pleasure to Sarah. But also, Mari was invited to the party and would be looking glamorous, mainly for Charles . . .

'All right, and thank you very much.'

'Don't thank me, child. I shall love helping you choose a dress for my party.'

They went into town the following day, Juley having rung Charles to say she would not be seeing him as she and Sarah were going shopping.

'Again?' That he was frowning into his receiver was not

difficult to imagine and naturally Juley felt a surge of happiness that he should be so eager for her company. 'When can I see you, then?' His voice was curt and she had the impression that he was irritable and she had to smile to herself.

'I do happen to have a job of work to do,' she teasingly reminded him, and heard what could only be described as a snort coming over the line.

'If it's this morning you are shopping then what about this afternoon?'

Before Juley could answer Sarah came into the bedroom from where Juley was speaking.

'Charles?' she enquired.

'Yes, I'm telling him we're going out today, shopping.'

'You seem to be embarrassed.'

'No, I'm not—'

'Charles is disappointed at not being able to take you out?'

Juley nodded her head; Charles was speaking, so she took her hand from the mouthpiece.

'You want to speak to Sarah, you say? Well, she happens to be here beside me.'

Sarah took the receiver and Juley's eyes opened wide as she heard her say, 'You can meet us in town and buy us both a lunch, seeing that you want to see my companion today.'

Juley heard a laugh and then just caught the words, 'It will be my pleasure. What time, and where?'

Sarah made the arrangements and then, with a twinkling glance at her companion, 'Juley will be free from lunchtime. Perhaps you'll be so kind as to see her home. I have some business to attend to and shall be using the car.'

'Business,' said Juley, not thinking. 'You never mentioned anything about having business to attend to.'

'The business has nothing to do with you. I need the car – we're being driven in one of Ramos's cars, as you know

– and so Charles must bring you home. However, I shan't be needing you until half past six at the earliest.'

'Oh . . . well, thank you very much.'

'He's smitten! And if you don't exploit the situation then you're a fool.'

'Mari—' began Juley when she was interrupted with, 'He's not in love with her. It's just the money, but unless my woman's intuition disappoints me it is you who will have the ring on your finger.'

'Sarah, please . . .' A deep sigh came from the very heart of her. 'Please don't be so optimistic. Charles will never marry me; it's impossible.'

'Nonsense. You're attaching far too much importance to this thing between him and Mari. I've told you, it was her estate and bank balance that has attracted him, but only up till now.'

Up till now . . . Charles must not fall in love with her – he *must not*!

Sarah's party was in full swing, with the same people invited as before but with two additions: Mari and her distant cousin Stephen Metcalfe, who had come over from England for a holiday, more for a rest, he had told Ramos, as he had been working so hard that, according to his doctor friend, he was going to be ill himself if he did not slacken off or, better still, take a rest. So he'd agreed and the obvious place was Mexico, since he had always been on good terms with his cousin. They were not blood relatives, having become cousins when a relative of Mari's married Stephen's second cousin – which made him and Mari second cousins, several times removed.

Stephen seemed at once to notice Juley, who looked very young and attractive in an evening gown of turquoise organza fitting as if it had been made specially for her figure. She was regal, too, with her mid-length hair taken back from her face and secured with a ribbon of the same colour as her dress.

After the meal there was dancing and it was to Juley that Stephen came at once, as if already he had chosen her as his first partner whenever the dancing should begin. Charles had obviously had the same idea but somehow Stephen managed to move in front of Charles and reach her first. Mari, mouth compressed, witnessed this but gave Charles a dazzling smile when he turned to her, and she did not let him see that she had noticed the quick scowl that had come to his face as Stephen claimed Juley for the waltz.

Later Sarah said gleefully, 'Charles is jealous of Stephen. This is going to be interesting.'

'Sarah, please . . . I've tried to convince you that Charles and I are only friends.'

'And without success – your trying to convince me, I mean.' A strange little smile hovered on her lips but she kept any further comments for another time.

Meanwhile, Charles made sure of the next dance. Juley felt tremors ran through her, as they always did when he held her. Soon she was floating on air and it seemed as if she and Charles were quite alone, that the rest of the company had melted away to some distant land – or perhaps they had never been in this heaven with her and Charles at all. He touched her hair with his lips and she admonished him.

'Sarah will be watching us,' she warned. 'She's been saying things.'

'What kind of things?'

'I have an idea she suspects we're having an affair.'

He held her away momentarily and she saw he was frowning.

'Surely she didn't mention such a thing to you?'

'No, not an affair, exactly. But she thinks you're falling in love with me.'

'Does she, now?' They were swinging to the edge of the floor and she guessed they would be outside in the gardens soon, as they were that very first night.

111

'I think she would like to see me settled—' Juley cut off, not meaning to have voiced anything like that.

'And would you like to be settled, Juley?' Again he held her from him; she suddenly became aware of two dark eyes staring venomously at her from across the huge banqueting hall. It was as if they burned into her and swiftly she turned away, so swiftly that Charles asked if anything was the matter.

'No . . .' And this time it was she who suggested they go outside.

'A good idea,' he smiled. 'I was about to make the same suggestion myself.'

Juley gave a small sigh. Mari would be furious about this, but Juley felt she could not bear that look focused on her another moment.

'It was so warm,' she said by way of an excuse but Charles laughed and teasingly told her she had no need to make excuses for wanting him to kiss her. 'You have such an inflated ego!' she countered at which he swung her slender body to him and kissed her till she was gasping for breath.

'Are you enjoying the party?' They had strolled over to a little log cabin facing the small pool where ducks could be heard but not seen, their having gone to roost for the night. The loungers were soft and dry and Charles drew Juley close up to him, his arm strong about her shoulders. 'Have I told you how beautiful you look tonight?'

A rhythm of rapture was set within her heart, and with it a medley of yearning on which she refused to dwell since there was no future for her with Charles or any other man. She was doomed and this was a temporary reprieve, this interlude of loving and making love.

'Yes, you have told me I – I look nice, and thank you, Charles.'

'How formal,' he laughed. 'Juley, you're very sweet.' He kissed her again, then caressed her face and hair.

She said reluctantly, 'We'll have to go back; we'll be missed.' And Mari, fuming . . .

'If that is what you want.' He rose, pulling her up with him. 'Is it what you want?'

She shook her head without hesitation.

'I'd stay if it were possible.'

'I'd take you to the casa if it were possible.' He was teasing yet serious, and she thought he looked very young, almost boyish. Yet the next moment as they walked back to the house and she cast him a slantways glance she saw all the familiar strength in his features, the strong, out-thrust jaw, the hard inflexible line of the chin. A man to respect, she thought, remembering with profound clarity his fury when she gave him up.

'Is he going to murder me?' she had asked herself during one terrifying moment when he swore she was his – hadn't he made her his? The disappointment when she never became pregnant must have been devastating for him. And often recently she had dwelt on what would have been the result had she been going to have his child and they had been married. Today he would know he did not have her for very long, that she was going from this world and leaving him and their child – or maybe there would have been other children as well.

They were back in the hall only a matter of minutes when Stephen came to ask Juley to dance. Mari had already come up to them and the three had begun to chat when Stephen appeared and took Juley away. She was conscious of Charles's eyes following her and wondered if he were jealous. Well, he need not be; he would never lose her to another man.

But it was not to be denied that Stephen was taking an extraordinary interest in her and when the late refreshments were served he was there beside her. Mari was making sure that Charles did not get far from her and so Juley, feeling rather cast out, was glad of Stephen's company, his interest being a sort of soothing balm to the hurt she was suffering in seeing the way Mari monopolized Charles, adopting an 'I own him' kind of manner.

Juley could not in any way blame Charles; he had brought his girlfriend to the party and it was only to be expected from everyone that he would be with her more than with anyone else.

'I wonder,' mused Agatha who had come to sit beside Stephen, 'if we shall be celebrating an engagement before very long.'

'My cousin and Charles?' Stephen nodded. 'I guess so; it's been on the cards for some time. When Mari was over in England recently she told me she expected to be married to Charles this year.'

'Well, they both would benefit from a union; their estates could be one then, a huge one.'

'They both seem to have the same temperaments, too,' observed Stephen. 'Neither appears to be romantic.'

Juley could have told him differently – very differently. Charles was definitely romantic – but this thought brought in its wake the doubts she had about him and Mari being suited. Materially yes, and in any other ways which did not include love and warmth and tender caring.

Agatha went off to join her sister and the small circle of guests with whom she was chatting. Juley saw Stephen's eyes following Charles and Mari, who were going back to the ballroom; he seemed preoccupied and Juley was searching for something to say to end the silence. All she could think of was: 'Are you staying long with your cousin?'

'About a week, perhaps a little while longer,'

'The rest will do you good.' She picked up a tiny strawberry tart and nibbled at the pastry, then put it down. 'You work in the hospital, but do you live there also?'

'No, I have an apartment close by.'

'It must be rewarding work. I believe you are very clever.'

114

He smiled and she thought he was a reasonably handsome man, as fair as Charles was dark and almost as tall. His eyes were blue with the kind of lashes and girl would envy. His mouth was full, compassionate, and she looked at his hands – long slender fingers, a surgeon's fingers that had saved many lives.

She dwelt on his work and naturally envied patients who had gone to him and were successfully operated on. If only her own case had not been so hopeless. Altogether three specialists had examined her, because Dr Blount had advised it, though it was just the one who had given her own doctor the report. She was beyond the stage where an operation was possible. It was too late.

'It is rewarding, yes.' Stephen accepted something from a tray offered to him by an immaculately dressed man-servant, and he had his glass topped up. 'I have an aunt who was most eager for me to become an artist, but it was medicine that drew me.'

'And you must be very glad you followed your own desires?'

'Of course. I'd not be happy in any other profession.' He smiled at her and after his eyes had swept the room to see if Mari and Charles were anywhere about he asked Juley to dance again.

He was a very good dancer and their steps harmonized so well that soon Juley noticed they were the centre of interest to the people who were not dancing, but sitting around watching the dancers.

'Can I invite you to have lunch with me tomorrow?' he asked. 'That is, if Mrs Greatrix will spare you?'

'I'm not sure . . .' She did not want to make him feel uncomfortable by refusing him, but on the other hand, if she were to be free, it was Charles she wanted to be with. 'I can't say if I'm free until I have asked Sarah. She might just want me and if she does, I would have to refuse your offer, but thank you for asking me,' she added graciously

115

and with a smile. He was looking down into her face with a strange expression in his eyes.

'I hope you are free, Juley. But if not, when is your day off? You must have one?'

'Not as such,' she answered truthfully. 'I'm free just when Sarah tells me – you see, I never really know until the actual day.' She felt she was being slightly dishonest, since it was very rarely that Sarah wanted her during the daytime. However, it was true that Juley was never quite sure until the actual morning, when Sarah would say, 'I don't need you until about half-past six, so you can go off and do whatever you like.'

'I do hope you and I can see something of each other, Juley.' His tone was serious and the blue eyes had an earnest quality about them. Did Stephen find her attractive?

She said guardedly, 'I'll have to see, Stephen. Being an employee of Sarah, I'm naturally committed to her wishes.'

He held her from him.

'Will you phone me if and when you are free? I would very much enjoy taking you out somewhere, whether it's to lunch or dinner. Mari has made one of her cars available, so perhaps we could have a drive around. I haven't seen much of the countryside around here as it isn't any fun going off on one's own.'

She promised to phone him but did stress that she did not think it would be possible for her to go out with him. He seemed disappointed but by no means dejected.

It was much later when, the four of them having found a table and were sitting chatting, Ramos came up and asked Charles if he were staying the night again.

'You can have the same room, on the same corridor as Sarah and Juley. So you can go off as early as you like without disturbing anyone because no one else sleeps anywhere near there. You were certainly off early last time. You're welcome to stay if you like?'

Charles shook his head, but before he had time to murmur

a polite refusal Mari was asking, 'You stayed here before?'
Her eyes slid to Juley, who felt sure little spots of colour
had tinted her cheeks.

'It was so that I could have wine,' he explained, his
manner cool and impassive. 'But I won't stay tonight,
Ramos, thank you. I have driven Mari and Stephen here in
my car, so I have to take them home.'

'I had no idea you'd ever stayed here.' Mari spoke as
if she just had to, and again she slid a glance in Juley's
direction.

'You wouldn't,' from Charles and now his tones were
crisp and distinctly brittle. 'You were away at the time of
Ramos's party, so how could you know?' It was a snub
which brought a little surprised gasp from Mari and the
colour rising in her cheeks. Stephen was puzzled and Juley
most uncomfortable. It was only Charles who appeared to
be cool and unaffected. For Juley, it was a relief when Sarah
came over to say she was going to bed and, suspecting she
would tell Juley to stay as she did not need her, Juley cast
her a swift warning glance and said she would come up
with her at once.

'What was going on?' demanded Sarah once they were
in her bedroom. 'There was a distinct atmosphere one could
cut with a knife, and then your being so anxious to get
away.' She was taking off her earrings while Juley was
already laying her nightdress on the bed.

'Charles . . .' Juley was reluctant to explain but, judging
by the look on her employer's face, she decided to take the
line of least resistance. 'He snubbed Mari – it wasn't very
nice of him but she did ask for it.' Juley expanded on this,
aware of the glimmer of satisfaction in Sarah's eyes.

'She did ask for it. What has it to do with her that Charles
stayed here that night . . . ?' She tailed off, her eyes widen-
ing. 'Why were you looking so embarrassed if it was Mari
who had been snubbed?'

Juley gave a start; she was totally unprepared for anything

like this and she now cursed herself for saying as much as she had. In an attempt to extricate herself and prevent any further questions she returned with a light laugh, 'Me – embarrassed! Whatever do you mean? No, it had nothing to do with me – it was Mari, being snubbed as I told you. I felt sorry for her, that's all.' She went over to the dressing-table and took a hairnet from a drawer. Sarah always slept in a net because, she maintained, a woman who wakes up to untidy hair loses her dignity. 'Is there anything else?' she asked casually and put up a hand to stifle a yawn. 'Gosh, but I'm tired!'

She was moving to the communicating door when Sarah commented dryly, 'You're trying hard, my dear, but not succeeding. That stare you gave me plainly said you were anxious to come away . . . to escape from the awkward-ness. But if it was only Mari who was embarassed . . . ?' She tailed off again, this time significantly and Juley coloured up.

'Sarah, I don't know what you are getting at, but you did promise not to probe into my affairs.'

The reminder fell on deaf ears.

'That night – when Charles stayed, you—' She broke off abruptly after her eyes had strayed to the door which had been locked, the door between their rooms. 'Never mind,' she added unexpectedly. 'But I'm beginning to suspect. Juley, that there was much more to that past friendship as you called it, than meets the eye.'

'Sarah—'

'I'm sorry if I'm talking out of turn, but this mystery about you and Charles vexes me. I cannot see your reason for such unnecessary secrecy. You and I have come close – oh, I know you would like to remind me of the short time we've known one another, but what has time to do with it when two people are kindred spirits? I have told you about my daughter; you must know that I want so much to regard you as my daughter, that there will be no parting when

118

Maisie comes back.' She stopped but Juley was dumb, too full for framing words, too close to tears because of the way Sarah was soon to be hurt. She suddenly knew a sense of contrition about her secrecy for if she had confided in Sarah at the start then she would have known there was no future for her and Juley together and that the association was, as it had been intended to be, only temporary. Sarah went on when she did not speak, 'There *was* more than friendship between you and Charles all those years ago. You were very close, and something came between you. He has never married – a man as handsome as he who must have had dozens of women running after him. Was there some question of marriage between you and him, Juley?' Sarah had moved over to a chair. She indicated another and automatically Juley sat down. She felt drained, saddened by the fact of what Sarah was going to suffer before very long.

She looked at her, aware of her shrewd eyes fixed upon her and she could not lie.

'Yes, Charles did want to marry me. I was only seventeen and Charles was only twenty-one. His father was very wealthy and it was he who parted us. He threatened to cut his son – his only child – out of his will if he married me.'

'What were his objections?'

'I don't really know, but as I say, he was very wealthy and I was a mere nobody. I guess Mr Burke wanted his son to marry into an equally wealthy family. I had to give Charles up; it wouldn't have been fair to marry him.'

'Your parents – did they object too?'

'It was only my father. He would have let me get married, I think.'

'I believe Charles's father is dead now, so he inherited a fortune from Ireland as well as from Mexico. Lucky man.'

'His father cut him off anyway.' She began to wonder what Charles would say if he knew she was giving away information about him. 'It was a cruel act but Charles doesn't seem to worry at all about the loss.'

'He's wealthy anyway.' A pause and then, with a frown: 'Charles doesn't strike me as a man who would allow himself to be dictated to. Was he so ready to let you go?'

Juley grimaced and described the scene when she told Charles she could not marry him. She naturally left out the scene at the cottage.

'You were a fool to give him up – but I expect you know that now.' An air of enquiry hung on the air. All Juley said was that, as things had turned out, it had all been for the best.

'As things have turned out?' with a frown of bewilderment. 'What do you mean?'

Juley shrugged her shoulders.

'I can't say more – and do please stop asking me questions. Believe me, it was for the best.' Yes, it certainly was, since if she and Charles had been married then he would soon be suffering the kind of heartbreak and loss which she would never wish upon him.

'I hope,' said Sarah with crisp deliberation, 'that you are not going to flirt with Stephen.'

'Flirt . . . ?' Wide-eyed, Juley shook her head. 'Whatever gave you an idea like that?'

'Tonight. You and he were together quite a lot, and I don't mean just dancing. You talked a lot and Charles was glowering at times. Don't do anything to make him jealous,' she warned, 'or you could suffer another such scene as you've described to me – only probably much worse.'

'I have no intention of trying to make Charles jealous! Besides, there can be no jealousy without love, and Charles does not love me.'

He's told you so?' asked Sarah curiously.

'Not in so many words, naturally. But he's talked about the time when you and I shall be going home and he is very casual about it.'

'He is?' with a gathering frown of puzzlement. 'He doesn't care that you'll be leaving here – I mean, he hasn't mentioned anything about keeping in touch afterwards?'

'No, he hasn't. And just to put you completely into the picture, he has talked about marrying Mari.'

'Well . . .' A deep sigh escaped the older woman. She seemed bitterly disappointed by what she had heard. 'They are totally unsuited,' she snapped presently. 'And a man of his intelligence should know it!'

'You're wrong, Sarah. They are suited. Her estate joins his. She has the kind of aristocratic personality which will be an asset to Charles in his business dealings—'

'Rubbish!' cut in Sarah repressively. 'A man like Charles would look for more than material gains and snobbery when choosing a wife.'

'You might think so, but I know—'

'Oh, for heaven's sake, Juley, shut up!'

Startled by this untypical behaviour, Juley stared disbelievingly at her employer. 'I was only stating a fact,' she murmured placatingly at last.

'Why must you be so secretive?' demanded Sarah. 'It makes it much harder for me to understand anything!'

Juley drew an impatient breath.

'If you would only accept the situation as it is, without wanting to know more – asking questions I can't answer—'

'Not can't – *won't*!'

'Very well, have it your own way. I assure you there really are things which I must keep to myself – I really must, Sarah, so please don't make me feel embarrassed by this curiosity which I cannot satisfy – I'm sorry.'

The plea went home after Sarah had gazed steadfastly into Juley's eyes for several seconds. But for all that her tones were stiff and chill as, changing the subject, she said she wanted to go to town in the morning.

'I want to buy some presents for people at home.'

Juley glanced swiftly at her.

'We're going home soon?'

'I didn't say so,' was the smoothly accented reply. 'I just

want to get the chore over and done with. I never enjoy looking for presents when I'm on holiday. It's always so difficult.' Her eyes wandered to the bracelet on Juley's wrist. 'I remarked on that bracelet. You said you'd had it before coming here but I have my doubts.' She was watching her companion closely, saw the tell-tale blush and said with ruthless disregard for her feelings, 'You were lying, weren't you? Charles bought it for you.'

Juley swallowed, becoming angry with Sarah for her total lack of diplomacy.

'Yes,' she muttered, 'he did buy it for me.'

'A costly gift.'

'Sarah, please . . .'

'Not the kind a man usually gives to a girl he's so casual about parting from.' There was a significant emphasis on the word 'casual' but Juley made no comment nor did she meet her companion's eyes. 'All right,' sighed Sarah resignedly and changed the subject, much to Juley's relief. 'What time can you be ready in the morning? I want to be off early as I've a hair appointment at two, so I want it all done by half past twelve at the latest, then we'll have time to relax over lunch.'

'I can be ready to suit you,' returned Juley obligingly. 'Nine o'clock?'

'Fine; it will give me three hours – well, a little less since it takes about forty minutes to get to town.'

Seven

Agatha decided to go to town with them and it was her chauffeur who drove the Bentley into the *Zocola* where the three women got out. The older two had talked unceasingly and Juley wished she had not been forced to come and it was a relief when Sarah, realizing she was bored, said she could go off on her own if she wished.

'We'll meet you back at the car at about – four?' She glanced at her sister. 'Will that be all right with you, Agatha?'

'It'll suit me fine. We'll have afternoon tea when you come from the hairdresser's. But, lunch – do you want to join us, Juley?'

'I think I'd like to have a snack somewhere.'

The two went off and Juley sat down on a seat, enjoying the sunshine and the flowers. The square was busy with brown-faced people hurrying and scurrying or just gossiping and laughing. Life was everywhere – vibrant, throbbing life . . . The tall trees and the flowers, the occasional bird or butterfly, the children, bright-eyed, loud-voiced; a dog tugging at its leash, and all had life . . . and a future. Try as she would she could not control her thoughts and this led inevitably to tears she was too tight inside to shed. She should have stayed with Sarah and her sister. It was not good to be alone any more. Her heart and mind seemed dead already; despair took on a physical drag so that she felt as if she were carrying a leaden weight within her. Why should this be happening to her? What had she ever done to deserve such a fate? Her thoughts flitted to her baby and then the tears did come, tears of anguish, rolling down her cheeks. What was James doing at this moment? Being fed? Or perhaps bathed, kicking in the water, laughing and perhaps showing the tip of a little white tooth. His first tooth; his first step, so wobbly that loving hands must be there to catch him before he fell. But then must come his first fall, a tear, before the same loving hands – and perhaps lips – to make him laugh again.

'All this would have been mine,' she whispered. 'James *is* mine!' She was so carried away by her imaginings that she had not noticed Stephen taking a seat beside her until she heard his voice.

'Hello, Juley.' He looked at her curiously. 'Can I ask who James is?' His tone had begun as a bantering one but at the tears he stopped rather abruptly and then asked concernedly, 'Whatever is the matter, Juley? You're crying.' He was all doctor and she his patient. 'You seem dreadfully upset about something.'

She was colouring painfully at the knowledge that he had heard those last three vehemently spoken words.

'It's nothing, Stephen – but oh, I am very glad to see you! Are you free? I mean, I'm on my own and shouldn't be, not the way I feel—' She stopped, biting her lip. 'I'm sorry; I just feel a bit depressed, and need company.'

His keen gaze was fixed on her face for a while before he let his eyes travel over her whole body.

'Tell me what is wrong,' he encouraged. 'I might be able to help.'

At that she closed her eyes tightly and shook her head. Her shoulders drooped and her voice was little higher than a whisper.

'No one can help me, Stephen,' she quivered. 'No one can do anything at all for me.'

Why was she speaking like this to him? It must be because he was a doctor – but she had had no intention of confiding in him. She must stop now, before she said enough to help him make an intelligent guess that there was something seriously wrong with her. He had moved away a little, in order to see her better.

'I don't understand. That was a cry of despair if ever I heard one. You're obviously in some kind of trouble. One usually has a very good reason for feeling the way you do.'

Good reason. Should she confide after all? Being a doctor he would respect her wish for strict secrecy. Yet on the other hand he might just consider it to be in her best interests for him to put her employer in the picture.

'I can't tell you anything,' she decided at last. 'It's very private, really, and I must keep it to myself.'

Stephen frowned and his deep-set eyes were narrowed.

'I think you should tell me what is wrong, Juley. It's something physical, isn't it?'

She started at his perception, then found herself admitting that a doctor's thoughts would quite naturally turn to what was physical.

'I can't answer that,' she returned without stopping to think what her words would imply.

'You have answered it,' was his instant and significant reply. 'Just what is wrong, Juley? I know we are only of very recent acquaintanceship, but I hope we shall become friends. Please regard me both as your doctor and your friend.'

She bit her lip. Last night he had seemed quickly to become interested in her; he had danced with her several times, and they had had supper together and, as Sarah had mentioned, they had talked together. She had no wish that he should come to like her too much – but how could she tell him she loved Charles to distraction?

However, she was weakening under his persuasion – and perhaps his subtle charm – but she drew on sufficient willpower to say, 'I would like you as my friend, Stephen, but I do not need you as my doctor.'

'I see.' His mouth tightened and she realized he could be

stern when necessary. He was obviously concerned for her but vexed by her stubborn attitude. 'You do realize that, as a doctor, I have already guessed that what is wrong with you is serious, for otherwise you wouldn't be so reluctant to confide.'

'I'm sorry.'

'Mari says you've been seeing a lot of Charles – she was talking about it this morning at breakfast. Are you and he more than acquaintances?'

She turned to look directly into his face.

'If Mari was talking about us, then she would have surely told you that we are not mere acquaintances. We knew each other years ago, when we were both very young.'

'You – were in love?'

Anger lit her eyes.

'That,' she quivered, 'is not a question I would have expected you to ask! We met only last evening, remember.' She half rose but to her surprise he took hold of her hand and pulled her back on to the seat.

'You are quite right; it is not a question I should have asked.' He smiled then, as if asking her pardon. 'But I admit I am not happy about your refusal to confide regarding what is wrong with you. However, you did say we could be friends so I am asking you to have lunch with me.'

Her eyes lit up. She had brought out a handkerchief to dry her tears but for the moment held it idle in her fingers.

'That will be lovely.'

'For me as well. I am on holiday, remember, so hope to make the most of it.'

With her? Was this a subtle move to pave the way for other invitations? Well, first things first, and this particular invitation was more than welcome. She wondered why he had come to town in the first place, and so early in the morning. As though reading her thoughts, he told her he had come to pay a call on a friend, a doctor who was with him when they were training.

'I had the idea of surprising him, but the visit can keep. It's too early for lunch, so what would you like to do in the meantime?'

'I'd like to walk about – if that is all right with you? I haven't explored the town properly yet.'

'Walking it is, then.' He stood up and she followed suit. 'You've been to Mexico City?'

'Yes; Charles took me. I loved every moment.' She spoke eagerly, not realizing the impression she was giving to him. 'Charles knows the city well, so knew where to take me.'

He said nothing for a while but later they chatted conversationally with intervals of quite companionship and by the time Stephen took her into a restaurant she was again at peace within herself. No doubt about it, Stephen's presence was soothing.

'I'd like to go to the powder room first.' She glanced around but it was Stephen who pointed the way.

'I'll be here in the lounge. What cocktail would you like?'

'I'll just have a dry sherry, please.'

In the powder room she used her blusher and lip-rouge and felt much better as she combed through her gleaming hair. She had felt she looked awful, after that bout of tears.

When she returned, smiling as she sat down, Stephen thought he had never seen a lovelier girl, or one so sad.

Sad . . . He watched her pick up her glass. There was more than one secret carried within her heart, he had decided, and more than ever wished she had been able to confide in him.

The restaurant was one of the most patronized in town, very plush, with a quartet playing soft classical music from a raised dais at the far end of the dining room.

The table was private, in a corner but with a view to the other tables. And no sooner had Juley and Stephen sat down than she noticed Charles and Mari at a table by the window. Charles had phoned very early this morning, only to be told, sadly, that they could not see each other today as Sarah wanted Juley to go shopping with her. Charles, as disappointed as she, asked if there was any chance of lunch, should he come to town. Juley, not knowing what her employer's plans were, but assuming she and Sarah would be lunching together, as at that time Agatha had not said she wanted to come, Juley had said a definite no, she could not have lunch with him.

And now here she was . . . with Stephen.

Following the direction of her gaze he remarked wryly, 'I rather think I shall be coming over again quite soon, for a wedding.' He looked then at Juley, probably recalling his remarks about her and Charles seeing a lot of one another. This, however, seemed not to make any difference to his optimism about a wedding. 'I'd like to see Mari settled. She isn't in her first youth.' He paused thoughtfully. 'She used to go about, have her flings as you might say, but since Charles came to live so close she's never looked at another man. I do hope they get together.'

Juley, her mouth dry suddenly, took up the glass just filled with water by the young waiter. She took a long drink, then replaced the glass on the table.

'They're not even engaged yet,' she just had to say. 'Do you really believe they are suited?' She was upset, wishing Stephen had not chosen this particular restaurant.

'That's a strange question to ask,' he laughed. 'Only they know the answer to that. However, they have a lot to offer each other, materially.'

'And what about love?'

'Love?' he seemed faintly amused. 'I don't think love between those two is so very important. From what I gather from Mari's letters, and from conversations we've had while I've been staying with her, I'd say that if they do marry it will result from the main consideration of mutual material gain.'

'Love is far more important in marriage than material gain.'

He laughed and said they would change the subject.

'Tell me, how do you come to be working for Mrs Greatrix?'

Juley paused, suspecting he had some ulterior motive for the question, not unconnected with his curiosity about her problem.

'I wanted a change of scene after my husband's death,' was all she replied.

'It was a sad business.'

'We were having a divorce. Perhaps I mentioned it last night.'

'It was a pity you didn't have children. I know from the experience of my profession that when a woman is either widowed or divorced, children are a wonderful comfort in most cases.'

Her lips trembled and as she was looking at Charles she missed her companion's keen and alert scrutiny.

'Hadn't we better be looking at the menu?' she recommended, anxious to change the subject. 'The waiter is staring at us.'

It was towards the end of the meal that Charles became aware of her presence. Their eyes met when for some reason he turned fully her way and she looked into his face rather than his profile. She saw his mouth compress as he noticed her companion.

'Charles has seen us,' with a sign from Stephen. 'I suppose we ought to have acknowledged their presence before now.' He stopped, his eyes smiling and a little amused. 'I didn't want company, you see.'

She let that pass, saying lightly, 'It was nice lunching together, but now perhaps we had better all go together to the lounge for coffee.'

'I expect so,' he nodded reluctantly. 'I'll go over and ask them to join us when they are ready.'

When Charles and Mari joined them in the lounge a short while later there was a distinct stiffness in the way Charles greeted Juley. His eyes flicked to her companion, then returned to her.

'So you were free it would seem.' And he added just as if he had to, 'It's a remarkably cushy job you have with Mrs Greatrix.'

She blushed and lowered her lashes. She wanted to explain but decided that here was not the place. But she was inexpressibly hurt by Charles's manner and his comment and as he continued to treat her coldly she was impelled to tell him how she came to be free after all. Waiting for a suitable opening she found one when in the course of conversation he again alluded to it.

'As a matter of fact, I came into town with Sarah and Agatha because they wanted to do some shopping, but then Sarah said I could go off on my own if I wished. Stephen happened to notice me as I sat in the park.'

'How convenient,' smoothly and with a sardonic curve of the fine lips.

Stephen was clearly taken aback and even Mari looked startled.

'As it happens,' responded Stephen curtly, 'it *was* rather fortunate that I happened to come along since Juley was feeling far from happy at being on her own.'

'No?' For a moment Charles's eyes examined Juley's face, but she was angry now and so her expression was one of defiance. So perhaps it was not surprising that Charles again spoke with an edge of sarcasm in his voice.

'Well, as you say, Stephen, it was fortunate that you happened along.'

Juley shot him a wrathful glance, then inserted a silky inflection into her voice as she enquired, 'Have you two been shopping?'

'We've been looking at engagement rings,' was the prompt and triumphant reply from Mari.

'You . . . ?' Juley felt as if powdered ice were being slowly poured over her body. She would never know how she recovered so quickly. 'Oh, but this is wonderful news! Congratulations, Charles. Much happiness, Mari . . .' She tailed off, because of the unfathomable expression on Charles's face as he looked at her, and then there was an even more unreadable expression as he turned his dark head to look straight into Mari's eyes. She coloured and glanced away and Charles's mouth curved with contempt. What was it all about? Of course, Juley realized now that she had been somewhat previous in her congratulations since no engagement had actually been announced. She herself coloured up now, as embarrassment swept over her. She had made a *faux pas*, apparently, but any attempt to rectify it would only result in further awkwardness for them all, so she remained silent, wishing the floor would open up and swallow her, or at least that Stephen would suggest they go, now that their coffee was finished.

'What the devil happened?' Stephen was saying when at length he and Juley were on their own again, strolling back to the square. 'Charles seemed angry at Mari's mention of engagement rings. I wish I understood those two! There are times when Mari convinces me they will marry, but there are also times when I have my doubts – and this is one of these times. I'm sure Mari will receive a telling off from Charles.'

'I was too impulsive with my congratulations,' admitted Juley, perturbed. 'I felt awful when I saw Charles's expression.' She was naturally very puzzled by the whole thing, because had she herself been free today then Charles would not have been with Mari, so there would have not been any looking at engagement rings.

'It was Mari's fault if it was anyone's,' Stephen was saying. 'But they must have been looking at rings or she wouldn't have said so. And if they were looking at rings why that attitude of Charles? He must have asked her to marry him. The whole thing doesn't make sense!' he ended explosively.

'I expect Mari will explain it all to you later.'

'Charles was in a foul mood before that happened,' recollected Stephen thoughtfully. 'He resented the fact of you and I being together – and that is yet another puzzling factor in what is becoming something of a mystery. You say you and he are old friends—'

'We knew each other several years ago,' broke in Juley, hoping to prevent any awkward questions. 'But we lost touch. I married and he travelled for a few years and then settled here. It was sheer coincidence that we met again, and I suppose it was natural that we should have the odd lunch together and chat about old times.' She looked sideways at him as they walked, saw him regarding her through narrowed eyes when he turned his head. He was deep in thought, appearing to be grappling with something he totally failed to understand. She could easily guess what it was.

'The odd lunch . . .' Stephen stopped by a seat and they sat down. 'Today . . . it was you he should have been with; I see that now. I was puzzled by his attitude and his sarcastic comments. Then, later, you were anxious to placate him by explaining how it was you came to be free. I suggest,' he added slowly and deliberately, 'that he'd had a disappointment, that he had hoped you would spend the day – or part of it – with him?' Juley said nothing; she could find nothing that would not lead her further into the maze. 'Did he phone you this morning asking you to go out with him?' demanded Stephen almost harshly.

'It is no business of yours—' she began when he interrupted her.

'Mari's feelings are my concern. She and I get along very well and I don't want her to be hurt unnecessarily.'

Looking at him, Juley rather thought there was more than his cousin's feelings involved. *There were Stephen's own.*

'He can't be falling in love with me after only a few hours,' she whispered to herself, staggered by the idea. And yet . . . he had shown a deep interest in her from the moment

132

of being introduced; even Sarah had commented on this interest, had told her not to try to make Charles jealous.

She said quietly, 'I can promise you that Mari's feelings will never be hurt because of me. I feel sure she and Charles will marry eventually. Also, I shall be gone from here within the next few weeks and Charles and I shall never meet again.'

He was silent, thoughtfully so, and it was a relief to Juley when, glancing at her watch, she was able to say, 'I must be off. I'm to meet Sarah on the car park at four o'clock.'

Her promise to Stephen had seemed quite a natural one to make at the time, but the more Juley thought about it the more she realized that she ought not to see Charles any more. Mari suspected they were spending time together and was upset about it. Juley mentioned this to Charles when he phoned later that day. Juley was just getting ready for dinner when the call came through to her bedroom. Charles was apologetic over his curtness.

'It was anger,' she corrected.

'Disappointment. I was mad at seeing you with Stephen.'

'So it *was* anger.'

'Both. Juley, are you free tomorrow?'

She paused, so long that he asked if she was still there.

'Yes. Er – Charles, I feel that you and I should call it a day – not see each other any more, I mean. It – it upsets Mari . . .' She closed her eyes tightly to prevent tears from falling. Her heart was breaking. Surely it would not do any harm to Mari if she gave her love to Charles for just a little while longer. Sarah must surely be thinking of leaving soon.

'I've told you, Mari doesn't know—'

'She does, and it matters. You must have been looking at rings—'

'So that's it,' he cut in. 'Well, I'll explain that when I see you. As for this idiocy about our putting an end to our affair, well, I don't believe it is what you want at all.'

'Perhaps not what I want,' she conceded, 'but what is right.'

'Where are you now?'

'In my room, getting ready for dinner.'

'Go and ask Sarah if you can dine with me.'

'Now?'

'No time like the present for righting wrongs. I'm not having your head filled with false impressions. Now, do as you're told and speak with Sarah.'

'I can't do that, not at this time.' Her heart was beating wildly. Charles was not intending to end their affair – even for Mari!

'Very well,' was the grim rejoinder coming over the line. 'I'll be there before you have time to sit down and I'll talk to Sarah myself!' And before she had time to make any further protest the line had gone dead. She had to smile as she imagined his dashing out to the car, then breaking all speed limits in order to arrive here before dinner was served.

She looked at the communicating door, wondering if Sarah had already gone down for pre-dinner drinks. She had done her hair, had laid out her black, sequin-trimmed evening dress on the bed, then come to her own room to shower and dress. She had chosen the pretty dress Sarah had bought for her; she had washed her hair and it gleamed, its natural highlights accentuating its beauty. On her wrist was the bracelet bought for her by Charles and on her finger a diamond solitaire – her mother's engagement ring given her by her father on her wedding day.

She hesitated by the door, then knocked quietly.

'Come in – there's no need to knock every time.' Sarah was dabbing perfume behind her ears. 'You look charming, my dear. However, you must let me buy you some more dresses.'

Ignoring that, Juley explained, albeit in halting accents, that Charles had rung and wanted her to dine with him.

'This evening?' Sarah looked surprised as well she might. 'It's short notice, isn't it?'

Juley nodded.

'He told me to ask you if it was all right and when I said it was too late for a change of plan he said he would come and see you himself, and he rung off straightaway, so I expect he went out to the car immediately and he's on his way.' She felt embarrassed but Sarah was smiling in the most satisfied way.

'You know very well it would have been all right,' was her reassuring comment. Then she added with a slightly puzzled frown, 'I thought you said he always saw Mari in the evenings?'

'Most evenings, but it seems he isn't seeing her this evening.' She paused a moment and then with sudden resolve, 'I didn't mention it to you but I met Stephen this morning and we walked for a while, then had lunch. Charles and Mari were there . . .' She tailed off, already regretting her confidence.

'So?' curiously as Sarah put the stopper back in the perfume bottle.

'Well, as he was with Mari then, he must have decided – er – have thought—'

'That it wasn't necessary to see her tonight as well. Very odd. But I was right when I said those two will never marry.' She stood up, her eyes on the mirror as she patted her hair. Then she picked up her earrings from the dressing-table and Juley saw that she had forgotten to put them in. 'What time will Charles be here?' She fixed one earring and then the other.

'It won't take him long,' was Juley's half-amused reply. 'He was in a hurry.'

'So it seems. Well, you had best get into a wrap and be ready when he arrives.'

'It's all right, then?' She was quivering with excitement and joy. An evening with Charles, dining by candlelight in that charming room in which she had dined the first time. 'Thank you very much, Sarah.' She would have liked to add, 'You don't know what it means to me,' but of course she did no such thing.

Charles arrived within half an hour of the phone call; Juley was ready and waiting, Sarah having said she would make her excuses to Ramos and Agatha.

'I wonder what they'll think?' she murmured. 'They know that Charles and Mari are more than friends.'

'Are they more than friends?' Sarah was in the hall with her and she sounded exceptionally sceptical. 'I wouldn't care to bet on it.'

When Charles arrived she merely greeted him and told him to take care of Juley.

'I'll certainly do that.' He soon had her in the car and as soon as he was off the hacienda property and purring along the road he said quietly, 'You seemed quite overjoyed at the idea of an engagement between Mari and me.'

'I've always known you and she will marry.'

'You haven't known anything of the kind. What do you mean by "always"? You haven't been here five minutes yet.'

She turned to slant him a glance.

'There is much I do not understand about you,' she told him rather pettishly and he was swift with the riposte that this made two of them.

'There is a lot I do not know about you, either.'

She said tentatively, 'You seemed annoyed about the ring.'

'What ring?'

Juley drew an exasperated breath.

'Mari said you had been looking at engagement rings – if you remember,' she added sarcastically.

'I remember. I also remember that you took a lot for granted.'

'Well, you'd not be looking at rings unless you were intending to become engaged!'

'It so happens,' he said tersely, 'that *I* was not looking at rings.'

'You mean . . . ?' She frowned at him as he turned his head. 'Mari was looking at engagement rings.'

'I'm not in control of how she entertains herself.' He swung the car from the main road into the narrower lane which was now so familiar to her. 'Mari and I met only a few minutes before we went in to lunch. She was in town shopping; I was there visiting an old man who used to work for my aunt. She had left instructions that he was to be cared for and in addition to the money she left, for him to receive every month, I now and then have my housekeeper make up a parcel of provisions and I deliver them myself, just to make sure he is all right as he lives alone. Had you been free, of course, I'd have chosen another day to go and see him.'

'So – why was Mari—? Oh, no wonder Stephen says he cannot understand any of it!'

'Mari often looks at rings – I believe most women look at rings as perhaps you do?'

'Not now,' she answered without thinking, 'as it isn't any use.'

'No use?' His dark head came round swiftly. 'What do you mean by that?'

She shrugged with assumed carelessness.

'I'll not be wanting an engagement ring seeing that I haven't a boyfriend, even.'

He said nothing but she somehow could not let the matter of the engagement ring drop.

'Mari must have had some hint from you that she should be looking at rings.'

'We have a certain understanding,' he admitted but the words came slowly as if he were reluctant to utter them. 'But if I do marry her I shall not be pushed into it and as far as I am concerned there is no hurry.'

'You sound less than lukewarm,' she could not help observing and he merely laughed softly and concentrated on negotiating the narrow bends as they neared the casa gates. He swept through them and brought the car to a halt on a brilliantly lighted forecourt.

'You look adorable,' he was saying after handing her cloak to a manservant who had opened the door, then stood waiting for Juley to discard her cloak. It was Charles who took it from her and as soon as the man had gone he bent and kissed her on the lips.

'Shall we forget Mari for tonight?' he smiled. 'There are plenty of more interesting topics you and I can converse about.'

'Charles, you don't seem to have the respect for Mari that you should have – if you intend to marry her.'

He looked down into Juley's eyes and said slowly, 'What is it to you how I feel about her?'

'I want you to be happy, that's all.'

'And you fear I shall not be happy with Mari?'

'I worry about it,' she sighed, thinking this was a most unusual conversation. 'I do want you to be happy, Charles, so please make sure you marry someone who will give you love and whom you can love.'

A tense, electric silence followed before Charles broke it rather abruptly by saying, 'I thought I said we'd forget Mari for tonight. Come on into the salon and we'll have drinks before dinner. I ordered it to be delayed until nine o'clock.'

It was only half past eight, so they had half an hour – a delightful half-hour for Juley as they listened to classical music. They were close, on a deep, softly cushioned couch and Charles's arm was about her shoulders, its warmth exciting on her bare flesh.

At dinner they sat opposite one another in saffron candlelight with silver and cut-glass gleaming and scintillating as the flames quivered. Roses sent off a heady perfume and two silent-footed manservants performed their duties with the food and the wine. Juley could not control swift-winged memories which took her back to the home she had shared with Barry and his mother. How different from all this! Yet she would have been content, as she always had been since her marriage, with her lot had Barry only been able to forgive her for the accident which had killed his mother.

She thought of Mari and tried to visualize her as mistress here. Of course, it would be no change since she had a similar home of her own.

'What are you thinking about?' Charles's smiling voice brought her back and she gave him a lovely smile.

'I was thinking, at first, of my home in England, and how different it was from this—' She swept a hand. 'But it was cosy and we had it very nice.'

'And you looked after your invalid mother-in-law.' His tone had changed dramatically, being taut now and faintly angry. 'No one should sacrifice their life for another person – not in the way you were sacrificing yours. You couldn't have had much pleasure, being tied all day.'

'I became used to it. She was a highly intelligent woman and we had interesting talks.'

Charles flicked a hand to have her champagne glass topped up.

'You mentioned "at first", so what were you thinking about after that?' He was smiling again and, reluctant as she was to see that smile disappear, she knew without doubt that Charles would have an answer from her.

'I was thinking of Mari, as being here—'

'Forget Mari!' He looked at her sternly across the table. 'We'll talk about you instead. Why were you unhappy at being on your own in town?'

'I felt – lonely and wished I'd stayed with Sarah and Agatha.'

'So you were glad to see Stephen?'

She nodded.

'Very glad.'

'And I was not very nice with you.' He sighed regretfully,

then immediately sent her a wry smile. 'I was jealous, you see.'

'Jealous?' It was said there was no jealousy without love. 'You've never been jealous before.'

'How do you know? I might as well tell you, my girl, that I could have punched Stephen on the nose last night.'

'But you were fully occupied with Mari,' she pointed out and saw his mouth go tight.

'If you mention Mari just once more,' he warned, wagging a finger at her, 'I shan't be responsible for my actions.'

She had to laugh.

'Oh, Charles, are you threatening me with violence?'

'Perhaps.' He glanced over his shoulder and found the two menservants were temporarily out of the room. 'But instead I shall make love to you as I'm sure we shall both enjoy that much more than if I were to beat you.'

Again she laughed, but this time it was a cracked, embarrassed little attempt which plainly afforded Charles some amusement.

'You're still shy.' He shook his head disbelievingly. 'After being married for four years, and after our having made love here, several times . . .' He tailed off; she could have finished for him,

'. . . and after that night, that first time. Oh, yes, I was shy then.'

For a long time they lay luxuriating in the aftermath of bliss, his hand enclosing her breast, his lips close to hers. A deep sigh escaped her. 'Once more and once less'. This is all so transient, she thought bleakly, and then it was with her, a blinding headache that had fallen almost without warning – just a small ache and the blast of agony to seer her head and cruelly strike her eyes.

'Oh . . . God, the pain!' She had not wanted to cry out but the throbbing torture was more than she could bear.

'Juley, dear Juley – what is wrong?' Charles had leapt up

and stood naked above her, his own mouth convulsed as he saw her agony. 'Your head – where are your tablets?'

'In my bag – I'll get them,' she added urgently for if he looked at that bottle he would know its contents were not ordinary aspirins. Even in her burning torment she told herself she must buy some aspirins and use the box for her tablets. Yes, she would not allow herself to be in a panic like this again. Charles had her bag; she managed to sit up and asked him to hand it to her, which to her relief he did without attempting to open it. He was probably a bit concerned that he would fumble and waste precious time; in any case, naked as he was, he went to the bathroom for a glass of water and handed it to her before even thinking of a dressing-gown. But soon he had one on and was finding another for her. 'I'll be all right in a moment.' She could have screamed out with the pain. It had never been as bad as this before and she was terrified she would die here, in Charles's divan bed.

'Juley, there's something seriously wrong and I want to know what it is.'

She shook her head, and leant back on the pillow, willing the tablets to act swiftly and put her out of this agony. She had put them back in her bag; she saw Charles looking at the bag and, afraid he might decide to look inside, she drew it to her again and clutched it in her hand.

'It's just a headache, like I've had before . . .' The pain was easing, so she could speak more steadily now. 'I'll put the dressing-gown on for a few minutes.' He helped her into it after she had slid from the divan, his eyes wandering all the time from what he was doing, to the handbag on the bed.

'You say you take aspirins. Can I see them, Juley?'

So he was no fool. He knew she was keeping them away from him.

'Why do you want to see them?' She feigned surprise and a casual mien. 'They're ordinary aspirins; there isn't anything to see.'

The shrewd eyes, the colour of pitchblende now, were focused upon her and his voice was penetratingly deep as he said, 'You're lying to me, Juley. Those are not ordinary aspirins, are they? Come on, I want the truth!'

'Charles, I'm prone to headaches—'

'As severe as this?'

'Some people are – many people have migraine, you know very well they do. I'm just unfortunate, that is all.'

'And for these very severe headaches ordinary aspirins are adequate,' he commented sceptically. 'I've said you're lying to me and I mean to see that bottle in your bag!'

'You shall not go into my handbag!'

On the point of snatching it from her he stopped himself.

'Very well. But you have admitted, by your very refusal to show me the bottle, that what you have in there are definitely not aspirin tablets.' He took up his clothes but still stood there for a moment before leaving the room.

'It's better?'

'Yes, almost gone altogether.'

'The tablets work swiftly,' he observed and even yet again his dark eyes flickered to the bag she was clutching.

'They're very good, yes.'

'You have them specially prescribed by your doctor?'

'I've told you, Charles, they are ordinary aspirins!'

'Don't lie! Haven't I said you've admitted they are not aspirins!'

By not allowing him to see the bottle. Fool that she was, not putting the tablets into a bottle labelled 'Aspirin'. It was so simple to buy some— Oh, to the devil with it! What business was it of his anyway?!'

When he returned she was dressed and on looking in the mirror she saw with relief that there was little sign of the pain she had so recently suffered. She felt sure that had there been any evidence and that she had looked ill, Charles would have made her stay the night, and that would have been disastrous since Sarah would have then learned that

Juley had had a serious pain and this would inevitably lead to questions which Juley felt she would have been forced to answer truthfully. She saw that Charles was not now too troubled about her but he did say, when they were in the car on their way to the hacienda, 'You ought to see a doctor about these headaches. They are far too serious for my liking.' Slanting her a glance, he went on, 'Just when are you going to come clean, Juley, and let me into your confidence?'

'There's nothing to tell.' She stared out of her window to a soft and gentle landscape bathed in stardust and moonlight. A romantic night with perfumes drifting into the car, carried on the zephyr of a breeze coming in from the sea. 'This apparent concern is quite unnecessary—'

'*Apparent* concern?'

'Real concern, then,' she conceded. 'But it really is unnecessary, seeing that, any day now, you and I could be saying goodbye.'

He gave a visible start.

'Any day? Sarah has plans to go home?' His voice was sharp, grittily so. 'Why didn't you mention it before now?'

'She hasn't actually said she's planning to go home.' Juley felt somewhat foolish at having mentioned something which had not yet even been discussed.

'Then what do you mean?' Charles sounded impatient, she thought.

'Well, when Sarah decided to come here we were on the plane the next day, so it seems she can make a decision and carry it out immediately.'

'So you feel you'll not have much warning when she does make up her mind to leave here?'

'Yes, that's right.' They had come away from the original subject and she was glad. For the rest of the journey Charles was strangely quiet, almost broodingly so, and as Juley felt she should not break into his thoughts, neither spoke at all until they were saying goodnight.

'I'll phone you early in the morning,' he stated and there was something inexplicably grim and determined in his manner. 'Sleep well, Juley, and I advise you to think seriously about seeing a doctor about these headaches.' His eyes fixed hers. 'I am certain you are lying when you tell me that the tablets you have are aspirins. I cannot fathom the reason for your secrecy, but—' He broke off so abruptly that she was startled into flashing him an interrogating glance. He was smiling, but thinly, and after bidding her goodnight again he turned to his car, leaving her with the manservant who had opened the door.

Eight

Although it had occurred to Juley that Charles might just speak to Sarah about the headaches, she had no answer ready when, the following morning at breakfast, she was tackled.

'Charles rang me early this morning telling me about the severe headache you had last night while you were at his home.' The compassionate eyes were a little hard now, as if Sarah were angry – and determined. 'It is time, Juley,' she went on abruptly, 'that you told me what is wrong with you. We are not all stupid, you know. Charles is anxious about you; I am anxious about you, and my sister is worried, too, about these headaches.'

'I haven't ever had any when she was there.'

'I told her about them.' A pause and then, 'You owe it to me, Juley, to confide.'

Juley said at once, 'There is nothing to confide – at least, nothing I want to talk about. We've been over all this before, Sarah,' she reminded her with a hint of censure. 'and I thought we'd come to a tacit agreement about my privacy.'

'Charles believes you are lying when you say you take nothing stronger than aspirins.'

'Charles should mind his own business; he ought never to have taken it upon himself to phone you.'

'Juley, he worries about you! Can't you see, he's in love with you?'

'He isn't! He mustn't be! No, I know he intends to marry Mari . . .' Her voice trailed away to silence as she recalled his indifferent attitude last evening when the girl was being discussed.

'You're not blind,' snapped her employer, exasperated. 'A woman knows when she is loved.'

'No – oh, why do you say such things?!' Distraught, all Juley could think about now was getting away – away from all these questions which, if answered truthfully, would result in the pity which she had been so determined to avoid. Away, too, from Charles, for although she felt sure that if he did love her he would have told her so, she knew that it was for the best if she tore herself away from him, too. It would leave the situation between him and Mari just as it was before she came here and agreed to have an affair with him. Yes, to get away was the wisest thing she could do, now that it was becoming more and more difficult to fob both Sarah and Charles off regarding her headaches. 'I'm going to my room.' She rose from the breakfast table, her food practically untouched. 'I want to think.'

'No, please sit down and finish your breakfast.' Sarah spoke persuasively and it was plain that she was regretting some of the things she had said. 'I've upset you and I'm sorry. We'll talk some other time – do please have your breakfast.'

With a sigh, Juley complied, but her mind was totally occupied with the idea of returning to England and going into a nursing home for the rest of the time left to her. Sheer desolation clutched at her heart as she visualized this move, away from those who cared about her – Sarah cared deeply, and Charles cared or he would not have phoned Sarah this morning.

Sarah said worriedly, 'What are you thinking about, Juley?'

'Nothing important.' She dug her spoon into her grape-fruit. 'I wish Charles hadn't rung you.' It was his action which had brought about the situation whereby Juley was contemplating leaving Mexico.

'He was troubled about you. It was natural that he would ask me if I knew what was wrong, seeing that you refused to admit that you had anything more than a normal headache – and were taking aspirins for it.' There was a certain significance in the last few words which only strengthened Juley's idea of leaving. The headaches would become more frequent and more severe, so that inevitably she would have to tell Sarah what was really wrong with her. Yes, looking at the position from every angle, Juley felt the only sensible course would be to make a final decision, and keep to it. Sarah spoke again, saying that Charles had asked her if Juley was free today. 'I told him you were free until about half past six, but if he wants to take you somewhere special I don't mind at all. I am capable of getting myself ready for dinner – I admit I'm not too good with my hair but it'll do for once.' Her tone was persuasive, almost as if she knew that Juley was in two minds about seeing Charles today. 'He said he'll be here to pick you up at ten o'clock.'

Automatically Juley glanced at the clock. She had about an hour to make up her mind . . . but already she was telling herself that as she could not very well leave immediately, she might as well enjoy what time was left to her here and go out with Charles.

'I'll go out with him.' Juley looked directly at Sarah. 'But if he even mentions my headaches, or tries in any way to question me, I shall come straight back here.'

As she was getting ready about twenty minutes later she heard Sarah on the phone in her bedroom. Juley made an intelligent guess: Sarah was warning Charles not to mention the headaches.

It was the following day and Sarah was glaring at her companion.

'Leave me? You can't leave me! And the reason you've given is absurd! The climate doesn't suit you? I've never heard such rubbish!' They were in the garden by the lake,

147

sitting on loungers and for a while had been watching the waterfowl preening themselves, their colourful plumage gleaming in the sunlight. Ducks on the water ruffled its surface, creating more light and shade, and in the flame of the forest tree above their heads an avian bustle intruded into the silence. It was a beautiful day, with flowers all around, and statuary of white marble contributing an air of opulence in keeping with the magnificent façade of the hacienda.

'I'm sorry you're so angry.' Juley spoke at last. It had been difficult enough broaching the subject; now it was going to be even more difficult, from what she could see. 'After all, you have plenty of company here, and there's nothing to prevent you from staying right up to the time of Maisie's return.'

'I demand a reason for this sudden decision to leave.' She had deliberately ignored Juley's words. 'It's been done for *some* reason, obviously, and I have a right to know what it is.' Undoubtedly she was both puzzled and upset and it was only what Juley had expected, but she hoped she could remain firm in her resolve. Very early this morning she had been up, writing a letter to Dr Blount, explaining that she was returning and asking if he would arrange for her to go into a nursing home as soon as she arrived. She would send a telegram when her final preparations were made, to tell him the time of her arrival at Heathrow Airport. The letter, in its envelope, had been slipped into a drawer, just in case Sarah should come into the room and see it. Juley had also bought aspirins when she was out with Charles yesterday, so her tablets were disguised now, by the new and innocent label: 'Soluble Aspirin'. 'It seems to me,' Sarah was adding wrathfully, 'that this decision's been taken without much thought at all.'

'Not without thought,' argued Juley. 'I have given it a good deal of thought—'

'Since when?' demanded Sarah. 'You had no thought of leaving me when we were talking yesterday morning.'

'I want to go home,' returned Juley pettishly. 'So can we let the matter drop?'

'No we can't. You said your house was sold.'

'It is, but I shall – shall have a place to go to.'

'Where?' persisted Sarah and it was very plain to Juley that she had no intention of abandoning her investigation. She had a set, almost aggressive expression on her face which came as a complete surprise to Juley, who had always seen the gentle side, the calm and dignified mien, the smile, the liquid softness of the eyes. 'I want to know where you will go – *if* you go from here, which, I can tell you, you will certainly *not* be in the very near future!'

'I shall find somewhere,' began Juley, ignoring the latter part of her employer's angry speech. 'It's really my business and I do not think you should trouble yourself about my – my future.'

'Not my business?' The vivid blue eyes now flashed bright as lightning. 'You know I have come to care about you, regard you almost as a daughter. Didn't I say I wished you were my daughter?'

A deep and trembling sigh escaped Juley.

'We've only known each other a few weeks—'

'Time! What has time to do with anything? Who cares about time – short or long? I shall not take your notice unless you can convince me you have a home to go to and, more important, unless you can provide me with a feasible explanation of this extraordinary and totally irrational decision!'

'It may seem irrational to you,' sighed Juley, 'but, believe me, it does have a logical purpose.'

'One you can't – or *won't* – explain?' gritted her employer.

'That's right,' was Juley's quiet reply. 'An explanation is impossible.'

The older woman looked at her angrily, but on noticing the desolation in her face, Sarah's whole manner changed.

'My dear, by your own admission I know you are all alone in the world. Your life recently has been one of disillusionment and trauma but since coming to me you appear to have found peace . . . and a niche of your very own. It would be stupid to leave me when I'm so concerned about your welfare and want so much to help you to find happiness. You won't even give me a reason for wanting to leave, so can you blame me if I can't make sense of any of it?'

'I'm sorry.' Juley half wished she had not come to Sarah like this but that she had just gone off, leaving a note of apology. How much easier it would have been, and why did she not think of it before now? 'I'd have left when Maisie returned—'

'No, you wouldn't. Do you suppose I'd want to lose touch with someone I've come to love?'

'Love . . .' Juley shook her head, thinking of what was soon to happen to her. 'No,' she cried fiercely, 'you mustn't love me – no, I don't want you to!'

Silence, deep and smothering, like a blanket of fog dropping over the whole area.

It was Sarah who at last broke through, to say slowly, her eyes narrowed and fixed as they looked into Juley's, 'You don't want love, either from Charles or from me. Can you give me a reason?'

Juley's whole body sagged. How much easier it would be to make a full confession and put an end to all this. An end to this but the beginning of pity, and with it the continual awareness that her end was close. As it was, up till now while she had been with Sarah, and especially since her meeting with Charles, she had been able to put that knowledge of doom from her for quite long periods of time, but if these people were to learn her secret then there could be no forgetting.

'I must leave you, Sarah,' she said, overcome with a strange fatigue which had nothing to do with her illness. She felt an inability to cope and knew she must escape. She rose from the lounger. 'I'm going inside . . .' Her big eyes, far too bright, looked down into those of the woman who had just said she loved her – and whom Juley knew she had come to love – and said with deep contrition, 'I'm so sorry. Sarah, to cause you pain, but it's unavoidable. One day – one day—'

She could not go on and, turning, she fled to the house and up to her room. But she had heard Sarah call after her, 'Charles will be here to take you out to lunch. He rang me this morning quite early. He had some business to attend to but he'll be finished by . . .' That was all Juley heard because she did not halt, or even turn her head.

But after she had calmed herself, dried the tears that had fallen, and changed into a pretty, flowered summer dress with shortish skirt and nipped-in waist, she decided to seek Sarah out again to see what time Charles was coming for her. She would go out to lunch with him today, and see him whenever he wished, until the day of her departure. Naturally she wondered if Sarah would tell him that she had said she was leaving, and knew she would not be in the least surprised if she was tackled about it by Charles, but she hoped she would not be. All she wanted for the next week was peace, and a little pleasure with Charles. She thought of Stephen, whom she had not seen for two days, but Charles had told her he was staying for about a fort-night, having decided a week was not long enough to put him back into shape.

'So you're back.' Sarah lowered her book on to her knee. Juley looked down at it, to see the same page at which it had been open when she left Sarah almost an hour ago.

'I came to ask what time Charles will be here.' She sat down on the lounger and rested her head against the cushions. 'It's so lovely here, and peaceful.'

'Yet you want to leave it.' No response and Sarah told her that Charles would be here at half-past twelve or thereabouts. 'He couldn't say exactly, but he's booked a lunch at the Hotel Reforma.'

'Thank you.' Juley was subdued, deeply affected by the knowledge that Sarah loved her and was so soon to be hurt. She would have been hurt anyway, even had Juley not decided to leave.

'You're very formal.' Juley said nothing to that and her silence seemed to anger her employer. 'You do realize you can't leave without giving me three months' notice?' she snapped and Juley shot her a startled glance. Three months . . . Anything could happen in that time.

'You can't enforce that kind of notice, Sarah, and you very well know it.'

'I can! And I shall, so you can resign yourself to adhering to *my* wishes, and to – to the devil with your own!'

'Sarah, what is the matter with you—?' Juley's voice jerked to a stop as Agatha appeared from behind a clump of pink oleanders. She was in a beach robe and it seemed she was intending to go over to the pool for a swim. Small and slender, she looked rather younger than her fifty-three years, although her eyes were neither as vivid or as lively as those of her sister, nor was her mouth so youthful.

'What's going on here?' she wanted to know, glancing from one to the other. 'I could hear you half a mile away, Sarah.'

'The garden doesn't go for half a mile!'

Surprise looked out of Agatha's eyes.

'Something's got into you all right. Surely you're not quarrelling with Juley?'

'Of course not,' from Juley, swift to come to Sarah's rescue. 'Are you going in for a swim?' she added, changing the subject and hoping Agatha would not reintroduce it.

'That's right. What I popped over here for, though, was to say that Stephen will be coming in about an hour. I had a pain in my side and thought that as we had a doctor friend in the area I might as well make use of him, so I phoned Stephen. He was very obliging and said he'd come and take a look at me.'

'But it's people's heads he's interested in.' Sarah looked faintly anxious. 'What's wrong with you, anyway?'

'That's what I am hoping Stephen will tell me. I know he's a neurosurgeon but all doctors can diagnose about other things.'

'The pain isn't troubling you too much,' observed Sarah, 'seeing that you're going for a swim.'

'No, it isn't much, but I might as well let Stephen take a look.' Her eyes flicked to Juley. 'Why don't you come along to the pool. You don't swim enough, dear. Run up and get into your costume.' She went off, pulling her robe together after it had come open, to reveal a pink and blue swimsuit.

Sarah looked apologetically at Juley and said, 'I'm sorry about screaming at you like that. And thanks for shutting Agatha up; she'd have gone on and on probing if you hadn't adroitly changed the subject.'

'It's all right.' Juley's eyes followed Agatha's figure thoughtfully. 'She's going to ask you plenty of questions when I leave, isn't she?'

'You are not leaving.' So quiet now the statement but just as compellingly spoken as before. 'There is no sense in it at all.' She paused and an electric current seemed to shoot through the air around them. 'I'm going to say something at the risk of your turning on me, Juley, and at the risk of embarrassing you. But first, I want you to know that I think no less of you, and that I care very much for you.' Another pause filled with tension and then, 'That first night we were here and Charles stayed – he was with you, in your bedroom—'

'Sarah!' Juley half rose from the lounger, her face crimson. 'Mind your own business, please!'

'It's too late for me to cut myself off from your affairs.'

153

There was a resolute, emphatic inflection in the older woman's voice and a determined glitter in her eyes. 'I've already made it my business. A girl alone in the world needs someone to care, to take an interest in her and what she is doing. I do wish you would regard me as – if not a mother – then a sincere and anxious friend who doesn't need to be overendowed with intelligence to have grasped the fact that you have a grave problem on your mind, such a grave problem that you should not be tackling it alone, and I want to help.'

Deeply touched, Juley wanted to cry . . . on Sarah's breast. Alone, Sarah had said. Little did she know that there was no way of grappling with her problem than alone. Turning, she regarded Sarah with a dull and vacant stare. For the past few minutes she had felt a tinge of pain and it was now increasing.

'I don't want you to concern yourself about me—' She stopped abruptly, wincing as the pain shot to the back of her head. 'I must go!' she decided urgently. 'I must go!'

'It's your head again . . . Juley . . .' Sarah rose from her lounger, her anxious eyes following Juley's retreating figure. She caught her up. 'What is it? Surely you can tell me?'

'I feel – sick – something I've eaten – sorry, I must run!' Surely that would prevent her employer from following her to her room. She hoped she had fobbed her off, since the last thing she wanted was for Sarah to realize just how bad the pains could be. She turned her head as Sarah fell behind and breathed a sigh of relief; Sarah was no longer following her. In fact, she was now going in the other direction.

After taking her tablets, Juley came from the bathroom with the intention of lying down on the bed for a while and she hoped that Charles would be a little late, just to allow her time to recover properly so that the agony would no longer whiten her face and dull her eyes. But to her surprise she came from the bathroom to see Sarah standing by her dressing-table, her face devoid of expression.

Unreasoning anger made Juley ask sharply, 'Why are you here?'

'I was naturally worried about you,' came the reply, spoken rather too casually, Juley thought, though without, however, attaching any undue importance to it. 'I wonder what it was that caused your tummy upset?' She glanced to the door of the bathroom, which was wide open. 'Feel better now?'

'Yes, thank you, Sarah.' She felt ashamed of her anger and the sharpness of the tone she had used. 'I feel very much better.' The pain was still there, but she managed a shaky laugh. 'I shall have to be more careful of what I eat for the next few days.'

'A wise precaution,' approved Sarah, then, in a voice lacking expression, 'You've been – er – sick in there?' Again her glance went to the bathroom.

'Yes, horribly!' She stopped, eyeing her employer curiously. Sarah seemed a little breathless, as if she had been hurrying. 'How long have you been here, in my bedroom?' she just had to ask.

'Oh – only a moment or two. I came through the door just as you were coming from the bathroom.' Her smile was thin and enigmatic. 'Don't worry, child, there's no need for embarrassment. I did not hear or see you vomiting.'

Juley blushed but relief swept through her. For one awful moment she thought she had been caught out in a lie.

Sarah asked if she was coming out into the garden again.

'You might as well be out there in the fresh air until Charles comes.'

'Yes. I'll be down in about ten minutes.' The pain should be gone completely by then. 'How long do I have? I might take your sister's offer up and go for a dip.'

'I'll join you, then.' Mechanically her eyes went even yet again to the bathroom. 'Well, I'll see you when you're ready – and don't forget about Charles.' She paused. 'Perhaps you haven't time for a swim—' She broke off and began coughing. 'Oh, dear . . . can I get a drink of water from your bathroom? 'It's nearer than my own.'

'Of course. I'll get it for you—'

'No, dear. I'll get it myself.' And she smiled as she went past Juley. 'I don't know what is wrong with my throat, it feels so dry.'

Automatically Juley heard the tap, the clink of a tumbler against porcelain and could visualize Sarah over the basin. But it seemed then that a long silence ensued before Sarah emerged, smiling again.

Juley watched the door swing closed as she went out, then she walked over to the bathroom to get the box of tablets she had left on the shelf. The label, covering the correct one, read: 'Soluble Aspirins'. What a good idea it had been to cover the original label, thought Juley. Yes, because otherwise Sarah would have surely noticed the original label. Juley put the tablets into the handbag she was intending to use, one that matched a pair of yellow leather sandals. She glanced at the clock and decided she had time for a quick dip. It would refresh her, she decided, and went off to join Agatha in the sunlit pool. Within a few minutes they were joined by Sarah and a pleasant twenty minutes followed.

Fully refreshed, she came from the pool just as Stephen came striding across the lawn towards the patio surrounding the pool.

'Hello, there,' he greeted Juley with a ready smile. 'You look as if you've been enjoying yourself.'

She nodded, returning his smile.

'I have. It's marvellous in there – but I suppose Mari has a pool you can swim in when you feel like it?'

'She does, a real beauty.' He glanced over her shoulder. 'I've come to see Agatha. She phoned to say she has a pain, but she seems to be swimming all right.'

Agatha came out followed by her sister.

'Sorry,' she laughed swinging her head after taking off her cap. 'I'm fine now.'

'So I see.'

'That should have cost you,' censured her sister. 'You can't just call a doctor out and not pay him.' She was regarding him with an unfathomable expression but spared a glance for Juley which fleetingly interrupted the long, fixed stare.

'Oh, I know,' from Agatha. 'My own doctor makes extortionate charges.' She sent Stephen an upward glance. 'But I expect you know how to charge as well. All doctors do.'

He made no comment on that; Juley noticed the glint in his eyes and knew he was far from pleased with Agatha.

He asked Juley if she were free that evening to come out to dinner with him. Sarah, aware that if Charles followed his normal pattern he would bring her back at around half-past six, but also not wanting Juley to go out with Stephen, said at once that she was sorry, but she could not spare Juley that evening. That Juley was surprised was plain by the start she gave. She knew that had it been Charles who wanted to take her out to dinner Sarah would have been more than willing to let her go.

'Perhaps some other time,' he said resignedly. 'I'll be going, then, seeing that Agatha doesn't need me after all.' He seemed to stop rather abruptly and when Juley looked at him he was staring at Sarah . . . staring in a very strange manner, as if some sign from her had puzzled him.

A hint of a frown knitted his brow and he was about to speak when Sarah, having picked up a towel, said tonelessly, 'As long as you are here, Stephen, I wonder if I could take advantage, and ask your advice?'

'About what?'

She was drying herself. 'I don't think it's serious.'

His frown deepened.

'Are you saying you have something wrong with you?' He looked her over and seemed to draw an impatient breath.

'Sarah, what – you never mentioned anything to me.'

157

Agatha was all concern as she, too, let her eyes travel over Sarah's figure.

'Nothing very terrible, but a trifle annoying.' She looked up into Stephen's face. 'I'd like you to have a look at a strange little swelling I have on my hip.'

'Swelling? Is it painful? It's probably a case for your own doctor when you get back home.'

'Oh, but, it must be examined, Stephen,' declared Agatha firmly. 'Sarah, how long have you had this swelling?'

'Not very long – about a week—'

'A week?' Juley was eyeing her curiously. 'Why didn't you say something to me? Is it painful?' she asked anxiously.

'Stephen's just asked me that. No, it isn't painful, but all the same, I'd feel more comfortable, Stephen, if you would take a look at it and give me your opinion.' She paused, avoiding the two pairs of eyes staring at her and concentrating on Stephen instead. 'I agree it is a case for my own doctor, but it's annoying me because I'm conscious of it all the time. After all, I shouldn't have a swelling on my hip, should I?'

'Well, no. It could be a cist.'

'Then you'll take a look, and tell me?'

He agreed and Juley watched them as they went into the house.

'Darned funny business,' frowned Agatha. 'Why hasn't she mentioned this before? A swelling – on her hip—' She shook her head and repeated, 'Darned funny business. A cist? On her hip?'

'I believe cists can grow anywhere – well, in lots of places.'

'Let us hope it's nothing serious.' Agatha's eyes were following the two as they proceeded towards the house, Stephen's head bent as if Sarah was whispering something to him. He turned his head to look at Juley, then turned it back again swiftly. 'Sarah and I have always enjoyed the very best of health and it would come as a severe shock to us if either ever had anything serious come our way.' She smiled at Juley. 'You're another who obviously enjoys good health. But then you're young so nothing's going to happen to you for a very long time.'

Juley turned to take up a towel. Agatha had already dried herself and she shook out her brown hair, sprinkled very lightly with grey. Her figure too was that of a much younger woman. Yes, both she and Sarah had enjoyed good health and it was apparent in their looks and vitality. It would be very sad if Sarah's swelling turned out to be serious, mused Juley. She would hate to think of her suffering in the same way she herself was doing, existing through a period of hopelessness and despair, to say nothing of the pain. She fervently prayed that Stephen would be able to reassure them all by finding that the swelling was nothing to worry about.

It was when she was back in her bedroom and almost ready to go down and wait for Charles, that he phoned, full of apologies, to say he could not make it after all.

'I've some business to attend to that can't wait,' he went on to explain. 'It's something unexpected and urgent which must be attended to at once.'

'That's all right, Charles. I understand.'

'I'm sorry and disappointed. However, shall you be free this evening? If so, we'll make up for the lost lunch by having dinner together.'

Her eyes lit with anticipation. For although Sarah had told Stephen she would not be free this evening, Juley felt she could be fairly certain a very different answer would have been forthcoming had it been Charles who wanted to take her out to dine.

'I'll ask Sarah and phone you back.' she promised.

'I feel sure it will be all right.' There was confidence in his voice. 'I'll be along for you at seven o'clock.'

'Oh, but I must ask her first—'

'I must go, Juley. See you this evening.' And on that he was gone, leaving the line dead.

She had to smile at his confidence, yet could understand it. He was undoubtedly a great favourite with Sarah and so could foresee no reason for her not allowing Juley to go off this evening.

When Sarah reappeared with Stephen she was smiling.

'It's nothing serious,' she was quick to reassure Juley, who was again in the garden, with a book. 'Charles not here yet?'

Juley shook her head.

'He's just rung to say he can't make it.'

'What a shame.' Sarah was frowning. 'What's wrong that he can't make it?'

'A business appointment, something unexpected.' Juley was aware of Stephen's sudden interest and was not surprised to hear him ask if he could take her out to lunch. This time Sarah seemed to think it was a good idea.

The hotel to which Stephen took her was one of the most luxurious she had even seen and she just stood as they entered the lobby, temporarily speechless with awe and appreciation.

'It's just out of this world,' she breathed at length. 'Have you been here before?'

'Yes, with Mari.' He gave a grimace as he took her arm and led her to the lounge. 'Only the very best is good enough for Mari. I'd never dream of taking her to anything less than this.'

'She's lucky . . .' Juley spoke with a sigh in her voice and as she was still looking around her she missed the strange, slantways glance her companion gave her. 'This place,' she said again, determinedly shaking off the depression that had descended on her for a moment. 'That centre-piece of Venetian glass – it's so beautiful. I suppose it is Venetian?'

'Yes, it is, and it gives an illusion of a cascade made possible by the lighting effects. I'm told a great deal of thought and planning went into the creation of this lobby.' But now they were passing through the high archway leading into the cocktail lounge. 'We'll have a drink in here while we study the menu.'

'Oh, but this is really living!' Although she would have preferred to be with Charles, she was glad she had had the experience of this wonderful hotel. 'Really living!' She settled back in the armchair, but her smile faded as she noticed the expression on Stephen's face. His eyes had darkened and his lower lip was caught between his teeth. 'Is something wrong?' she enquired anxiously.

'No, dear, nothing.' He had recovered instantly from what had upset him but Juley was still watching him in some puzzlement. There must have been some very serious reason for an expression like that to descend on him so suddenly.

'Don't look so worried.' He laughed; she knew it was forced. 'If you must know, an unpleasant memory crossed my mind but it is gone now.'

As she continued to watch him, as he gave the order to the waiter who had come along. Juley was not at all satisfied with his explanation. Yet, why should he lie to her? Suddenly impatient with her bewilderment, she picked up the menu which had been put before her, and opened it. But somehow she could not study it, and she realized it was owing to the intense scrutiny to which she was being subjected by the man opposite to her. However, it did not last for long, not after he saw that she had noticed. He discussed the menu with her and ordered.

'I'm so glad you found nothing serious in that swelling of Sarah's,' she was saying once they were at their table. 'Both Agatha and I were dreadfully worried. Thank goodness it didn't last long.'

'You'd have been troubled if there had been something seriously wrong with her?' There was a curious inflection in his voice which could not escape her.

'Of course. I've become very attached to her.' She paused,

then added. 'With a swelling one naturally thinks of a malignant growth, a frightening growth.'

Stephen took a bread roll from the silver basket and put it on his side plate. His silence seemed deliberate and Juley had the impression that he was weighing his next words before speaking them.

'You say you've become attached to her, yet you want to leave her.'

She glanced swiftly at him.

'Sarah told you that?'

'It's obvious, isn't it?' Juley merely nodded and he went on, 'It was when she and I had gone to her room so I could look at the – swelling.'

Why the slight hesitation? wondered Juley.

'What did she say exactly?'

'That she did not want you to leave her. She was mystified, saying you had not given her any logical reason.' He picked up his knife and fork, then stayed the intention to fix her gaze instead. 'Why do you feel it is necessary for you to leave, Juley? You have no one to go to, no family, no home.' He was troubled and his expression revealed it.

'She told you that as well?'

'We were – er – chatting about you. It came out; it was natural that it should.'

Again a hesitation. Why? She asked curiously, 'Why are you taking such an interest in my affairs?'

'Because I like you very much,' was his unhesitating reply and it was natural that she should colour, and lower her lashes. 'Don't be shy with me, Juley,' he added in gentle tones. 'The last thing I want is to embarrass you.' He paused; she made no comment and he said finally, 'I can say I like you, surely?'

Her face broke into a winning smile.

'Of course you can, Stephen.'

'And – do you like me?'

'I wouldn't be here if I didn't,' she rejoined with a hint

of coquettishness in her tone. But if she expected to produce a laugh from her companion she was mistaken. His face remained sober and she realized he was far more serious and thoughtful this afternoon than on any occasion when they had been together and she was fast reaching the conclusion that he had something very troublesome on his mind.

'We've strayed from what we were talking about. Will you tell me why you want to leave Sarah's employ?'

'I can't explain, but I can tell you that it is necessary for me to go back to England.' She was pale and her eyes were sad. 'It's my own private affair, Stephen,' she added after a space. 'I know what I am doing, and why.' Her wide gaze fixed his for a moment. 'Please do not ask me any more about my decision.'

But he shook his head at once and said quietly. 'You're all alone in the world, so surely it would be wise to stay with someone who cares about you, and your welfare. Sarah has developed a sincere affection for you – in fact, she has grown to love you as a daughter.' So serious and with a most obvious degree of concern.

His persuasive words and manner had a profound effect on her and it was very difficult to say, 'I've made my decision, Stephen, and I must keep to it.'

'Must?' He seized on the word. '*Must*, Juley?'

She gave a small sigh, not of impatience but merely because she wanted to explain, yet could not.

'There are times in one's life, Stephen, when decisions have to be made and kept. I have reached this particular time and, therefore, I am determined to keep firmly to the decision I have made.'

He looked at her, an unfathomable expression in his vivid blue eyes. Then to her surprise and relief he shrugged his shoulders and changed the subject. However, it appeared to prey on his mind because after they had left the table and were having coffee in the lounge he brought it up again.

'I hope you'll forgive me, Juley,' he began, fixing her

gaze across the low, glass-topped table to which they had been shown by the waiter who had then brought their coffee, 'but your plight troubles me—'

'Plight?' she broke in swiftly. 'That is an odd word to use.'

'Perhaps.' He spoke quickly as if correcting a slip of the tongue. 'Your situation, I ought to have said. And I revert back to Sarah's feeling for you. It seems totally illogical to me that you should hurt her by leaving—' here he broke off to wag a finger at her – 'without an explanation and when you yourself have no home to go to.'

'Stephen, please—'

'Surely it isn't so urgent that you leave?' he broke in with a frown of impatience at her manner. 'You know, dear, it is good sometimes to confide, to unburden oneself.'

'I agree, but this is a time when confidences cannot be made. I'm sorry . . .' She felt almost ready to pour our her very soul to him – or to someone, for the burden was becoming more than she could bear alone. Anger rose as she realized that this persistence on Stephen's part was the cause of how she was feeling; he was depressing her, reminding her as it did, of the position she was in.

Stephen said seriously, 'There are others who worry about you, Juley. I myself am anxious and I'm sure Ramos and Agatha have an affection for you and they will be troubled at learning of your intention to leave Sarah when you have no home in England to go to.'

She paused, closer than even to bearing her soul. She gave herself a few seconds to ponder the idea, then, sure that it would get to Sarah, then to Charles, she shook her head. All she wanted for the short time left to her was to live a normal life but with her secret revealed she would be faced with pity, with treatment usually meted out to those who are ill or to others who needed pity. This was not for her. And in any case, it was best that she should tear herself away from Charles. At present it was on the cards that he would marry Mari, but there were occasions when it seemed he was near to thinking more about Juley than would in the end be good for him.

'I can't confide,' she quivered at last, a distinct catch in her voice. 'I want to leave in about a week's time but Sarah says she wants more notice than that.'

'It wouldn't be fair to leave her at such short notice. I am in full agreement with her about that.'

Faintly she smiled.

'Sarah does not need a companion. Stephen.'

'But she needs you. You don't seem to appreciate just what you have done for her. She told me about her daughter, what a disappointment she has been to her. Juley, please stay with Sarah – for the present, at least.'

The last five words seemed to be spoken with a strange inflection and a slight frown of puzzlement creased Juley's brow.

'You really want me to stay, don't you?' Only when the question was asked did she realize how silly it was.

'That's surely obvious by now,' was his rather sharp reply.

She nodded her head, reaching for the cream. She poured some on to her coffee and raised her eyes as she replaced the silver jug on the table.

'Perhaps I shall give Sarah more notice,' she sighed at last. 'Though I cannot see that it is at all necessary.'

Ignoring the last sentence, he told her he was very glad she had made the concession. And there was a silence after that, heavy and tense. It seemed to be reflected in the strange, sad irony of his tone as he added, 'I hope you and I shall see a lot of each other while I am here.' A pause and then, 'I am not leaving as soon as I intended. There is no hurry as there is adequate help at the hospital and I've had a letter from a doctor friend to advise me to prolong my holiday for another week or two.'

'That will be nice.'

'And we will see one another?'

'If Sarah gives me time off, it might be possible.' If she was staying, she mused, then it was Charles she wanted to be with, this despite her firm conviction that she ought not to continue with their affair. She was dining with Charles this evening and it was most likely that they would make love, that once more she would be living – yes, living life to the full!

Stephen was murmuring as if to himself, and this brought her from her reverie.

'Your house . . . you sold it so soon—' He broke off on becoming aware of her eyes flying to his. 'Er – it was very soon after your husband's death, I mean.'

She could find nothing to say; her nerves were tingling as it struck her forcibly that it was possible that Stephen had made an intelligent guess . . . and reached the sort of conclusion only a doctor – and especially a neurosurgeon – would reach.

'The house was too large for one person,' she offered, managing a smile. 'I shall have to – to look for something smaller.' She was agitated, unknowingly crushing the soft leather of her handbag in hands that had groped for it without her own volition as it had lain on the vacant chair beside hers. Stephen's eyes slid downwards in the deep silence following her words.

'We've finished our coffee, Stephen, so we can go now.'

He nodded but made no answer. His eyes were still fixed to her bag and as she glanced down she noticed her knuckles shone white, so tightly was she clutching the bag. Slowly she relaxed, profoundly aware now of his fixed interest, and of the unnatural silence, heavy and oppressive. She swallowed, and quite unconsciously closed her fingers tightly on the bag again.

'We must go,' she said but as she was about to rise Stephen leant over to release her fingers. Juley was so taken aback that she made no protest even when her bag fell to the floor. All she uttered was, 'Oh . . .'

'I'm so sorry.' Stephen rose swiftly to retrieve the bag. 'I'm afraid it has come open, Juley, and the contents are spilled. But I'll get them.' He was collecting them up and his body was between the bag and Juley, who waited for him to hand it to her. He was apologizing as he collected up her compact, comb, handkerchief and other items like her pen and diary, and a small, suede-backed copy of Omar Khayyám which she invariably carried around with her so that she always had something to read. 'Forgive me,' he said, handing her the bag after snapping the clasp shut. 'Your hands were tightly clenched – a sure sign of nervousness and strain and my doctor's instinct was to release your fingers so you would relax . . .' His eyes had caught something he had failed to see; the tiny book of Omar Khayyám was lying just underneath the chair on which he himself had been sitting. He bent to pick it up, and as if by instinct he opened it at the place where the ribbon was marking a page. Juley froze as she watched him reading the verse which was flowing through her own mind as well:

Ah, fill the Cup: – what boots it to repeat
How time is slipping underneath our feet:
Unborn TO-MORROW, and dead YESTERDAY,
Why fret about them if TO-DAY be sweet?

And underneath, neatly in pencil she had added: 'Sweet, with you, my beloved Charles.'

She wanted to snatch the book from him, then realized it was too late and merely waited for him to hand it to her. His blue eyes never left her face as he did so. His expression was enigmatical and he did not speak as he watched her open her bag and slip the book inside. She had blushed, then gone pale; she heard Stephen's voice at last, taut and somehow strangled.

'I'm sorry, Juley – about letting all your things fall out.

It was clumsy of me.' No mention of the verse but the hint of a smile now on his lips.

'It isn't important,' she returned with a lightness which she guessed did not deceive him. 'There's nothing break-able in my bag.' She glanced around, asking if he had made sure to pick everything up, while at the same time auto-matically feeling through the silky leather for the small porcelain-lidded box into which she had put a few of the tablets from the bottle marked. 'Soluble Asprins'. Stephen was looking into her eyes but she saw his gaze fleetingly interrupted and she knew he had seen her action. But by now she was almost admitting that Stephen had made the intelligent guess which had previously worried her.

It was only later, when she was in her room, placing the handbag on a chair, that it struck her that this was not the kind of bag to fly open easily. For one thing, the leather was very soft and for another the clasp was of the kind which lifted over, from one side of the frame to the other. Strange, she mused, that it had come open. Then she shrugged; it *had* come open and she thought no more about it.

Nine

Charles came for her at half-past seven and was in earnest conversation with Sarah, in the hall, when Juley came down from her room. She was dressed in a flowing cotton skirt colourfully embroidered round the hem, and the blouse was of moss green to match the green in the embroidery. Her hair shone with health; her cheeks were aglow as were her eyes. It was plain to the two standing there, and whose attention had been attracted as she reached the bottom of the stairs, that she was happy. Sarah sighed suddenly and it seemed to July that a frown had been suppressed and a smile appeared instead.

'You look wonderful.' Charles's smile sent her heart leaping. How attractive he was! Tall and dashing and superbly masculine.

Dashing . . . ? She smiled and when he asked what had amused her she found herself saying, 'I thought you looked dashing, then decided it was not very mature to use a word like that.'

'I hope,' he returned with a laugh, 'that it isn't merely a schoolgirl crush you have on me.'

He was funning, of course, and she fell into his mood.

'Could be, Charles. For I sometimes feel not very grown-up at all.'

Sarah was looking on, her expression taut, unsmiling. Juley turned to her, thanked her for allowing her the evening off, then added anxiously, 'We are friends again, aren't we – now that I've agreed to stay on for a while longer?'

169

Sarah nodded and said yes, they were friends again.

'So off you go and enjoy your evening. Charles, take good care of her and drive slowly on your way back.'

'I'll do that,' he laughed and took Juley's arm. Sarah opened the front door and stood aside to let them pass. Impulsively Juley turned and kissed her on the cheek.

'Thank you again,' she whispered huskily and went with Charles to his car.

The evening was wonderful and with every moment Juley was telling herself how lucky she had been in finding her dear Charles again, so that her last weeks could be happy ones. It was like a miracle, fate having given her this magic interlude, this sunlit brilliance before the terrible, frightening darkness that was to descend upon her, smothering her into oblivion.

Charles had asked if she would like to dine at a restaurant, but said that he had left orders for a dinner to be cooked at his home.

'The choice is yours, Juley,' he smiled. 'Home or a restaurant?' And she had without pause chosen his home. Because after dinner they would go up to his suite and make love.

It was after midnight when he brought her back to the hacienda and Sarah had gone to bed. But when Juley put out her light she noticed the narrow shaft of light coming from under the door between her room and that of her employer. Should she call 'goodnight'? For some reason she was unable to understand, Juley remained silent and moments later she was asleep.

The following morning she awoke to sunshine peeping through the chinks of the long satin drapes and she sprang out of bed, stretching luxuriously as she moved towards the window. But Sarah's voice stayed her progress and she glanced at the clock. Half-past eight! They had both overslept. She listened, waiting for Sarah to call again, then realized she had not called her in the first place. She was talking on the phone and Juley heard, 'You managed to get another one? Was it necessary? You had the one I gave you analysed . . .' A pause and Juley moved with the intention of going into her bathroom but she stopped again. 'I see. You want to make absolutely sure. And you want me to get hold of . . . Look, Stephen, I'm not able to talk any more just now. I'll do my best to get hold of it and phone you in about an hour.'

Juley knocked and entered, saying she was sorry she had overslept. She saw her employer's expression, a startled expression and said rather casually, 'I heard you on the phone to Stephen. Is something the matter?'

'You heard?' sharply. 'What did you hear?'

Juley shook her head, bewildered.

'Nothing important. You mentioned Stephen's name so I wondered if anything was wrong – that swelling? It wasn't serious, after all?'

'No. Fetch me my morning tea, please.' Sarah looked relieved, obviously as a result of Juley's answer to her question. 'I can't abide that maid with the dirty yellow face.'

'I'll just get into a pair of slacks and a top and go down for a tray. Just tea, of course?'

'I'd like toast as well.'

Juley swung around.

'Toast?' This was the only time Sarah had asked for toast. She hated eating in bed, she maintained. 'Aren't you going down for breakfast, then?'

'No, I'm not very hungry. Toast will do nicely – oh, and some black cherry jam. Lay me a dainty tray, Juley. And there's no hurry.' She ended with a smile which Juley strongly suspected was forced.

'No hurry?' on a curious note.

'Take half an hour if you like.'

'You're quite well?'

'Fine, but lazy this morning. Not like me at all, is it?'

'No,' replied Juley smoothly, 'not a bit like you.'

As she donned the slacks and a blouse Juley was puzzling

over her employer's strange behaviour – for it certainly was strange. In the kitchen Juley was given a free hand in getting the tray ready. When she returned Sarah was sitting up against the lace-trimmed pillows, her hair neat and short, the net having been taken off. Her nightdress of ruched pink nylon and lace was off the shoulders and Juley thought she looked very glamorous for her age and wished she would find a nice kind man for company, and perhaps even get married.

'That looks lovely. Thank you, Juley. And now you can run along and see to yourself. Go down to breakfast. I'll not be getting up for a while. You were late in bed last night but so was I – and even when I was in bed I couldn't sleep. I'll see you in a couple of hours or so.'

This straying from the customary by Sarah naturally occupied Juley's mind while she took her bath, got herself dressed in white linen slacks, marine blue over-blouse and white leather strapped sandals. She made a hearty breakfast of paw-paws and pineapple slices, with scrambled eggs and toast to follow. Sarah usually ate well at breakfast, too . . .

With the meal finished Juley found herself at a loose end, as Agatha was away for the whole day with her husband, who had an important business lunch in Mexico City and all the men had their wives with them.

It was the first time since coming to work for Sarah that Juley felt lost – alone and with nothing to do, no one to talk to. Juley knew Sarah would not want her in the afternoon because she usually liked to be on her own with a book, though sometimes she would take a siesta, as many people did in this part of the world.

Juley strolled for half an hour in the hacienda's magnificent grounds, where trees and flowers lavished the gently moving air with a perfume as delightful as any of the world's exotic fragrances. The sun was warm but not too hot; the sky was brittle clear and sapphire blue with a mere sprinkling of lacy cirrus floating like intricate silver webs meticulously spun by some magical hand. It was sheer bliss, a heaven on its own, far removed from the grime and smoke and industrial horror-blocks of concrete reaching to the overcast sky, naked and gaunt, evilly scarred with the pollution of man's supreme achievement: Progress!

Juley decided to explore the countryside just outside the grounds for she had not seen much of it except from the windows of the various cars in which she had travelled. She strode out briskly, into the immediate precincts, alive to the clear crystal air, the sunshine and the various smells and sounds drifting to her as she hurried along. Birdsong and insect humming, the soughing of a zephyr of a breeze, the stirring of leaves to scatter the scent of pines and oleanders lining the winding, uphill road. Not a person in sight, nothing human at all other than herself. Only what Nature provided.

She had been walking for some twenty minutes when the sound of a car, a mere purring from behind, caused her to turn and at the same time to veer to one side and mount the grass verge. Charles! Her heart leapt for joy and a lovely smile lit her face.

'Charles . . .' Excitement flared within her, accelerating her heartbeats, quickening her pulses. It was almost always like this and she did wonder sometimes if this ecstasy would have continued indefinitely had it been possible for her and Charles to marry.

With a slight screeching of brakes he brought the car to a standstill. He asked her what she was doing out here, walking all on her own. His gaze was all-examining and so she gave a laugh which lit her own eyes and took the anxiety from his. He had been remembering her headache but she knew that at present she gave a picture of perfect, youthful health and vigour.

'I'm at a loose end.' She came to the open window and explained about Sarah's wish to stay in bed.

'Then get in,' he said but leapt out and hurried round so as to open the door for her. She smiled up at him; he bent to kiss the tip of her nose. 'If you look at me like that,' he said dryly, 'you could be asking for trouble.'

'Oh, I wouldn't call it that,' she shot back, adopting his mood. 'And I don't think you would, either.'

'You're an abandoned little wanton.' He kissed her again, this time on the lips. She asked where he had been, watching those slender hands on the steering-wheel as he prepared to set the vehicle in motion again.

'I've been into town – had to be there early.' He paused and then, 'Mari and I had a tiff last night—'

'Last night!' exclaimed Juley. 'But it must have been after one o'clock when you got back from bringing me home.'

'Nevertheless, she phoned me – had been trying since half-past eleven. She's found out that you and I have been seeing each other every day, often spending the whole day together and she's furious. The green blades of jealousy stabbing at a woman's heart. Thank God I was born a man!' His sneering contempt for the girl he had been expecting to marry caused Juley to flinch. He seemed not in the least upset about the 'tiff' as he called it. Juley rather thought it was much more than that. She recalled Mari's anger in the café when she had told Juley she knew that she had been out with Charles on several occasions. Now she knew, apparently, that they had been seeing one another regularly – every day, in fact. Surely she had now suspected there was more than mere friendship in the situation existing between them. Juley was sorry for her, but she knew she would feel glad if a permanant rift took place since Charles deserved someone far warmer and more sincere than Mari.

She felt she must say she was sorry and ask if Charles wanted to end their relationship. He smiled at her, turning his head swiftly.

'End our wonderful affair? Not likely! I told you I would not be pushed into marriage and I hope I also convinced you I would not tolerate a clinging woman. We did have a certain understanding but it was tacit – never discussed. I expect I'd have had to make up my mind one day but as it is – well, it would seem that Mari has made up my mind for me.' He turned with a smile. 'Are you free now, for the rest of the day?'

She shook her head.

'I left Sarah in bed, as I told you, but she said she would see me in about two hours' time; that was around a quarter past nine –' She glanced at the clock on the dash. 'She should be up by now.'

Charles brought the car smoothly to a halt on the semi-circular forecourt and came round instantly to open the door for Juley to alight.

'Go and find her and ask if you are free.' It was an imperious order and Juley's chin lifted a fraction. He seemed amused at the gesture and, giving her a slap, told her to do as he bade her.

'I feel a fraud,' she frowned. 'I certainly do not earn my salary.'

'If Sarah is happy, why should you care?' He sounded so casual, so unheeding of what she had said and as she went into the house she was thinking of his attitude towards Mari's anger at his taking another girl out every day. The undisguised contempt, the satirical amusement that contained no hint of humour in its true sense – just male mockery, derision for the opposite sex. His behaviour had acted as a cankerous irritant on her, she recalled, for here was a side of her adored Charles which was new to her, and which she did not particularly like.

Sarah was not about and soon Juley was seeking out Agatha, who, said one of the maids, was in her bedroom.

'Sarah's gone out,' was Agatha's surprising reply to Juley's enquiry. 'Didn't she tell you she was intending to go to town?'

Juley shook her head.

'I left her in bed. She said she hadn't slept very well, but told me she would see me at eleven o'clock.'

Agatha shrugged her elegant shoulders, her smile untroubled as she said she had no idea when her sister would be back.

'She didn't give you any idea when she'd be back?'

'None – come to think of it,' mused Agatha, 'she was acting rather strangely, sort of abrupt with with me and noncommittal.'

'I wonder if it's that swelling? It proved to be a cist, didn't it?'

'That's right. But it wasn't serious and Sarah isn't in any hurry to have it removed. She said she'd see to it when she got back home.'

'Have you seen it?' enquired Juley curiously and the older woman shook her head, frowning darkly.

'She refused to let me take a look. Not like her at all.'

Juley sighed, more with exasperation than anything else. She strongly suspected Sarah of deceit regarding that swelling. Yet why on earth should she put on an act? Stephen had seen it, so it must be there. Yet why couldn't Sarah let her sister see it? Had Sarah merely invented a swelling just to have a private talk with Stephen?

'I suppose I'm free, then,' was all she said.

'You're going out with Charles?'

'He wants me to, yes. He's waiting. He gave me a lift.'

'Lift? Where from at this time of the morning?'

'I'd been for a walk, passing time until Sarah should get up.'

'She was up and out by a quarter past ten.'

A quarter past ten . . . And yet she had told Juley she would see her at eleven . . .

'It's all right, then?' Charles noticed that Juley now had her handbag and a large straw hat as she came to where he was standing, by his car. He opened the door for her. 'Sarah's a real brick, letting you off every day like this.'

'Sarah,' returned Juley on a dry note, 'is not in. She went out at a quarter past ten, to town, according to Agatha.'

'Out . . . ?' Charles looked puzzled. 'I thought you said she was to see you at eleven o'clock?'

'So she did. And she also gave me to understand she was having a lie-in because she hadn't slept well. I did see a light in her room last night when I got to mine, so she was awake then.'

'But she didn't lie in after all?'

'No. And as it was nine o'clock, or a bit later, when I took her breakfast tray in – while she was still in bed – she must have wasted no time at all in eating her toast, having her bath and getting ready to go out. Sarah usually takes a long time getting dressed and making up her face, because she's so particular. Well, you must know that?'

He nodded instantly.

'She always looks as if she's ready to do some modelling, I agree.' He shrugged then and told Juley to get into the car. 'I'm taking you to a restaurant for lunch and then we'll go back to the casa. Suit you?'

'Of course.' She was still puzzled by Sarah's behaviour but happy to be with Charles, so a smile soon appeared, to erase the slight frown that had previously settled on her brow.

'I thought it would be a treat, and a change for you. We've been lunching at home a bit too much.'

'I love it. Charles, just as much – no, even more than a restaurant.'

'It's cosy. I admit. Nevertheless, eating out is always a pleasant change.' He drove then in silence while Juley looked from the side window to admire the scenery – hills and a valley and the glimpses of the sea when bends in the road were taken.

He had booked their table but they decided to have a drink in the lounge first. A waiter took their drinks order while another presented them with a menu each.

'Lord!' About to open the menu Charles made the exclamation which brought his companion's head up with a jerk.

'There's Sarah – with Stephen! With Stephen . . .' he repeated in a most puzzled and quiet tone.

The couple were deep in conversation, a coffee tray on the low table at which they were sitting, opposite to one another.

'It looks as if they've had lunch together and come in here for coffee.' Why should Sarah be here with Stephen? Was it a prearranged meeting or was it made only this morning? In either event, it was obvious that the subject under discussion was serious. Charles was staring curiously at her as Juley brought her attention from the couple who were sitting not far away at all.

'Aren't you going over to them?' asked Charles, an odd inflection in his voice. He was just as puzzled as she as to why those two should be here in the hotel lounge. Juley swung her head again. They were so intent on their subject that neither looked up, or away from the other, so had not discovered the presence of Charles and Juley.

'I don't think so,' replied Juley. 'I can't say why, but I'm reluctant to intrude.'

'I understand, because that is just how I myself feel. Come on, let's go straight into the restaurant. Our drinks will be brought to the table. We can have them there.'

Once sat down Juley looked at Charles and said, 'You're just as puzzled as I, aren't you?'

'It surely can't be that they've become attached to one another?'

'Sarah's twenty years older than Stephen!' she exclaimed.

'It wouldn't be the first time such a thing has happened.'

'No,' returned Juley emphatically as she recalled Sarah's confession that she had never married because she was still in love with her husband's memory. 'With Sarah it couldn't possibly be anything like that.'

'Well, maybe you are right, but – have you no idea at all why they should be here, talking together like that, so engrossed they might be engaged in some conspiracy?'

'I have no idea at all,' she answered, shaking her head. 'It's most odd, since if Sarah had a date with Stephen why didn't she mention it?'

'I expect there is some quite logical explanation which Sarah will tell you about when she sees you later today.' He opened the menu and began to glance over it. Juley did likewise, agreeing with Charles's tacit indication that as there was no answer to their questions they might as well stop asking them. As he stated, Sarah would no doubt enlighten Juley later in the day.

But it was to transpire that Sarah was to remain secretive concerning her lunch date with Stephen. Juley, having gone into her bedroom in answer to her call, was asked instantly to find something plain for her to wear for dinner that evening.

'I'm too tired to bother dressing up. There isn't anyone coming to dinner this evening.'

After doing as she was told Juley took up the brush in readiness to do her employer's hair.

'I came back for eleven o'clock,' she said, 'but you'd gone out.'

'Yes,' briefly and without expression.

'Did you have a nice day?'

'Not too bad.' Sarah moved to sit down on the stool which Juley had drawn out from beneath the dressing-table. 'What did you do with yourself?'

Juley began brushing Sarah's hair. She found she was no more inclined to be informative regarding her movements than was Sarah.

'I went for a walk before eleven. Charles came along and gave me a lift back.'

'And you spent the afternoon with him, of course?'

'You weren't there to ask—'

'You knew it would be all right. You must see him just whenever you want.'

'Thank you. We do enjoy being together.'

Sarah had no comment to make, much to Juley's surprise

179

as she had expected the usual comment that Charles was in love with her and she should exploit the situation and oust Mari. Juley had no intention of telling her about the tiff, but she did have the idea of phoning Stephen to find out something. She could phone on the pretext of wanting a chat. She decided against it for she suspected that any subtle questions by her would be bypassed, that Stephen would be as secretive as Sarah was being.

However, having slept on it she had second thoughts about phoning Stephen. But when she did phone it was to be told, to her utter astonishment, that he had caught a plane last evening for England.

'He's gone?' Dazedly she stared at the receiver, waiting for the manservant at the other end of the line to speak.

'It was very sudden, *senhorita*. There was a phone message waiting for him when he arrived home yesterday afternoon and he asked me to get the airport for him and he began to pack at once.'

A phone message . . .

'Thank you. 'Juley replaced the receiver on its hook and turned away, her wide brow creased in a frown. Just what was going on? Not that it was any of her business, but she was interested for all that. There was too much of the mystery about the several incidents and she would not have been human had not her curiosity been aroused. She rang Charles to see if he knew anything about it. He was as staggered as she by Stephen's hasty departure.

'It sounds like an emergency at home,' was all he could think of. 'A family matter – or crisis.'

'He has a family?'

'Of course. Parents and a sister.'

'One of them could have been taken ill.'

'Well, it isn't our business, as you remarked, Juley. All the same, there seems to be a mystery. What did Sarah say about her date with Stephen yesterday?'

'She never mentioned it.'

'She . . . ? You didn't tell her we'd seen them?'

'No. I was expecting her to say something but when she didn't I realized she was keeping it a secret from me, so naturally I didn't mention that we'd seen them together.'

'Strange and even more strange.' He became thoughtful before asking, 'Does Sarah know Stephen has left?'

'She didn't mention it at breakfast. The manservant at Mari's home who told me about Stephen's departure said the phone message had come yesterday afternoon, so that would be after he had lunched with Sarah. He went off in a great hurry.'

After a pause Charles suggested she should mention it, casually, to Sarah and see what her reaction was.

'All right, I will.' She broke off, grimacing to herself. 'We're dreadfully nosey about things which are not any concern of ours.'

'Agreed, but there have been several mysteries lately and I have a strong suspicion that they could be linked in some way.' There was a distinctly odd inflection in his tone. Juley was reminded of the several times Charles had accused her, Juley, of being mysterious. However, she was confident that Stephen's departure had nothing at all to do with her own problem, simply because there was not the remotest possibility that it could have been. Charles was speaking, asking if she were free today.

'Sarah hasn't given me the day off, but I expect her to.'

'I'll come over in about an hour – maybe an hour and a half.'

Juley had to smile. This confidence had never once let him down; Sarah must be about the best employer who ever breathed.

'I feel like telling her to keep my salary for this month.' Juley's thoughts were spoken aloud and resulted in a laugh drifting over the line.

'I'll see you later,' was all he said, though, and the line went dead.

Ten

'**D**id you know that Stephen had left, gone back to England?' It was a mere five minutes after talking to Charles that Juley was asking her employer the question. She had found her in her bedroom, seated at a small writing desk by the window, which was wide open, so that the scent of the flowers on the terrace invaded the lovely room. Sarah looked regal, sitting there at the antique desk, her hair immaculate, her dress of a superlative cut, her make-up expertly applied. Her head shot up as Juley phrased her question.

'What did you say?'

'He's gone back to England—'

'He can't have done!' Sarah's voice was unfamiliarly harsh, and raised, which was not like her at all. 'He wouldn't do a thing like that after promising—' She stopped abruptly, colouring up. 'Just what are you talking about?' she demanded after a swift recovery. 'What makes you think that Stephen has left and gone back home?'

Nerves tingling, Juley stared at her for a long moment in silence. Why had Sarah reacted in that way on hearing that Stephen – with whom she had secretly lunched yesterday – had cut short his holiday and rushed back to England? True, she had seemed to make a swift recovery, but Juley felt sure the calmness was only a veneer, for Sarah's chest was heaving, as if she were breathless . . . or affected by some strong, uncontrollable emotion. In answer to her query Juley said at last, 'I've just phoned Mari's home because I

182

wanted to have a chat with Stephen. I was told there was a phone message waiting for him when he got home yesterday afternoon and he rushed away—'

'Without telling me!' Sarah was plainly both bewildered and very angry. Her eyes met those of Juley and it was evident that the older woman was now in a quandary. Would she come out into the open, wondered Juley, and explain what was going on?

'What made you phone Stephen?' she wanted to know and Juley repeated that she felt like a chat. But her lids came down so that the long lashes hid her expression. Sarah's eyes narrowed.

'You're holding something back from me,' accused Sarah and this brought forth the soft echo of an impatient sigh.

'That,' said Juley sharply, 'makes two of us.' She widened her eyes to give Sarah the benefit of a full and direct stare. 'I might as well tell you that Charles and I saw you with Stephen yesterday. You seemed as if you'd been lunching together. When we saw you you were drinking coffee in the lounge. I know it isn't any of my business, but you've reminded me many times that you regard me as a friend rather than a mere employee. I would have thought you'd have mentioned this date with Stephen.'

Sarah was silent, busy with her own thoughts, which were far from pleasant, judging by the frown that darkened her brow.

Juley came closer to the desk and stood looking down at her. And Sarah broke the silence after a while to say in a voice which sounded hoarse and cracked, 'Yes, I was secretive about my meeting with Stephen . . .' She paused as if groping for the right words with which to express herself. 'You see, Juley, I – well, the fact of the matter is that I just had to find out more about these headaches. Charles has been troubled as well, but you must know that.' She looked up into Juley's white face. 'Surely you've had some slight suspicion of what was going on?'

'Stephen phoned you early yesterday morning, so you sent me off to make coffee and toast so that you could search my room—' Juley broke off, shaking her head. 'I still cannot piece it together,' she cried. 'You will have to begin at the beginning.'

'Very well.' There was a firmness about Sarah now, a resolution, and the first thing she said was, 'I make no excuses for my interference, Juley. I have come to love you; I know Charles must be close to loving you. We care, Juley! Don't you see, people *care* about you!' Juley merely nodded her head and sank down into a chair that happened to be close. 'The first thing was to get hold of one of these tablets and this I did by the ruse of wanting a drink from your bathroom. You see, love, I knew very well you hadn't rushed in there to be sick. I gave the tablet to Stephen and he had it analysed—'

'That swelling,' interrupted Juley but then had no need to say more for Sarah admitted there had never been a swelling; she merely wanted to have a private few words with Stephen about these headaches suffered by Juley. 'He cares too,' she added, 'perhaps more than is good for him. However, that is by the way. He had the tablet analysed but wanted another, just to be sure, and this he obtained by spilling the contents of your handbag.'

'He took a tablet from my box?'

'That should be obvious; the bag was let fall on the floor deliberately.' She paused a moment but Juley had no further interruption to make and she went on, 'He phoned me yesterday morning to tell me of his suspicions, but asked me to try to get hold of the name and address of your doctor in England. Hence my sending you off – yes, I wanted to search for some clue about your doctor. I hoped to find a letter, which I did, and I immediately rang Stephen back. He had said it was very urgent and when I gave him Dr Blount's name, address and telephone number he said he would phone right away. He did this and then phoned me to arrange to have a talk. I met him in town and we had lunch. We didn't notice you and Charles at all.'

'You were too engrossed.'

'I was begging Stephen to examine you with a view to operating. He on the other hand was trying to convince me that your case was hopeless—'

'It is hopeless. Three doctors saw me and I was given the verdict after they had consulted together.' Juley felt drained of all feeling. She thought: all this and not even a twinge in my head. It would come later, no doubt, and probably be worse than anything she had had before. Her eyes strayed to the tranquil view through the window, of hills and meadow to the right, and the calm turquiose sea to the left.

'I couldn't accept any of it!' Sarah's voice was determined, obstinate. 'To me it's a case of while there's life there's hope – it is as simple as that! Doctors! I'm only in my present perfect health because I've steered clear of them all my life and so has Agatha. We don't believe in them!'

Juley had to smile.

'Yet you are asking Stephen to operate on me?'

Sarah had the grace to blush, but maintained that surgery was different.

'We need men like Stephen, but it's these idiots who come out with absurd statements that someone is going to die. How the hell do they know?'

'Sarah, I've never heard you so angry,' began Juley. 'I do appreciate how you are feeling about me, but—'

'But nothing!' She was glowering owing to her thoughts. 'I can't understand Stephen's going off without a word of explanation. He had almost weakened, because I kept reminding him of the fame he was attaining worldwide owing to the miracle operations he'd been performing; he was succeeding where others had failed. Yours would not have been the only case he'd tackled which had been declared hopeless, no, not by any means. And now he has gone, without examining you as he promised.'

'He did promise, then?'

'Almost. As I said, he was weakening; he said he'd have another talk with Dr Blount and one with the specialist who gave his verdict, then he would decide. I know he'd have examined you – if he'd stayed here, that is!' She was furious but, judging by the sparkle in her eye, not defeated. She was thinking madly and Juley, her heart pounding now as she dwelt on all that had been said, waited, not very patiently, for Sarah to resume. 'I don't know what to think . . .' She shook her head and Juley heard her teeth grit together 'I must find out more about this sudden flight. There must have been some very urgent reason . . . Yes,' she mused, calmer now and of softer voice. 'I'm not giving up, Juley. You mean too much to me now for me to let you die without doing everything in my power to have you cured.'

'Cured . . . Oh, Sarah. I have never even thought of such a possibility. Do you suppose – but no, it seems to me that Stephen has left because he doesn't want to be involved. He's afraid that if he did operate and I died he would be blamed.'

'Stephen's not a coward. He has some other reason for leaving and I shall find out what it is.' She rose from the chair and stood looking down at the girl she had come to regard as her daughter. 'Dearest Juley, we have to try. One doesn't give up like this. It's sheer defeatism, an attitude of mind I cannot understand and certainly not accept. You must know how Charles is feeling—'

'No! Sarah, he mustn't begin to care! I don't want him to care!' Tears sparkled on her lashes and she turned away, fumbling with the catch of the patio window. 'I need air!'

'You're ill – why have I caused this situation? Juley, it isn't your head?' Fearfully she stared but Juley reassured her.

'I just want to be outside – I want to think.'

'So much is explained,' mused Sarah. 'I can now see why

186

you didn't want either Charles or me to love you.' She could see it threatened to be an emotional scene which would end in their both being in tears, so she added briskly, 'Off you go and enjoy yourself with Charles – I expect he's coming for you?'

'Yes, he is.'

'Then use the blusher and put on a pretty dress. I'll sort out why Stephen has left.'

They had strolled through the lovely grounds of the casa hand in hand; they had lunched on the patio, and all the while Juley had her mind fixed on the possibility of a cure. One moment she was telling herself not to be foolish while the next moment she found her spirits soaring as she thought of all the successful operations performed by Stephen. But then she would remember his hasty flight and would feel sure he was escaping from the insistent persuasions of Sarah. Charles had twice asked Juley where her thoughts were, why she was so preoccupied and each time she had managed a swift smile and a light, 'It's nothing. I'm just happy, that's all.'

'Something is on your mind.'

'All people have things on their minds.'

He gave up, at least outwardly, but she somehow felt sure he was thinking of her headaches and she wondered just how much, and how often, she had been discussed between Charles and Sarah.

He stopped to kiss her as they reached a shady spot well away from the house and the probability of servants' prying eyes. Would he soon be telling her he loved her? Juley sighed as she recalled the several times Sarah had maintained that he loved her – or at least was well on the way to loving her. Juley now toyed with the idea of telling him about her condition and as the happy hours passed the idea became an intention. Yes, and she would tell him about her little boy, the baby she had been forced to part with and

Charles would realize the heartache she had suffered and he would draw her to his breast and comfort her, dry her tears. She glanced around as they began to walk on again. Everywhere life was pulsing – brightly plumaged birds chirping and darting, butterflies hovering above bushes gently swaying in the breeze, insects with iridescent wings catching the sunlight. By the ornamental pool birds similar to those seen at the hacienda preened themselves, while in the pool itself fish of every exotic colour darted about among the vivid green of the aquatic vegetation.

'This place is heaven—!' Juley's exclamation was cut short by a bright flash of sunlight reflected on metal – the long sleek bonnet of Mari's car. Juley's heart sank; she did not want any intrusion into this blissful interlude. Besides, now that she had decided to reveal her secrets to Charles she felt the urge to do it at once.

'Mari's back already?' Charles's tone was sharp and impatient. 'She went to England; I expected her to stay for at least a week.'

'She's been to see her aunt again? You didn't mention that she had gone away.'

'I forgot,' casually as if it was of no importance whatsoever.

Juley asked, 'You want to talk with her? Shall I leave you?' Reluctant as she was to leave him, Juley admitted it was the thing to do.

Charles nodded and said, 'Yes, please, dear. I shan't keep you long. Go into the sitting room and I'll join you in ten minutes or so.'

'Yes . . .' Juley's thoughts were confused; she somehow knew that Charles was about to tell Mari something she would not like to hear, and while this was gratifying, mainly because she, Juley, had been terribly troubled that Charles was making a mistake by marrying Mari – that was, if he really meant to, which seemed to be the case at first – and that he was bitterly going to regret it, since all Juley could see for his future was unhappiness. Then there was the

188

thought, inspired by Sarah, that Stephen could save her life
. . . and if that were possible then Juley was sure she and
Charles would marry. So much confusion, so many thoughts
flitting about that they coalesced to form the kind of muddle
with which she was quite unable to cope, so it was with
relief that she looked forward to a few quiet moments on
her own. She and Charles were watching the smart chauffeur in blue uniform moving round the car to open the door
for Mari, who looked superb in a cream linen suit and pure
silk matching blouse. Her hair immaculate and her hands
beautifully manicured, she seemed to have stepped right
down from the platform of some exclusive fashion parade.
She strode with confidence towards them, the smile on her
face strangely triumphant and Juley felt the fine hairs on
her forearms rise inexplicably.

'Good afternoon, Mrs Allen – Charles.'

'You're back rather quickly,' began Charles when he was
curtly interrupted.

'I don't remember saying how long I would be away.'
Her eyes raked Juley's figure with an expression of malice
and contempt.

'I'll go, Charles—'

'No, Mrs Allen, do stay to hear what I have to tell Charles
about you. It will provide you with the chance of denying
it, if you hear it at first hand, won't it?' The soft purr of
the accent was like that of a cat feeling particularly
contented with life. Charles looked frowningly from one
girl to the other.

'What is this all about, Mari? It almost sounds as if you
are threatening Juley.'

'Not at all, Charles,' she denied silkily as she turned her
attention to Juley. 'I wonder, Mrs Allen, if you have told
Charles about your baby? If so, then I'm wasting my time
but, somehow, I feel you would never confess to giving
away your baby as soon as your husband died. You wanted
to have a good time, no doubt, spread your wings and look

for another husband. The encumbrance of a young child would have restricted you—'

'Mari,' broke in Charles, who had listened with growing bewilderment to what Mari had to say, 'what is all this? Juley doesn't have a child.'

'I found out by sheer chance that she had had her baby adopted. A maid of my aunt's knew the couple who took the child – the details are of no consequence,' she put in impatiently. 'So now, Charles, you must judge this woman for yourself. I know you've preferred her to me. I guessed you'd been more than friends in the past. Well, you are welcome to her. If you are willing to marry a woman who callously gave her baby away before its father was cold in his grave, then you deserve all you get.' With that she swung around and strode to her car. The chauffeur sprang to the alert, opening the door for her. Charles looked down into Juley's ashen face and had no need to ask, 'Is it true?'

She swayed as an agonizing pain shot through her head. Charles had turned his attention to the car as it swung towards the long avenue of lime trees that led to the road and to Mari's home.

'Yes,' faltered Juley, 'it is true. But there was a reason, and – and if she hadn't come I was going to tell you everything – yes, now.' She raised her eyes, trying not to think of the searing agony in her head. 'I'm telling the truth, Charles . . .' She tailed off at the harshness of his expression.

'A reason?' with a lift of his brows. 'An excuse – is that what you are telling me? What possible excuse could you have had?' His gaze was coldly accusing and after a few stammered words which she realized were totally unconvincing, she broke down and cried. 'Those two snapshots, you remember them?' Charles's tone matched the glacial expression in his dark eyes.

'Yes, of course I remember them.'

'You said they weren't yours, but they were. You had your baby adopted to get rid of the encumbrance. You didn't

want it. You let it go without a qualm, and even the snapshots were of no sentimental value to you, apparently, since
you left them there, to be thrown away.'

She could not speak for several seconds. Her heart was
crying at what he had said. So many hurting accusations
but somehow his comments about the snapshots having no
value to her were the most wounding of them all. For she
would have given every penny she owned just to have them
in her possession, so she could look, and pretend, or use
her imagination as to what her precious baby was doing.

She whispered brokenly, 'I can – can explain . . .' But
her head was throbbing unbearably and all she wanted was
to get back to the hacienda because she was afraid, terribly afraid, that this was the end.

So much for the hopes inspired by Sarah . . .

Soon, though, Charles would know all the truth and it
crucified her to think of his self-condemnation, and his
heartache, for she knew he loved her.

If only Mari had not come – or even had she come later
– then Juley's confession would have been made and
Charles would have heard her version instead of the warped
and malicious one submitted by Mari.

'Please take me home,' she begged. 'I – I want to be with
Sarah.' Dear Sarah, who knew more than Charles, yet did
not know about little James, not yet.

'Does Sarah know about this child?' His voice was a rasp,
his eyes marble-hard.

'No – please take me to her.' Her face was as white as
his shirt but he could feel no pity for her at this moment
of disillusionment and he told her curtly that he would send
out a manservant to drive her home. 'You – you won't
t-take me yourself . . . ?' He was gone; she scarcely saw his
swiftly retreating figure for the tears that blurred her vision.

When the servant came along she was by the fountain
where, having taken a tablet, she was cupping her hands to
collect water with which to wash it down.

'Are you ready, *senhorita*?' he asked respectfully. She nodded and was handed into the car. The pain had gone by the time she reached the hacienda, so she readily agreed when Agatha asked her to join her for afternoon tea. Not that Juley wanted anything to eat, but she needed a drink of tea, and she needed the company. Agatha chatted in her usual lively way even while interrupting the flow now and then by deploring the absence of her husband.

'I always go with Ramos on these business trips but I can't leave Sarah – not for three days.'

'Where is she?' Juley had expected her to join them for tea. 'Is she out?'

'She's been trying to get someone on the phone. I don't know why she doesn't give up and leave it till some other time. She's secretive, too, and I can't get out of her whom she's trying to contact. All she says is that it's a friend. I can't imagine why it's so urgent. Still, it's her affair and she'd not thank me for poking my nose in.'

Agatha had a hair appointment, so she went off at a quarter to four, and Juley went to her room with the intention of lying down, but on hearing Sarah moving about in the next room she knocked and opened the door.

'Come in, Juley.' She stared. 'Is something wrong? I thought you'd be spending the whole day with Charles.'

'Sarah . . . you don't know everything about me even yet.' Shoulders sagging, she went over to the bed and sat down. 'You see, I had a baby a short while before my husband was killed. When I knew I was going to die I had him legally adopted – Dr Blount arranged it all for me. My baby's n-name is – is James – Oh. Sarah, I'm so unhappy!'

'A – baby?' Sarah went to her, deep compassion in her eyes. 'My dear child – my poor darling. You had to part with your baby? It must have torn you to pieces.'

'It did – no one knows what it means, Sarah, to say good-bye to your baby, for ever. But he has wonderful parents who adore him. Dr Blount sent me two snapshots.'

192

'Let me see them, love—'

'I lost them!' cried Juley distraught. She explained and saw Sarah's eyes fill with tears. 'But that isn't all,' went on Juley chokingly. 'What I want to tell you is that Charles knows and believes I gave James away without a qualm. He said I did – just think of that! My heart was breaking, and he said I gave my child away without a qualm, just got rid of him so I could have a good time, without the encumbrance. Just imagine my hearing my baby referred to as an encumbrance! I hate Charles!'

'How did he come to say a thing like that?' Sarah sat down on the bed beside the girl she had befriended and put an arm about her shoulders. Juley lifted her face to catch the breeze drifting in from the open window where dainty lace curtains were billowing into the room. 'I'm amazed at Charles – but there must be some explanation; he must be under a misapprension?'

'It was Mari—'

'Mari? What has she to do with it?'

'She was visiting her aunt . . .' Juley went on to give Sarah a full explanation. 'So you can see why he was so disgusted,' she said finally. 'I'd denied the snapshots were mine and – and he concluded I did not value them.'

'It was a pity you panicked over the snapshots, but yet it is understandable. If you'd told him about your baby you'd have had to give the reason why you parted with him.' She paused and frowned. 'You know, darling, it is a great pity you didn't confide in us all—'

'You'd have pitied me and I couldn't have endured that. I wanted to live a normal life. Surely you can understand that, Sarah?'

'Of course, dear . . . and yet . . . Time,' she murmured to herself. 'There'd have been more time.'

'But I had been told there was no hope, so time had nothing to do with it.'

Sarah gave a deep and impatient sigh, a sigh that she

193

considered the conversation was drifting away from what was immediately important.

'I can scarcely believe that Mari would do a dastardly trick like that. She must be poison.' Sarah's tone was harshly condemning. 'And you say Charles believed her without even giving you a chance to explain?'

'I admit I didn't persist in my effort. You see, the pain came on and I could scarcely think about anything but getting back here, to you, Sarah – in case – in case it was the end. I wanted to be with you.' Her eyes were brimming and so were Sarah's, but both soon dried their tears. 'It could be for the best that Charles hates me because there isn't a chance that I'll be cured.'

Another impatient sigh before Sarah almost snapped, 'Charles doesn't hate you; he loves you. As for no cure – Juley, I don't want you to accept what those quacks told you—'

'Sarah, they are specialists!'

'It's a defeatist attitude of mind,' continued Sarah as if no interruption had occurred. 'The reason I'm up here is because I'm expecting a call from Stephen. The lines have been hell this morning, with that stupid foreign voice coming on all the time, babbling in a tongue I cannot understand, telling me the lines are all busy!'

In spite of herself Juley had to smile.

'You say you can't understand, yet you say she told you the lines were busy?'

'What else could she be saying?'

'You say you're expecting a call from Stephen? You've contacted him, then?' Juley's heartbeats were increasing; it was amazing what even a glimmer of hope could do to one's nervous system.

'I did manage to get through to his hospital; someone there promised to get in touch with him and tell him to call me back. So now I'm waiting.' She pursed her lips. 'I cannot understand why he hasn't phoned me to explain why he went off so quickly. He left me in the lurch, so to speak.'

'Agatha is very curious.'

'Seething with curiosity would be a more appropriate description of how she feels.'

'She's at the hairdresser's now.'

'Good. She'll not be back for— That must be Stephen!' She flew to the phone and grabbed the receiver. 'Don't go, Juley – unless you want to lie down, of course.'

'In a moment.' She wanted to know what Stephen had to say.

'Yes, but . . . you've to find a hundred thousand pounds! But, Stephen, how did your sister manage to steal a sum like that?' A pause; Juley's eyes had widened interrogatingly but Sarah was listening intently and the whispered question on Juley's tongue was never uttered. 'I understand. No wonder your mother wanted you home. Won't this man your sister works for wait?' She turned to Juley and was about to speak but Stephen was answering her. Sarah's eyes flickered. 'You've been able to talk to Dr Blount with all this on your mind. Wonderful! I do appreciate it, Stephen, and now that you've explained I understand why you had to leave so suddenly – but I admit I was mad at the time.' Another pause. Juley read nothing from her expression at first but then her eyes came alive. 'I see. Shall you come back here or do you want me to bring Juley over there?'

Juley's heart leapt, and it seemed that every nerve in her body jerked at the same time. Her entire being seemed to be in the throes of continued movement, all beneath the skin. Her eyes were wide, her mouth mobile but dry – oh, so very dry! Deep emotion filled her. Hope had soared . . . but was there time? Sarah was so right. She should have told of her condition earlier than this . . . when there was still some time left. Now there was very little, according to what the doctor had predicted. 'All right,' heard Juley after what seemed an eternity of waiting. 'I'll bring her over – on the next plane. We'll be over by tomorrow even if I have to charter one. Pray for her, Stephen, as I shall.' Her eyes met Juley's as she replaced the receiver. 'No crying,' she admonished.

'N-no . . .' A silence fell, the vibrating hush that ends in hope. 'Thank you, Sarah.'

Sarah shook her head, wise enough to say, 'I want you to be optimistic, love, but do prepare yourself for Stephen to be in agreement with those others.'

Juley nodded her head but before she could speak Sarah was saying inconsistently, 'Forget that! Stephen will *not* agree with the others. He'll operate, and save your life!'

'Oh, Sarah, I'm too full for words!'

'So you're going to let me take you to England?'

Juley actually heard herself laugh.

'How can you ask? Sarah, if this gives me life, I have only you to thank.'

'No, dear, you will have Stephen to thank first, and your own courage and will to live next. After that, no matter.' She kissed Juley on the cheek and then in a determined tone, 'I'm going to talk to that idiot, Charles. He should know you had some very good reason for parting with your child.' But when she rang there was no reply.

'I've an idea that when he has time to think he'll reach that conclusion, mainly because I did tell him I was intending to make some kind of confession.'

It was to transpire that Juley's conclusion was correct but when Charles, contrite and ready to listen, arrived at the hacienda he was to be informed by Agatha that her sister had gone on a jaunt to London and taken Juley with her.

'One never does know what Sarah will do next,' she complained. 'I was having a shampoo and it seems she made up her mind there and then to take a trip to England and she managed to get two seats on a plane leaving in less than three hours, so off she went after having Arminda scurrying and hurrying to pack the suitcases. Ordered the car and away! Took only a small case each – no clothes hardly. I'm damned if I can understand such impulsiveness!'

'She left no message?'

'Just a line to say they were going to England. She told Arminda to tell me she'd phone when she got to the hotel. What hotel you ask? I don't even know the name or even if it is in London – I just assume it is, but it could be anywhere, knowing that sister of mine! Poor Juley, being hustled around like this. First coming here and now off – somewhere. What next? Can you tell me that?

'Can I use your phone,' asked Charles, ignoring her questions.

'Of course. Er – an important call?'

'To the airport. An enquiry about the next plane to London.'

Eleven

After the examination was over and the X-ray plates had been perused by Stephen, Sarah suggested that she and Juley go first to a café for lunch and then to Harrods for a quick look around before going back to the hospital to wait for Stephen's verdict. For her part, Juley could have gone straight back after lunch and sat there, waiting, but Sarah was having none of that. Brisk and more businesslike than Juley had ever seen her, she took full command, so that for the first time in her life Juley felt she had a mother to be concerned about her. It was a wonderful feeling and it seemed that with every minute that passed she was being drawn closer to the woman whose own daughter had proved to be such a disappointment to her.

The lunch was appetizing enough, but, on tenderhooks as she was, Juley could not enjoy it. However, she did enjoy Harrods, never having been into that legendary store before. Acres and acres of treasures both modern and antique; lovely things to buy – if one had that kind of money . . . and if one had a reasonable expectation of life. As it was, Juley contented herself with a toilet bag in flowered silk, her having come away without hers in the haste to get to the airport. In her thoughts there was always Charles, whom she knew would be hers if life was given back to her. That he would already be on his way to England never for one moment occurred to her.

Nor had she any idea of the strength of Mari's hatred for her . . .

*　*　*

Stephen was willing to operate!

'I can't believe it! I just cannot take it in!'

He looked troubled at her optimism. He felt he had to warn Juley of the risk, telling her that it would be touch and go – at best a fifty-fifty chance of success.

'During the op your life will hang on a thread, Juley,' he warned her seriously. 'Right through the entire time it takes. But that is not all, because even when it is over there will be no immediate cause for rejoicing.'

'I know all this, and I haven't a thing to lose.' She and Sarah had invited him to dine at their hotel in the heart of Knightsbridge, and they had just sat down at the table. 'It's wonderful of you, Stephen, because I know you have other, serious problems on your mind.'

'I've told Juley about your sister,' interposed Sarah, 'because, like me, she could not understand your hasty departure without a word to either of us. I know you won't mind. It's safe with Juley, you can be sure of that.'

'Lindy,' sighed Stephen, but his face brightened suddenly. 'It isn't as bad now as it was.' He looked at Sarah. 'As I told you, my sister got herself mixed up with a young man whose gambling was contagious and Lindy, handling all the firm's accounts, was tempted after getting herself deeply into debt. Like so many gamblers she thought she could win it all back if she continued. The result was that she was unable to put the money back because she lost it. Her employer gave her a month to find the money; if she failed she would be prosecuted.'

'And this would have ruined your father, you said?'

'That's right. He's probably the most respected and popular doctor in the district. Mother would of course have suffered, too, had Lindy been brought to court because the case would have made headlines in a small community in which they live. Local rags have no more consideration for people's feelings than have the tabloid scandal sheets. All journalists are out for sensationalism and people have been

driven to suicide by their vicious – and often quite untrue
– reports.' He became thoughtful for a space and then went
on, 'Naturally Dad sent for me and I left Mexico at once.
However, the situation is not now so bad; Mari has offered
to lend us the money so we can repay Lindy's boss. It's
going to take us all some time to repay Mari but we're more
than grateful for her offer.'

'Mari . . .' Juley felt that in some ways at least, she had
misjudged the girl. 'What a relief it must be to you all,
Stephen.'

'It is.' He smiled at her. 'One problem solved, and now,
let us hope that the coming operation will be a success.'

'I shall pray for Juley.' Sarah spoke softly and with tenderness in her eyes. 'If anyone deserves the right to live, she
does.'

Stephen looked at her.

'Sarah told me about your baby. Is he really legally
adopted?'

'Yes.' Juley's lip quivered. 'Even if I do live I think my
baby is lost to me for ever.' Neither could find anything to
say to that and soon Juley was bitterly regretting her action
in having James adopted quite so soon. 'I should have
waited—' she began, but Stephen interrupted her.

'No, Juley, you did the right thing with circumstances
being what they were at that time. You made sure he was
all right, his future assured with parents who will love him,
and I'm very sure that, at the time, you did what was the
very best for your child. So have no regrets, dear. James
will be all right.'

She felt sure he had discussed it all with Dr Blount, who
would have given a picture of the parents James now had.

'If I live, though, I shall always be thinking of him, and
wondering how he is faring, if he is clever at school—' She
broke off, too full to say anything more.

'You'll not be thinking about him all the time, Juley,'
Sarah assured her, trying to brighten up this little dinner

party. 'You'll have more children to think about and care for.'

Charles . . . Juley could not help but feel more cheerful knowing that, should the operation be successful, she would become his wife. True, he had not given her any real proof, but her woman's instinct told her all she wanted to know. Sarah was asking Stephen if Mari knew of the coming operation. It was a question that came out naturally, the follow-on to Sarah's thoughts about the girl's generosity, which she considered out of character.

'Or perhaps you haven't mentioned Juley's illness to her?' added Sarah, and Stephen said his father had mentioned it when he phoned to thank her for the loan of the money. He didn't think I'd mind if he spoke of my next "job", as it were.'

'She'd be surprised – that I was ill, I mean?'

'Father said she went very quiet, so quiet that he thought the line had failed. Then he said she sounded very strange when she asked him to get me to phone her as soon as possible.'

'Sounds rather odd.' Sarah's forehead creased in a frown. 'You do know, Stephen, that if the operation is successful, Charles and Juley will marry?'

He was silent for a while before submitting in a voice of resignation, 'I did suspect it, yes – in fact, I think I was sure.'

'Charles hasn't actually asked me to marry him,' Juley inserted. 'We might all be taking too much for granted.'

'I don't think so,' from Stephen with a wry smile. 'From what Sarah has told me there seems little doubt of Charles's being in love with you.'

'What did Mari say when you phoned her? You don't mind my asking, do you, Stephen?'

'I haven't phoned yet. The lines were busy, so as I hadn't much time to get ready for this date with you two, I decided to leave it till tomorrow. It will have to be tomorrow now owing to the time difference as she wouldn't be happy if I got her out of bed in the middle of the night.'

No more was said and the rest of the evening was spent eating the delicious meal and then chatting afterwards in the hotel lounge as they sipped coffee and cognac. Yet for Juley the atmosphere was tense and, glancing at Stephen from time to time, she had a strong suspicion that the coming operation was causing him as much nervous tension as it was causing her. After all, he was going against the verdicts of three specialists. He had examined her old X-rays and admitted that there had not been anything that could give hope. However, he believed there was a slight chance and, as Juley had told him, she had nothing to lose – well, perhaps a few weeks, but the risk was worth it, a million times! she had told Sarah.

The following morning they were out to get Juley things she would require for her stay in hospital. It was a strange kind of shopping and certainly not one either of them enjoyed. On their return to the hotel they were given two messages by the receptionist at the desk. Dr Blount and his wife had sent a letter wishing her luck, but it was the other message that sent Juley's spirits soaring.

'Charles – he's here! He's come to me! But how did he know where we were staying? He can't know why I'm here though – I mean, to have an operation,' she added with a puzzled frown. 'I can't understand . . .' She tailed off as she noticed Sarah's expression. 'You . . . But—'

'Let's sit over there and get ourselves a drink before lunch. A dry sherry for you?' Without waiting for an answer, Sarah was away to find a table, with Juley close behind. 'There, this is cosy.' She beckened for a waiter and ordered their drinks. 'And now . . . I phoned Agatha in the early hours, had to get up in the middle of the night owing to the time difference, and the urgency. Agatha wouldn't have been pleased had it been the other way round; you know what she is—'

'You were going to tell me about Charles,' broke in Juley with a hint of impatience. 'Please – what did you do?'

'I was about to explain, dear. I phoned Agatha to explain the reason why we came away, as I hadn't put anything about it in the note – there wasn't time anyway. She told me Charles had called to see you and when she told him you were on your way to England he used her phone to get himself a seat on the first plane out, which, like ours, was within a few hours. His plane arrived at Heathrow about two hours ago and I made sure I had a car there to meet him.'

'Sarah, you darling! You think of everything.' She stopped. 'But why didn't you tell me before now? And how did Charles find your driver?'

'He held up a card with Charles's name on it. I had told the driver we were staying at the Hyde Park Hotel and I managed to book him a room, and so Charles is now here, settled in, I hope, and hopping about his room, waiting impatiently for you to call him. I didn't tell you he was coming as I wanted it to be a surprise. Also, I wasn't sure he would be here. Agatha did say he had booked the seat but I felt it was better for me to wait until I was certain he had arrived before letting you become excited. It would have been too much of a disappointment had something occurred to delay his arrival.' She smiled affectionately at her. 'I left Charles a note at reception. He knows everything – why we are here, and I did add a bit about the reason why you parted with little James – but you have plenty of time to do your own explaining this evening. He must have gone to the hacienda as soon as he'd had a little think about the baby; he would know you would never part with him unless there was a very good reason. I guess you will find him contrite and apologetic and begging for forgiveness—'

'No, I don't want him to feel awful, Sarah.'

'I reckon he'll now be in as bad a state of nerves as I – knowing what you are to go through. He'll probably be able to hide his feelings, though. As for me—' Her voice broke unexpectedly and Juley stared at her, bewildered. 'For myself, Juley, I'm beginning to wonder if I'll break under the strain.'

Emotion flooding over her, Juley quivered, 'Do I mean so much to you, Sarah?'

'You should know by now, child, just how much you mean to me. A pause, reflective and faintly sad. 'I'd rather lose my own daughter than lose you.'

'Sarah!'

'So don't you forget it, my girl! There are two of us who will be praying very hard for your life – and others as well. So keep that courage flowing and don't let us down. The *will* to live is the most important thing.'

'Next to Stephen's skill.'

'All right. I concede. Next to Stephen's skill. Yet you just remember that the two complement each other.'

'I'll remember.'

'Good, and enough of this. Off you go and phone Charles in his room. I'll order another place at our table and we'll all have lunch together. I'm so glad he arrived on time. Oh, and don't be too long – I mean,' she said teasingly, 'don't you two keep me waiting a couple of hours or so for my lunch!'

Juley laughed and saw Sarah flick a hand to fetch the waiter.

'We'll be down before you've finished the other drink you're ordering,' she promised.

'I'll not bet on it. Off you go!'

Juley knew she would never forget that moment of reunion. She had phoned Charles, but he did not suggest he come down to meet her; she must come up to him instead. He was waiting with his room door wide open, and his arms open too.

'Juley, my own, my beloved girl.' He held her close as he drew her into the room, his lips touching her hair, his

breathing erratic. 'Dearest Juley, forgive me. Why didn't
you explain?'

'Someone might see us. We ought to close the door.' This
mundane interruption was just what was required to prevent
a scene that could have been so emotional, so profound,
that Juley would have been in tears, which was the very
last thing she wanted. Charles grimaced and closed the door,
then he opened his arms again and, gladly, eagerly, she
melted into them, rapture enveloping her as he kissed her
tenderly on the lips.

'Charles, dear Charles, you came to me, when I needed
you so much.' His ardour flared but he remembered in time
to be gentle, so very gentle. 'You were so quick!'

'As soon as Agatha said you and Sarah had left I
suspected something dramatic was afoot and I wanted to
know what it was. Added to this was my contrition over
the way I'd accepted Mari's accusation at face value –
God knows why for I'd known you in the past and you
weren't the girl to give your baby away merely to be free
of him. Your willingness to have an affair with me seemed
at first to need no further explanation than that you needed
a bedmate, being widowed so young. But very soon I was
pondering, thinking, frustrated at what was becoming
more and more a mystery. You were beginning to act as
if you were falling in love with me, yet suddenly you
wanted to end our affair. None of it made any sense, but
I know now that you didn't want me to fall in love with
you.' He looked tenderly into her shining eyes. 'I never
was out of love with you, my darling . . . and I am thinking that you never were out of love with me, despite your
marriage.'

'It seemed a happy enough marriage—'

'Only because you didn't expect much; you were content
with a dull routine, caring for your husband and his invalid
mother. That was not the life for you, dearest, and I intend
to make up to you for those wasted years. Get well, sweet,

and then our lives will really begin . . . yours and mine, together.'

'Yes . . . the operation . . . we can only hope, darling Charles, and pray. Stephen has a reputation for working miracles. Please make no mistake, Charles, it will need a miracle to make me well again. I've had the opinions of the cleverest brain surgeons in England, this in addition to that of the first man whose verdict was borne out by the other two. It was awful, but I did make myself face reality. I became resigned. Dr Blount wanted me to take a long holiday but I knew I must have a job and this one with Sarah was perfect for me for my last few mo—' She was stopped by a gentle hand over her mouth; Charles then drew his hand away and kissed her, over and over again, but always keeping his ardour well in check.

'You are no longer resigned, darling.' A statement. He spoke as if it were a question.

'No, dearest Charles. How can I be resigned when I have so much to live for?' Her heart throbbed with the consciousness of her love for him.

'That's my girl.' He gave her a gentle hug and she lifted her eager lips to touch his cheek.

'I'm trying to make myself believe in miracles.'

'Then just you keep on trying, my darling.' He drew her slender body close again and kept his strong arms around her. She nestled her face into his jacket. She wanted him, yearned for close and naked physical contact, but there was a restraint about him even in his kisses and when presently he held her away from him and gazed with tender emotion into her eyes, he said softly, 'I'm not taking any chances with you, my darling. I won't even hold you as I would like.' He paused a moment and she could hear the rapid beating of his heart. 'The operation – Sarah said in her note that it would take place tomorrow afternoon?'

She nodded her head. She felt she would rather not think

about it, not just now when she was with her beloved Charles, close to him, alone with him. Nevertheless she answered, 'That's right. Stephen is at the hospital getting everything prepared. Also, he's sent to some place abroad for a special drug which will be needed if the operation is successful. The drug is being flown in on what Stephen called a "priority one flight". It will help me to pull through after the strain of the operation.'

He was nodding slowly, his eyes vacant, a nerve pulsing at the side of his jaw.

'I'll be close my dearest, all the time it is going on.'

'It's wonderful to have you here. Oh, Charles, if I'd only known there might be a chance for me I'd have told Sarah and Stephen everything. Yes, Sarah especially for she is desperate for me to live.'

'You got yourself a mother when you went to her.' He grimaced. 'I guess she's going to be my mother-in-law before very long.'

'She'd love to be called that.'

'I wish you had confided in me, Juley, right in the beginning. I'd have been on to Stephen at once. When he came to Mari's, did you not think of asking his opinion?'

'I'd become so resigned that although I knew he was a neurosurgeon I never dreamed of consulting him or asking his help. I remember envying those whom he had cured but even then it never occurred to me that I myself might have a chance.'

'No one in England was willing to operate?'

'They said my case was hopeless.'

'Well, it isn't and never was. Just you remember that. And now, we must go down to Sarah,' he decided and bent to kiss her.

'She told me not to be long. I think she'll have gone to her room to wait.'

'She probably feared we'd be an hour or so. You can ring her room.'

'Sarah is wonderful,' she mused. 'What would I have done without her? She's made such a difference in my life.'

'You wouldn't have gone to Mexico . . .' Fate, he was thinking. Fate had parted them eight years ago and now fate had brought them together. Surely it would not be so cruel as to part them again . . . for ever.

'I don't believe it!' Sarah's face wore a look of horrified disbelief. 'No human being would be so callous!'

As Sarah's room phone was engaged when she rang at Charles's request, Juley had told him to go down to the lounge while she went along to Sarah's room, which was only half a dozen doors from the one occupied by Charles. When Juley entered her room Sarah's hand holding the receiver was shaking visibly.

'What is is?' whispered Juley close to her ear. 'You look – devastated.'

'Well, what is your decision, man! Are you going to let that woman blackmail you into abandoning what is your duty?' Never had Juley thought to see her employer in such a fury. Her face was purple, her teeth clenched together. 'Yes, yes, I know what the money means to your family, and I'd find it myself if I could in so short a time. We are talking of a life, man – a life!'

'Sarah . . .' Juley, white-faced and urgent, was pushed away before she could say more.

'Only the thread of a chance? So, you are willing to let that thread break without doing anything to save it? Stephen, I'm staggered that you would— Oh, go to hell – rot in hell!' Sarah slammed down the receiver, her whole body aflame and quivering with rage. 'What have I done?' To Juley's further bewilderment she put her face in her hands and wept.

'Sarah, dear, please tell me—' Juley, about to put an arm around her, turned at the gentle tap on the door. She was shivering, feeling icy cold, for she had understood enough to freeze the very blood in her veins. 'Come in,' she invited without thinking. Then she began to say, 'Sarah, Stephen won't operate, will—' But Charles was in the room and Juley said, 'Charles, something awful has happened. I don't think Stephen is going to operate, after all.'

'What! How do you know?'

'Stephen's dithering,' snapped Sarah between sobs. Juley's face drained of colour now that she had heard it come from Sarah's lips. Until then she had not been sure, had hoped her fears were imagined.

'Stephen won't help me . . . ?'

'What the devil's going on?' demanded Charles, glancing from Sarah's tear-stained face to Juley's ashen one. 'Tell me. Sarah!'

'Mari's threatened to withdraw her promise of the money if her cousin operates. It's diabolical – criminal!'

'Money,' repeated Charles impatiently. 'What money?'

'Charles doesn't know about Stephen's sister,' proffered Juley. She felt faint, drained with anguished disappointment, unable to believe that Mari would carry her hatred to these lengths, that she would rob Juley of her chance to live.

'Tell him. Juley; I can't!' Sarah left them to go to the bathroom to bathe her eyes, leaving Juley with the task of giving Charles an explanation.

'Stephen will have to give in to Mari's ultimatum because if that money isn't forthcoming his family will be ruined.'

'Do you mean to tell me that Stephen isn't going to operate because of money – *money*!' He shook his head. 'I don't believe it!'

'It's a hundred thousand pounds, Charles, and it has to be paid at once or Stephen's sister will be prosecuted and the family disgraced—' She stopped as, his face a mask of fury, Charles strode purposefully towards the phone. He was soon on to the hospital and Stephen was there.

'Hello, Charles. I'm afaid I'm busy – can't spare any time—'

'You'll spare time all right,' came the interruption through gritted teeth. 'What's this about a change of mind over Juley's operation?'

A silence followed. Juley was straining her ears and presently she heard, 'I'm operating, Charles.'

'You are? But, Sarah said—'

'Tell her I'm sorry for any upset I may have caused. I was so devastated by Mari's news when I phoned her that I've not been able to think clearly since. I was shattered. As you've obviously been put in the picture you will know just what I'm doing to my family by defying my cousin. I did a lot of mind searching but came at last to a decision. I'm a doctor; this I am putting before all else. The operation will take place as scheduled.' The next moment Charles was staring into a silent receiver.

'Charles, we can't let Stephen's family be ruined . . .' She tailed off. How stupid they were, she and Sarah. A smile broke even before Charles said, 'They're not going to be ruined, my love.' His expression underwent a dramatic change as he looked down into her big eyes and after taking hold of her icy cold hands he enclosed them within his own, passing on their warmth. 'Have you no imagination, my sweet?' Then dramatically he was in a black rage again. 'Mari – she must be Satan's daughter to have thought up anything like that! But did she believe she could succeed? Didn't it occur to her that I would pay the money?'

Juley wondered why she had not guessed at once that he would pay, and she was surprised, too, that this had escaped Sarah. Perhaps it was just shock, the devastating information that Stephen was not sure he would operate. Sarah had gone into a wild fury without stopping for a moment to think, to remember Charles, who was in love with Juley.

Sarah came from the bathroom, eyes swollen but dry.

'Charles is paying that money to Stephen,' Juley told her wryly. 'We should have known he would.' That was perhaps not the right thing to say but already Juley felt as if she

210

were Charles's wife. 'Charles has just spoken to Stephen on the phone.'

'Damn me!' swore Sarah, forcing a weak and shaky laugh, 'of course we should have known that Charles would pay.' She looked at him. 'You've told Stephen?'

Charles shook his head, a thoughtful expression on his dark and handsome face.

'Not yet. He has made up his mind to operate.'

'Without the assurance of the money?' Sarah looked surprised. 'But only ten minutes ago he as good as said he wouldn't do it.'

'I'd rather say he was in doubt, being so troubled about his family, but that doubt had gone by the time I phoned him.'

'I see. So he's decided to put his duty as a doctor first.'

Charles nodded his head, saying he would soon let Stephen have the money.

'It will ease his mind. I want no anxiety on that man's mind when he is doing the operation.' He paused to smile at Juley. 'I'm glad, though, that he had come to a decision *before* he knew he was to get the money. I like Stephen and have always regarded him as a man of honour and I really couldn't see him putting anything before duty.'

Consciousness came slowly, like the reluctant drifting of a mist over a hill when a breeze comes up. And Juley's first recollection was of the pain, the searing agony that had caused her to cry out only minutes after being admitted to hospital. She had optimistically hoped that no more pain would come before the anaesthetic was administered. Then this pain, and she was asking herself fearfully if this was the end. Charles was beside her stretcher when she cried out in agony; he had walked along as far as they would allow him. And, with Sarah, he had been at the hospital all afternoon and well into the night. Stephen's orders then had been that they should go back to the hotel and get some

211

rest, then they could come back. No, he could not give them any hope at all. The operation had taken place and he was not saying anything more at present.

'It's hell, Stephen!' protested Sarah, distraught at the uncertainty. 'You must have some idea of her chances? Surely you can tell us something.'

'I have. The operation has taken place.' He too was tired and Charles, with a hand beneath Sarah's elbow, urged her along the white-walled corridor and out to the car he had hired.

'He won't commit himself!' She was very close to tears and Charles spoke to her soothingly.

'Juley's been through a long-drawn-out operation which must affect her resistance. Stephen told me this. So that is the reason he won't commit himself.'

'He doesn't want to give us false hope.'

'Juley will pull through,' he returned and his confidence was catching.

'Yes, of course she will. She can't leave us both breaking our hearts.'

She looked at him as they came from the car into the lighted lobby of the hotel. She had never seen anyone so drawn and grey. His features seemed to have thinned in the last few hours, his eyes sunken deeply into their sockets. Undoubtedly the strain was telling on him as much as it was on her.

'There's nothing we can do but wait, as Stephen says.' Charles's voice was tired and low. Sarah knew that had he not been the strong man he was he would have broken down altogether and given way to tears.

They had a few hours' rest, then returned to the hospital. Yes, they could stay, said Stephen, but went on to add, 'You'll not be seeing her today, though, so don't either of you try to make me change my mind.' He was the stern physician in full charge, commander of a situation and his word was law. 'I'm going off duty for a few hours.' His

212

mouth curved in the ghost of a smile as his eyes met those of Charles. 'I hope I've saved her for you.'

There was nothing in his voice to betray what his feelings for Juley were, but Sarah's perceptive eyes read in his that which made her whisper to herself, 'I hope you find someone who will deserve you, Stephen . . . and somehow I feel sure you will.'

Stephen was there when Juley opened her eyes. There was this mist preventing any clarity of focus but gradually it thinned and her lips moved, slowly and with difficulty.

'You saved me . . . I'm alive.'

'How do you feel?' Stephen took her wrist between his fingers.

'In my body? It feels numb.'

He smiled faintly.

'You've lost all your hair, I'm afraid.'

Her eyes lit, just as if losing her hair was about the best thing that could happen to her.

'But not my life. Thank you.' she said simply.

'It was a job of work.' His voice was almost brusque. 'Which no other surgeon was willing to take on. Maybe it was the challenge. It often is with me, when I'm faced with what appear to be hopeless cases.' His smile deepened as he veered the subject a little. 'Do you remember coming round the first time? This is the second, you know.'

'I do remember, yes. It was misty just like this time. I must have drifted away again; I don't remember anything after the mist.' She stopped rather abruptly a question in her eyes.

'No, it'll not happen a third time, Juley.'

After a small pause she asked about Charles and Sarah.

'Are they here? Can I see them?'

'Not today, dear,' he replied gently. 'Tomorrow if you are up to it, but it will be for a few minutes only. I can't take any risks, Juley.'

She understood. The awareness of life having been restored to her was all that occupied her mind for a long while after Stephen had left her. She was aware of nurses, of course. of being given a drink, of having a warm flannel on her face and hands. But the one vital and profound sensation was that of salvation and it was like a miracle. For months she had been resigned, with growing fear and despair as the months dwindled into weeks and soon it would have been weeks into days she would not have dared to count.

Now she was alive with a future before her! This because of the faith in himself of one man. Stephen had saved her for Charles.

Stephen allowed two visitors, but one at a time came into the light and airy private ward where Juley lay, her head heavily bandaged. Charles asked Sarah to go in first and with a smile of understanding she nodded her head.

'He only let me stay for ten minutes,' she complained on returning to Charles. 'Maybe he had sympathy for your impatience – yes, she's fine, Charles, and eager to see you.'

Yet Juley had no words to utter when, after coming to the bed, Charles stood looking down at her, his glance moving from the bandages to her eyes, eyes brighter than he would ever see them, and on her lips a smile that was to charm him for the rest of his life.

'Juley,' he managed at last in a rush of gratitude. 'My own dear love—' But his voice broke then and she watched with a sort of fascinated disbelief the convulsive trembling of his lips.

'Everything's going to be all right,' she assured him tremulously. 'Stephen is confident that I'm out of danger.' Her face broke into that alluring smile again but it brought no response and she knew he was still deeply affected by emotion and gratitude. 'We can make those plans you mentioned, remember?' She was trying to bring him back to his normal cool and confident self, the man with an especial kind of charm that even his arrogance seemed to enhance.

'I remember. We'll soon be looking over the casa together and you'll be planning changes—' He stopped at her lovely smile. 'I love you so very much,' he said simply and for a few wonderful moments of silence they just held hands and looked into each other's eyes, conscious of the miracle operation which had given them a happy future together.

'I have an idea Stephen will be shooing me off in a moment,' prophesied Charles with a wry smile. 'So I'll . . .' He was about to kiss her when Stephen walked in and Charles straightened up.

'Your time's run out.' Stephen stopped, looked at them both and then, 'You can have another five minutes,' he conceded and went out. He returned when the five minutes had elapsed and they walked to the door together, both turning to give Juley a small salute and a smile before the door was closed and she was left alone. Once outside, Charles, again affected by emotion, forgot all he had planned to say to Stephen and instead murmured thickly, 'Thank you, Stephen. We shall both remember, all our lives, the gratitude we feel towards you.'

Stephen was already making an impatient gesture with his hand.

'It was a challenge, as I told Juley. I feel good in that I've done what others considered impossible. I don't want gratitude, Charles,' he went on seriously, 'just the promise that you'll take good care of her, always.'

'That,' returned Charles, 'is my intention.'

'And now it's my turn to thank you for the money. We're out of a horrible mess thanks to you – oh, yes, I understand it was the natural thing to do, but I and my parents thank you.' He paused then, before mentioning the girl whose conduct had shocked everyone. 'Let us hope this has taught my cousin that she can't go through life pushing people around. You had a narrow escape, Charles.'

215

There was a moment's hesitation, and then: 'Juley and I met eight years ago and would have married but for my father – no, he didn't dictate to me, no one could. But unfortunately Juley believed she was doing what was best for me. She refused to marry me after my father had told her he would cut me off if I did marry her. I am afraid I was brutal with her in my efforts to make her see that what she was doing was wrong. We parted, though, and fate sent her over to Mexico . . .' He tailed off, smiling at Stephen's expression.

'So it was meant to be, that you would marry.' He sighed then smiled faintly. 'I thought I had a chance at one time but I see now it must always have been you.'

Charles said nothing and the two went their separate ways, Charles to join Sarah where she was waiting in a small private room.

It seemed an eternity to them both before the day dawned when they were to bring Juley from the hospital. A week later they flew back to Mexico with Juley looking so brim-ful of health that anyone not previously having known her would never have believed that, so recently, her life had hung on a thread. She and Charles were to be married at the hacienda, married in its own private chapel, in fact, but Stephen said they would have to wait for about six months.

'Your hair won't be grown, I'm afraid,' he added with a wry grimace, 'but certainly you will by then have some hair.' He looked at the attractive turban-like cover which was in effect a pure silk scarf, one of several bought for her by Sarah. 'Of course, if you don't want to wear a wig for your wedding,' Stephen was saying in some amusement as his eyes flickered to Charles, 'you could wait for a year. Your hair should be quite lovely by then.'

'We'll settle for the wig,' was Charles's prompt rejoin-der but Sarah considered it time she intervened to remind the two men that Juley did happen to have some say in the matter.

'After all,' she added a little tartly, 'it is her lovely day.'

Juley looked at Charles, aware that, like her, he was remembering the years already lost to them and she was not long in saying, 'I agree with Charles. We'll settle for the wig.'

It was not the big, important wedding that would have taken place had Charles married Mari, but both Juley and Charles had agreed not to have any unnecessary fuss. In any case Stephen, though back in England. still kept a watchful eye on Juley and had made two visits to Mexico, staying at the hacienda. since the operation, and he had never been in favour of a big wedding for his patient. Juley was happy to have Dr Blount and his wife, Letty, as guests, and more than delighted that Sadie and her husband, Vic, would travel from Australia to attend their wedding. Stephen was of course to be best man, Sadie matron of honour, while Sarah seemed quite naturally to take on the role of substitute mother, while Ramos, delighted at having a wedding at the hacienda, gladly agreed to give Juley away.

Maisie was at the hacienda and it was she, along with Sadie, who helped to dress Juley in a beautiful creation of cream organza.

'You look beautiful!' exclaimed Maisie and Sarah said with a wry grimace that this was the first time she had seen Maisie animated about anything.

The day dawned warm and sunny, with the wisp of a breeze to stir the palm fronds and the flowers in the hacienda gardens, just enough to scatter pervasive perfumes which Juley knew she would remember all her life. Perfume, like music, was always nostalgic.

At last, dusk was falling and the guests beginning to leave. Stephen, Dr Blount and Letty, Sadie and Vic, were of course staying on at the hacienda for the night, as guests of Agatha and Ramos. Chatting went on and on and it seemed an age before Charles and his radiant bride were driving away, car rattling and streaming with bunting, towards the casa, since a proper honeymoon was postponed for the time being, this on the advice of Stephen, who did not want his patient to travel again yet awhile. It was as the car turned into the casa grounds that Charles turned to his wife and told her he had had words with Dr Blount about getting James back.

'You did mention that you would like to have him,' he added finally and Juley's heart leapt. But a moment later Charles was saying that Dr Blount did not think the couple would want to part with the little boy, nor did the doctor feel it would be a good thing to move him now even were his parents agreeable.

'He *was* legally adopted,' she murmured, aware of very mixed feelings, for on the one hand she knew her little boy was loved, and he had security. On the other hand, what a joy it would be to have him back, in her own care. 'I'm sure they wouldn't part with him now.'

'No.' Charles's hand left the wheel and she felt its warmth on her knee. 'Much as we would like to have James, darling, I do feel we should make no attempt to remove him – and frankly, I agree with you and the doctor that his parents would never part with him now.' He brought the car to a halt before the brightly illuminated façade of the casa. He turned to her and kissed her gently on the lips. 'You and I shall have children, darling. I know part of you will always cherish James, and that is how it should be, but you'll have ours to love, too. And remember always that James is happy—'

'But lonely. You once said an only child was a lonely child.'

'Because I had a father who had no interest in me at all. I might not have been there for all the notice he took of me when I was a child. But Dr Blount says James's father dotes on him, talks of the time when he'll be able to take him running and to football matches, teach him to swim and play cricket.' He paused then and for some reason Juley looked at him sharply. 'Another thing the doctor told me was that James's mother thinks she is pregnant.'

'But she couldn't have children! That's why they adopted James.'

'Surely you've heard how, quite often, a woman becomes pregnant after adopting a baby? It's a strange phenomenon – as if, once the couple have a child to love and care for, they become more relaxed, losing that "desperation" as Dr Blount calls it.'

'It will be wonderful if James has brothers and sisters!'

Charles smiled; he had been troubled lest she would have anxieties about James having his nose pushed out if other children, of their own, came to the couple. But she had no such worries. Such was her confidence in the couple who had adopted her child.

They alighted from the car and Charles carried his bride into the casa amid smiles from the servants who were lined up in the hall, despite the lateness of the hour. Wishes for their happiness came in English, and in Spanish as well.

Once in their bedroom Juley stared at her head after taking off the wig. She got undressed then looked at her head again.

'Be thankful you look like that.' Charles had come from the bathroom in a robe of emerald green silk under which his muscles rippled, suggesting the absence of any other clothing. Juley was in a creation of diaphanous nylon and lace bought for her by Sarah. The matching négligée lay across the back of a pretty pink bedroom chair but as she went to get it she was stopped by the advance of her husband. 'Come to me, my own love . . .' His arms were wide and gladly she let them enfold her. She had been yearning for this moment; he knew she craved his kisses and with a little exclamation of triumph he crushed her soft lips with his own. She quivered against him, thrilling to the tender warmth of his hand on her breast, to his roving mouth seeking the gentle curve of her throat, pressing kisses on it and moving lower, with his ardour rising all the time. He was a wonderful lover; this she knew so well. Tender and gentle one moment and fiercely passionate the next. For a while they stood together as if reluctant to separate even for the fleeting moment it took to get into the bed. But after slipping off her nightdress and his own robe, Charles lifted her in his arms and carried her across the room. The covers had been turned down; the drapes were open, to let moonlight stream in to shed a silver radiance across the bed. Charles smiled at the tight little curls clinging so closely to her head. 'A little pixie – a darling, tempting, alluring little pixie.' He bent to touch her lips before sliding beside her warm and eager body.

She quivered with rapture, and murmured huskily, 'Charles . . . I love you so much.'

'And I love you, my own dearest wife. Darling, it has been so long but now we have a wonderful future before us.'

She turned in his arms, melding her yielding body closer to his, using her hands in the way she knew would excite him as he was exciting her. Fulfilment came within seconds as they clung and gasped, moving in rhythm, carried aloft to the realms of Nirvana and floating there on a magic cloud, drugged by ecstasy and reluctant to return to earth.

'Dearest love,' murmured Charles a long time later, 'this is for ever.'

'For ever,' she whispered fervently, again offering him her lips. And, later still, she murmured sleepily, 'Charles, if ever I think of James and cry a little, you won't become impatient with me, will you, darling?'

'Juley, my love, don't be silly. Of course you will think of your son. How could it be any other way?'

She snuggled down happily.

'And do you know what we shall call our first son – yours and mine?'

He laughed softly.

'I don't suppose I shall get a prize for guessing that one. How can we call him anything but Stephen?'